D0554722

CAXTON'S BOOK:

A COLLECTION OF

ESSAYS, POEMS, TALES AND SKETCHES.

BY THE LATE

W. H. RHODES.

EDITED BY DANIEL O'CONNELL.

WITH A NEW INTRODUCTION BY

SAM MOSKOWITZ

HYPERION PRESS, INC.
WESTPORT, CONNECTICUT

Library of Congress Cataloging in Publication Data

Rhodes, William Henry, 1822-1876.
Caxton's book.

Reprint of the ed. published by A. L. Bancroft,
San Francisco.
I. Title.
PS2698.R43C3 1973 818'.4'09 73-13263
ISBN 0-88355-117-9
ISBN 0-88355-146-2 (pbk.)

Published in 1876
by A.L. Bancroft and Company, San Francisco.

Hyperion reprint edition 1974

Library of Congress Catalogue Number 73-13263

ISBN 0-88355-117-9 (cloth ed.)

ISBN 0-88355-146-2 (paper ed.)

Printed in the United States of America

THE SCIENCE FICTION HOAXES OF WILLIAM HENRY RHODES

By Sam Moskowitz

One of the most dynamic, yet least understood currents in the development of American science fiction is the hoax. This form of science fiction grew naturally in the newspapers of 19th century America. The great difficulty in tracing the continuous progression of American science fiction has been the misconception that it would be found primarily in hardcover books, or failing that, in the leading publications of the day.

It has been forgotten that only a tiny percentage of Americans of the 19th century had the income to buy books and up until the 1890s few could afford the quality magazines. It was no accident that Richard Adams Locke's impressively influential *The Moon Hoax* was serialized as *fact* in the first successful penny newspaper in the United States. *The Sun,* the New York City newspaper which carried the story daily in its editions from August 25, 1835 to August 31, 1835, saw its circulation shoot up in the space of three days to 105,000, larger by far than that of any newspaper in the world, including those in London.

Some years later, Edgar Allan Poe, in deliberate connivance with the publisher of the same paper wrote the story that is known today as *The Balloon Hoax.* It appeared in the April 13, 1844 edition of *The Sun.* Locke's story, which purported to discover a civilization on the moon with the assistance of a remarkable new telescope, and Poe's, which alleged to be a description of the first aerial flight across the Atlantic, not only created sensations but also convinced Jules Verne that he should begin writing science fiction. The date of origin of Edward Everett Hale's famed story of an artificial earth satellite, *The Brick Moon,* given in that author's introduction to his collected works as 1838, underscores his debt to Locke's hoax.

When Edward Page Mitchell began writing his landmark stories for *The Sun,* all his early tales were set up with headlines and decks in the manner of newspaper features. *Back From That Bourne,* an alleged tale of the return of a man from the dead as the result of a seance, was featured on the front page of *The Sun* for December 19, 1874. Mitchell's story, *The Soul Spectroscope,* in the December 19, 1875 edition, with its allegations of a professor who had discovered means of recording sound, constructing lie detectors and photographing odors, was presented in newspaper style as fact, with clues sprinkled throughout to reveal it as a hoax to the observant.

Just how many newspapers presented fantastic hoaxes in the manner of Richard Adams Locke and Edgar Allan Poe, has never been carefully researched. However, one of the most unusual and striking successes of this type of hoax was accomplished by a San Francisco lawyer, William Henry Rhodes, who wrote a series of fantastic newspaper hoaxes starting with *The Case of Summerfield,* which was published in *The Sacramento Union* for May 13, 1871, as having been submitted by its San Francisco correspondent whose initials were W.H.R.

The Sacramento Union had been, since 1850, the most powerful and influential paper in the state of California, particularly when it came to shaping legislation. Regular rail service between San Francisco and Sacramento brought it in to competition with a host of other dailies that had larger circulations and greater advertising. The political elements opposing the policies of the paper had thrown their full support behind a competitor established in 1867, *The Sacramento Record.* The publication of *The Case of Summerfield* was regarded by the Union's enemies as a desperate measure to stave off circulation decline.

Whatever impact the story had on circulation, there is no gainsaying its effect on the paper's readers. The Rhodes' concoction stirred up the inhabitants of northern California in 1878 in much the same way that the good citizens of northern New Jersey were scared out of their wits in 1938 by Orson Welles' famous radio broadcast of *The War of the Worlds. The Case of Summerfield* was a seemingly objective report, buttressed by very convincing legal depositions, of a man named Summerfield who had invented a chemical means of making the oceans of the world inflammable, and threatened to set the oceans afire if he were not paid one million dollars. The story, which leads off *Caxton's Book,* caused a state of near panic among many native Californians. Even though Summerfield was reported to have been killed, the very idea that a formula existed capable of consuming the waters of the world in an inferno of flame was understandably frightening.

Such important "news" could not be ignored, so the evening paper, *The Sacramento Reporter,* picked up the story and ran it complete the same day. Several days later, on May 16, 1871, *The Sacramento Reporter* exposed the story as a hoax. It had linked up the initials "W.H.R." with William Henry Rhodes, who already had a reputation of more than twenty years standing as a writer of fiction, articles, essays, columns and poetry under the name of "Caxton." There were few regular readers of the San Francisco newspapers and magazines who were not familiar with the literary efforts of "Caxton," so it was not unbelievable that he might indulge in this sort of journalistic deception.

Neither *The Sacramento Union* or William Henry Rhodes would initially own up to the hoax. To the contrary, Rhodes replied in the pages of *The Sacramento Union* for May 18, 1871 offering to show documentary evidence that would validate his story to anyone appearing at his office at 21 Wright Street in San Francisco. Also, instead of trying to allay the public panic, the newspaper set out to heighten it by running a sequel titled *The Summerfield Case Again* in *The Sacramento Union* for June 10, 1871. In this follow-up story, Black Bart, the most infamous outlaw to appear in California up to that time, was reported to have made off with a vial of the chemical that could destroy the world. Readers could only draw the chilling conclusion that the whole nation was now at the tender mercies of this merciless arch criminal.

Eventually, the newspaper confirmed that the well-known Caxton was indeed the author of both hoaxes. Oddly, the populace did not explode in anger at the hoaxer. Instead, he was applauded for his clever feat and even feted by his admirers. Rhodes had long been a popular local figure ever since his arrival in San Francisco in 1850.

The future "Caxton" was born on July 16, 1822 in Windsor, Bertie County, North Carolina; he was the son of Colonel Elisha A. Rhodes and the former Maria Ann Jacobs. Young Rhodes had been sent to study at Princeton, but he left, without finishing his schooling, when his father was appointed the U.S. Counsel at Galveston, Texas. However, in 1844, after completing two years at Harvard Law School, he began the practice of law in Galveston, where he served as a probate judge for one year. After a brief stay in New York City, Rhodes returned to his home town of Windsor, where he lived until 1850. His first published book, a small, well-illustrated volume of poetry, was intended as a tribute to the vanishing Indians. Titled *The Indian Gallows and Other Poems,* it was produced in 1864 by the press of Edward Walker, New York.

Rhodes was married on December 29, 1859 to Susan Harrison. The ceremony was performed in Oroville, California. At that time he had already established his reputation as a writer under the pen name of "Caxton." His writings appeared mostly in newspapers, but he also contributed to such magazines as *The Golden Era, The Pioneer, The Hesperian,* and to a short-lived publication that he edited, *The True Californian.*

He was best known for his participation in the much-publicized Vigilance Committee of 1856. This body of prominent San Francisco citizens took the law into its own hands for the purpose of cleaning up the bad element in that city. When a well-known jurist, Judge David S. Terry, was charged with attempted murder, it was Rhodes who prevented the vigilantes from executing the accused man. Despite this, Terry remained unforgiving and refused to ever see him again.

Though he achieved a certain measure of fame, Rhodes was never a wealthy man. He devoted too much time to his writing and too little to the practice of law. The net result was a loss of clients and a reduced income. Rhodes had four children — a daughter and three sons. He named one of his sons Arthur Pym after the character in Edgar Allan Poe's famous short novel. Much later, one of his great grandsons would carry the surname of "Caxton."

Spurred by the success of *The Case of Summerfield,* William Henry Rhodes continued to write new hoaxes, which were published in various San Francisco newspapers right up to the time of his death from Bright's disease on April 14, 1876. After he died, his friends hastened to collect these writings in a volume entitled *Caxton's Book,* which was published later that same year by Bancroft & Co., San Francisco. The proceeds realized from the sale of the book went to Rhodes' widow. The volume was edited by Daniel O'Connell, a well known San Francisco poet, author and editor. The revealing "In Memoriam," which is signed with the initials W.H.L.B., was written by another friend, the lawyer William H. L. Barnes, who helped ease the inhuman conditions of American seamen aboard sailing vessels when he won the famous "Sunrise Case."

A few of the pieces in *Caxton's Book* that are not science fiction were taken from Rhode's contributions to *The Golden Era* and other such publications. However, the bulk of the book consists of his unique science fiction tales, including *The Case of Summerfield, The Summerfield Case, Phases in the Life of John Pollefexen, The Aztec Princess, Legends of Lake Bigler, The Telescopic Eye, The Earth's Hot Center,* and the poem *The Avitor.* It is important for the reader to know that all the fiction were hoaxes and that they all appeared originally in newspapers. Any weaknesses we now see in them as stories stem from the author's attempts to hoodwink the public into believing that his outlandish tales were true. It is equally important to note that the science fiction hoax, which evolved over the years, formed a tradition of its own in literature and must therefore be judged by separate standards. To resolve any doubts about the existence of such a tradition and its orderly progression, the reader need only consult a tale in this book, *The Telescopic Eye.*

The story is about a young man who is thought to be blind. Then, astonishingly, it is discovered that his affliction is really an incredible farsightedness that enables him to view things at great distances with telescopic clarity. Thus, he is able to fix his gaze on the moon and see there in minute detail the existence of a lunar civilization. *The Telescopic Eye* ends with the youth shifting his super eyes from the moon and focusing them on Mars so he can begin describing that remote planet. It is apparent that in fabricating this tale Rhodes was influenced by Locke's *The Moon Hoax* and Poe's *The Balloon Hoax,* both of which must have been known to him. In 1844, when Poe's story was published in New York in *The Sun,* the yet-to-be "Caxton" was attending nearby Harvard where, according to a statement by Barnes in his introduction to this volume, "His fondness for weaving the problems of science with fiction, which became afterwards so marked a characteristic of his literary efforts, attracted the special attention of his professors." Rhodes himself exercised an influence on writers who continued the hoax writing tradition. Many of these authors, whose work invariably appeared in newspapers, had obviously been inspired by the literary deceptions of "Caxton".

It should not be supposed that Rhodes is a completely forgotten figure in American letters. To the contrary, in the history of California literature he is regarded as a minor classic. His "hoaxes" were reprinted frequently in various newspapers for years after his death. In 1907 a clothbound series of "Western Classics" was issued by Paul Elder & Co., of San Francisco and New York. *The Case of Summerfield* was the second work selected for the series. It had an introduction by Geraldine Bonner and a frontispiece reproduced from a painting by Gallen J. Parrett, which depicted a scene from the story. One thousand copies of this edition were printed. In April, 1939, the Book Club of California again reprinted *The Case of Summerfield* as the second in a series of six short stories by California authors. The Rhodes' tale was printed as a handsome brochure in a limited edition of 650 copies. More recently, Anthony Boucher, then editor of *The Magazine of Fantasy and* Science Fiction, reprinted *The Case of Summerfield* in the Summer, 1950 issue of his magazine. In his introductory note, Boucher wrote what may well serve as a fitting estimate of the inimitable "Caxton": "W. H. Rhodes was in this and other stories one of the great pioneers of modern science fiction."

PREFACE.

THE sketches and poems in this volume were written at a time when the author was engaged in the practice of a laborious profession. It was the intention of Mr. Rhodes to collect them from the various newspapers and periodicals in which they had appeared, and publish them in book-form whenever he could obtain a respite from his arduous duties. But before he carried out his long-cherished object he died, in the prime of his manhood and the ripeness of his literary life. Many of his poems were written for the monthly gatherings of the Bohemian Club. There, when Caxton's name was announced, his literary friends thronged about him, confident of the rich treat the brain of their beloved poet had provided for them. His wit was keen and sparkling, without a shade of malice; and many an anecdote, that began with some delightful absurdity, closed in a pathos that showed the great versatility of Caxton's genius. The Case of Summerfield, which is perhaps the most ingenious of the tales in that peculiar vein, was widely copied and warmly praised for the originality of its plan and the skill of its execution. The editor of this work has observed, as far as lay in his power, the intention of the author in the selection of those compositions which Mr. Rhodes had put aside for compilation. With such a mass and variety of material (for Caxton had been a busy worker) it was difficult to select from productions all of which were excellent. Few liberties have been taken with them; for, indeed, Caxton was himself so conscientious in the arrangement and correction of his manuscript, that, with the exception of some slight and unimportant alterations, this book goes before his friends and the public in the same order as the author would have chosen had he been spared to perform the task.

In Memoriam.

At the time when, according to custom, Mr. Rhodes's death was formally announced to the several Courts of Record in San Francisco, one of the learned Judges urged the publication of his writings in some form which would give the bar a permanent memorial of one of its most esteemed members, and to them their proper place in American literature. This has been accomplished by the present volume. It is sincerely to be hoped that while it will largely add to Mr. Rhodes's reputation, it may also serve to furnish a most interesting family some substantial aid in the struggle with life, from which the beloved husband and tender father has unhappily been removed.

William Henry Rhodes was born July 16, 1822, in Windsor, North Carolina. His mother died when he was six years old, and his father, Col. E. A. Rhodes, sent him to Princeton, New Jersey, to be educated at the seat of learning established there. Col. Rhodes was subsequently appointed United States Consul at Galveston, Texas, and without completing his college course, the son followed his father to his new home. There he diligently pursued his studies. He found many young men like himself, ambitious and zealous in acquiring information, and these he associated with himself in literary and debating clubs, where the most important matters of natural science and political economy were discussed. The effect of this self-bestowed education was most marked. It remained with him all his life. He was thoroughly versed in the political history of the country, and possessed an amount of knowledge concerning the career, motives and objects of politics, parties and public men, which, had he ever chosen to embark in public life, would have made him distinguished and successful. No one ever discussed with him the questions connected with the theory of our government without a thorough respect for the sincerity of his convictions, and the ability with which they were maintained. He was, in theory, a thorough partisan of the Southern political and constitutional school of ideas, and never abandoned them. But he advocated them without passion or apparent prejudice, and at all times shrunk from active connection with politics as a trade. He was an idealist in law, in science and government, and perhaps his early training, self-imposed and self-contained, had much to do with his peculiarities.

In 1844, he entered Harvard Law School, where he remained for two years. Here, as at home among his young friends, he was a master-spirit and leader. He was an especial favorite of his instructors; was noted for his studious and exemplary habits, while his genial and courteous manners won the lasting friendship of his classmates and companions. His fondness for weaving the problems of science with fiction, which became afterwards so marked a characteristic of his literary efforts, attracted the especial attention of his professors; and had Mr. Rhodes devoted himself to this then novel department of letters, he would have become, no doubt, greatly distinguished as a writer; and the great master of scientific fiction, Jules Verne, would have found the field of his efforts already sown and reaped by the young Southern student. But his necessities and parental choice, conspired to keep him at "the lawless science of the law;" and literature became an incident of life, rather than its end and aim. He never really loved the law. He rather lived by it than in it. He became a good lawyer, but was an unwilling practitioner. He understood legal principles thoroughly. He loved the higher lessons of truth and justice, of right and wrong, *fas et nefas*, which they illustrated; but he bent himself to the necessary details of professional life—to the money-getting part of it—with a peculiar and constantly increasing reluctance. The yoke of labor galled him, and always more severely. An opportunity to speak and write what was most pleasing to his taste, which set him free as a liberated prisoner of thought, his untrammeled and wandering imagination extravagantly interweaving scientific principles, natural forces, and elemental facts, in some witch's dance of fancy, where he dissolved in its alchemy, earth, air and water, and created a world of his own, or destroyed that beneath his feet, was of more value to him, though it brought him no gain, than a stiff cause in courts which bound him to dry details of weary facts and legal propositions, though every hour of his time bestowed a golden reward.

His early professional life was passed in Galveston. He was measurably successful in it, and won many friends by his gallant and chivalrous advocacy of the causes intrusted to him. His personal popularity elevated him to a Probate Judgeship in Texas. This office he filled with honor; and at the expiration of his term, he returned, after a brief sojourn in New York, to his native state and town, where he practiced his profession until 1850. In this year he caught the inspiration of adventure in the new El Dorado, and sailed for California. From that time he continued a citizen of this State. He was widely known and universally respected. He practiced his profession with diligence; but mind and heart were inviting him to the life and career of a man of letters; and he was every day sacrificed to duty, as he esteemed it. He was too conscientious to become indifferent to his clients' interests: but he had no ambition for distinction as a jurist. He was utterly indifferent to the profits of his labors. He cared nothing for money, or for those who possessed it. His real life and real enjoyments were of a far different sort; and his genius was perpetually bound to the altar, and sacrificed by a sense of obligation, and a pride which never permitted him to abandon the profession for which he was educated. Like many another man of peculiar mental qualities, he distrusted himself where he should have been most confident. The writer has often discussed with Mr. Rhodes his professional and literary life, urged him to devote himself to literature, and endeavored to point out to him the real road to success. But he dreaded the venture; and like a swift-footed blooded horse, fit to run a course for a man's life, continued on his way, harnessed to a plow, and broke his heart in the harness!

William Henry Rhodes will long be remembered by his contemporaries at the Bar of California as a man of rare genius, exemplary habits, high honor, and gentle manners, with wit and humor unexcelled. His writings are illumined by powerful fancy, scientific knowledge, and a reasoning power which gave to his most weird imaginations the similitude of truth and the apparel of facts. Nor did they, nor do they, do him justice. He could have accomplished far more had circumstances been propitious to him. That they were not, is and will always be a source of regret. That, environed as he was, he achieved so much more than his fellows, has made his friends always loyal to him while living, and fond in their memories of him when dead. We give his productions to the world with satisfaction, not unmingled with regret that what is, is only the faint echo, the unfulfilled promise of what might have been. Still, may we say, and ask those who read these sketches to say with us, as they lay down the volume: "*Habet enim justam venerationem, quicquid excellit.*"

W. H. L. B.

CONTENTS.

CAXTON'S BOOK.

I.

THE CASE OF SUMMERFIELD.

THE following manuscript was found among the effects of the late Leonidas Parker, in relation to one Gregory Summerfield, or, as he was called at the time those singular events first attracted public notice, "The Man with a Secret." Parker was an eminent lawyer, a man of firm will, fond of dabbling in the occult sciences, but never allowing this tendency to interfere with the earnest practice of his profession. This astounding narrative is prefaced by the annexed clipping from the "Auburn Messenger" of November 1, 1870:

A few days since, we called public attention to the singular conduct of James G. Wilkins, justice of the peace for the "Cape Horn" district, in this county, in discharging without trial a man named Parker, who was, as we still think, seriously implicated in the mysterious death of an old man named Summerfield, who, our readers will probably remember, met so tragical an end on the line of the Central Pacific Railroad, in the month of October last. We have now to record another bold outrage on public justice, in connection with the same affair. The grand jury of Placer County has just adjourned, without finding any bill against the person named above. Not only did they refuse to find a true bill, or to make any presentment, but they went one step further toward the exoneration of the offender: they specially *ignored* the indictment which our district attorney deemed it his duty to present. The main facts in relation to the arrest and subsequent discharge of Parker may be summed up in few words:

It appears that, about the last of October, one Gregory Summerfield, an old man nearly seventy years of age, in company with Parker, took passage for Chicago, *via* the Pacific Railroad, and about the middle of the afternoon reached the neighborhood of Cape Horn, in this county. Nothing of any special importance seems to have attracted the attention of any of the passengers toward these persons until a few moments before passing the dangerous curve in the track, overlooking the North Fork of the American River, at the place called Cape Horn. As our readers are aware, the road at this point skirts a precipice, with rocky perpendicular sides, extending to the bed of the stream, nearly seventeen hundred feet below. Before passing the curve, Parker was heard to comment upon the sublimity of the scenery they were approaching, and finally requested the old man to leave the car and stand upon the open platform, in order to obtain a better view of the tremendous chasm and the mountains just beyond. The two men left the car, and a moment afterwards a cry of horror was heard by all the passengers, and the old man was observed to fall at least one thousand feet upon the crags below. The train was stopped for a few moments, but, fearful of a collision if any considerable length of time should be lost in an unavailing search for the mangled remains, it soon moved on again, and proceeded as swiftly as possible to the next station. There the miscreant Parker was arrested, and conveyed to the office of the nearest justice of the peace for examination. We understand that he refused to give any detailed account of the transaction, only that "the deceased either fell or was thrown off from the moving train."

The examination was postponed until the arrival of Parker's counsel, O'Connell & Kilpatrick, of Grass Valley, and after they reached Cape Horn not a single word could be extracted from the prisoner. It is said that the inquisition was a mere farce; there being no witnesses present except one lady passenger, who, with commendable spirit, volunteered to lay over one day, to give in her testimony. We also learn that, after the trial, the justice, together with the prisoner and his counsel, were closeted in secret session for more than two hours; at the expiration of which time the judge resumed his seat upon the bench, and discharged the prisoner!

Now, we have no desire to do injustice toward any of the parties to this singular transaction, much less to arm public sentiment against an innocent man. But we do affirm that *there is, there must be,* some profound mystery at the bottom of this affair, and we shall do our utmost to fathom the secret.

Yes, there is a secret and mystery connected with the disappearance of Summerfield, and the sole object of this communication is to clear it up, and place myself right in the public estimation. But, in order to do so, it becomes essentially necessary to relate all the circumstances connected with my first and subsequent acquaintance with Summerfield. To do this intelligibly, I shall have to go back twenty-two years.

It is well known amongst my intimate friends that I resided in the late Republic of Texas for many years antecedent to my immigration to this State. During the year 1847, whilst but a boy, and residing on the sea-beach some three or four miles from the city of Galveston, Judge Wheeler, at that time Chief Justice of the Supreme Court of Texas, paid us a visit, and brought with him a gentleman, whom he had known several years previously on the Sabine River, in the eastern part of that State. This gentleman was introduced to us by the name of Summerfield. At that time he was past the prime of life, slightly gray, and inclined to corpulency. He was of medium height, and walked proudly erect, as though conscious of superior mental attainments. His face was one of those which, once seen, can never be forgotten. The forehead was broad, high, and protuberant. It was, besides, deeply graven with wrinkles, and altogether was the most intellectual that I had ever seen. It bore some resemblance to that of Sir Isaac Newton, but still more to Humboldt or Webster. The eyes were large, deep-set, and lustrous with a light that seemed kindled in their own depths. In color they were gray, and whilst in conversation absolutely blazed with intellect. His mouth was large, but cut with all the precision of a sculptor's chiseling. He was rather pale, but, when excited, his complexion lit up with a sudden rush of ruddy flushes, that added something like beauty to his half-sad and half-sardonic expression. A word and a glance told me at once, this is a most extraordinary man.

Judge Wheeler knew but little of the antecedents of Summerfield. He was of Northern birth, but of what State it is impossible to say definitely. Early in life he removed to the frontier of Arkansas, and pursued for some years the avocation of village schoolmaster. It was the suggestion of Judge Wheeler that induced him to read law. In six months' time he had mastered Story's Equity, and gained an important suit, based upon one of its most recondite principles. But his heart was not in the legal profession, and he made almost constant sallies into the fields of science, literature and art. He was a natural mathematician, and was the most profound and original arithmetician in the Southwest. He frequently computed the astronomical tables for the almanacs of New Orleans, Pensacola and Mobile, and calculated eclipse, transit and observations with ease and perfect accuracy. He was also deeply read in metaphysics, and wrote and published, in the old *Democratic Review* for 1846, an article on the "Natural Proof of the Existence of a Deity," that for beauty of language, depth of reasoning, versatility of illustration, and compactness of logic, has never been equaled.

The only other publication which at that period he had made, was a book that astonished all of his friends, both in title and execution. It was called "The Desperadoes of the West," and purported to give minute details of the lives of some of the most noted duelists and blood-stained villains in the Western States. But the book belied its title. It is full of splendid description and original thought. No volume in the language contains so many eloquent passages and such gorgeous imagery, in the same space. His plea for immortality, on beholding the execution of one of the most noted culprits of Arkansas, has no parallel in any living language for beauty of diction and power of thought. As my sole object in this communication is to defend myself, some acquaintance with the mental resources of Summerfield is absolutely indispensable; for his death was the immediate consequence of his splendid attainments. Of chemistry he was a complete master. He describes it in his article on a Deity, above alluded to, as the "Youngest Daughter of the Sciences, born amid flames, and cradled in rollers of fire." If there were any one science to which he was more specially devoted than to any and all others, it was chemistry. But he really seemed an adept in all, and shone about everywhere with equal lustre.

Many of these characteristics were mentioned by Judge Wheeler at the time of Summerfield's visit to Galveston, but others subsequently came to my knowledge, after his retreat to Brownsville, on the banks of the Rio Grande. There he filled the position of judge of the District Court, and such was his position just previous to his arrival in this city in the month of September of the past year.

One day toward the close of last September, an old

man rapped at my office door, and on invitation came in, and advancing, called me by name. Perceiving that I did not at first recognize him, he introduced himself as Gregory Summerfield. After inviting him to a seat, I scrutinized his features more closely, and quickly identified him as the same person whom I had met twenty-two years before. He was greatly altered in appearance, but the lofty forehead and the gray eye were still there, unchanged and unchangeable. He was not quite so stout, but more ruddy in complexion, and exhibited some symptoms, as I then thought, of intemperate drinking. Still there was the old charm of intellectual superiority in his conversation, and I welcomed him to California as an important addition to her mental wealth.

It was not many minutes before he requested a private interview. He followed me into my back office, carefully closed the door after him and locked it. We had scarcely seated ourselves before he inquired of me if I had noticed any recent articles in the newspapers respecting the discovery of the art of decomposing water so as to fit it for use as a fuel for ordinary purposes?

I replied that I had observed nothing new upon that subject since the experiments of Agassiz and Professor Henry, and added that, in my opinion, the expensive mode of reduction would always prevent its use.

In a few words he then informed me that he had made the discovery that the art was extremely simple, and the expense attending the decomposition so slight as to be insignificant.

Presuming then that the object of his visit to me was to procure the necessary forms to get out a patent for the right, I congratulated him upon his good fortune, and was about to branch forth with a description of some of the great benefits that must ensue to the community, when he suddenly and somewhat uncivilly requested me to "be silent," and listen to what he had to say.

He began with some general remarks about the inequality of fortune amongst mankind, and instanced himself as a striking example of the fate of those men, who, according to all the rules of right, ought to be near the top, instead of at the foot of the ladder of fortune. "But," said he, springing to his feet with impulsive energy, "I have now the means at my command of rising superior to fate, or of inflicting incalculable ills upon the whole human race."

Looking at him more closely, I thought I could detect in his eye the gleam of madness; but I remained silent and awaited further developments. But my scrutiny, stolen as it was, had been detected, and he replied at once to the expression of my face: "No, sir; I am neither drunk nor a maniac; I am in deep earnest in all that I say; and I am fully prepared, by actual experiment, to demonstrate beyond all doubt the truth of all I claim.

For the first time I noticed that he carried a small portmanteau in his hand; this he placed upon the table, unlocked it, and took out two or three small volumes, a pamphlet or two, and a small, square, wide-mouthed vial, hermetically sealed.

I watched him with profound curiosity, and took note of his slightest movements. Having arranged his books to suit him, and placed the vial in a conspicuous position, he drew up his chair very closely to my own, and uttered in a half-hissing tone: "I demand one million dollars for the contents of that bottle; and you must raise it for me in the city of San Francisco within one month, or scenes too terrible even for the imagination to conceive, will surely be witnessed by every living human being on the face of the globe."

The tone, the manner, and the absurd extravagance of the demand, excited a faint smile upon my lips, which he observed, but disdained to notice.

My mind was fully made up that I had a maniac to deal with, and I prepared to act accordingly. But I ascertained at once that my inmost thoughts were read by the remarkable man before me, and seemed to be anticipated by him in advance of their expression.

"Perhaps," said I, "Mr. Summerfield, you would oblige me by informing me fully of the grounds of your claim, and the nature of your discovery."

"That is the object of my visit," he replied. "I claim to have discovered the key which unlocks the constituent gases of water, and frees each from the embrace of the other, at a single touch."

"You mean to assert," I rejoined, "that you can make water burn itself up?"

"Nothing more nor less," he responded, "except this: to insist upon the consequences of the secret, if my demand be not at once complied with."

Then, without pausing for a moment to allow me to make a suggestion, as I once or twice attempted to do, he proceeded in a clear and deliberate manner, in these words: "I need not inform you, sir, that when this earth was created, it consisted almost wholly of vapor, which, by condensation, finally became water. The oceans now occupy more than two thirds of the entire surface of the globe. The continents are mere islands in the midst of the seas. They are everywhere ocean-bound, and the hyperborean north is hemmed in by open polar seas. Such is my first proposition. My second embraces the constituent elements of water. What is that thing which we call water? Chemistry, that royal queen of all the sciences, answers readily: 'Water is but the combination of two gases, oxygen and hydrogen, and in the proportion of eight to one.' In other words, in order to form water, take eight parts of oxygen and one of hydrogen, mix them together, and the result or product is water. You smile, sir, because, as you very properly think, these are the elementary principles of science, and are familiar to the minds of every schoolboy twelve years of age. Yes! but what next? Suppose you take these same gases and mix them in any other proportion, I care not what, and the instantaneous result is heat, flame, combustion of the intensest description. The famous Drummond Light, that a few years ago astonished Europe—what is that but the ignited flame of a mixture of oxygen and hydrogen projected against a small piece of lime? What was harmless as water, becomes the most destructive of all known objects when decomposed and mixed in any other proportion.

"Now, suppose I fling the contents of this small vial into the Pacific Ocean, what would be the result? Dare you contemplate it for an instant? I do not assert that the entire surface of the sea would instantaneously bubble up into insufferable flames; no, but from the nucleus of a circle, of which this vial would be the centre, lurid radii of flames would gradually shoot outward, until the blazing circumference would roll in vast billows of fire, upon the uttermost shores. Not all the dripping clouds of the deluge could extinguish it. Not all the tears of saints and angels could for an instant check its progress. On and onward it would sweep, with the steady gait of destiny, until the continents would melt with fervent heat, the atmosphere glare with the ominous conflagration, and all living creatures, in land and sea and air, perish in one universal catastrophe."

Then suddenly starting to his feet, he drew himself up to his full height, and murmured solemnly, "I feel like a God! and I recognize my fellow-men but as pigmies that I spurn beneath my feet."

"Summerfield," said I calmly, "there must be some strange error in all this. You are self-deluded. The weapon which you claim to wield is one that a good God and a beneficent Creator would never intrust to the keeping of a mere creature. What, sir! create a world as grand and beautiful as this, and hide within its bosom a principle that at any moment might inwrap it in flames, and sink all life in death? I'll not believe it; 't were blasphemy to entertain the thought!"

"And yet," cried he passionately, "your Bible prophesies the same irreverence. Look at your text in 2d Peter, third chapter, seventh and twelfth verses. Are not the elements to melt with fervent heat? Are not 'the heavens to be folded together like a scroll?' Are not 'the rocks to melt, the stars to fall and the moon to be turned into blood?' Is not fire the next grand cyclic consummation of all things here below? But I come fully prepared to answer such objections. Your argument betrays a narrow mind, circumscribed in its orbit, and shallow in its depth. 'Tis the common thought of mediocrity. You have read books too much, and studied nature too little. Let me give you a lesson to-day in the workshop of Omnipotence. Take a stroll with me into the limitless confines of space, and let us observe together some of the scenes transpiring at this very instant around us. A moment ago you spoke of the moon: what is she but an extinguished world?

You spoke of the sun: what is he but a globe of flame? But here is the *Cosmos* of Humboldt. Read this paragraph."

As he said this he placed before me the *Cosmos* of Humboldt, and I read as follows:

Nor do the Heavens themselves teach unchangeable permanency in the works of creation. Change is observable there quite as rapid and complete as in the confines of our solar system. In the year 1752, one of the small stars in the constellation Cassiopeia blazed up suddenly into an orb of the first magnitude, gradually decreased in brilliancy, and finally disappeared from the skies. Nor has it ever been visible since that period for a single moment, either to the eye or to the telescope. It burned up and was lost in space.

"Humboldt," he added, "has not told us who set that world on fire!

"But," resumed he, "I have still clearer proofs."

Saying this, he thrust into my hands the last London *Quarterly*, and on opening the book at an article headed "The Language of Light," I read with a feeling akin to awe, the following passage:

Further, some stars exhibit changes of complexion in themselves. Sirius, as before stated, was once a ruddy, or rather a fiery-faced orb, but has now forgotten to blush, and looks down upon us with a pure, brilliant smile, in which there is no trace either of anger or of shame. On the countenances of others, still more varied traits have rippled, within a much briefer period of time. May not these be due to some physiological revolutions, general or convulsive, which are in progress in the particular orb, and which, by affecting the constitution of its atmosphere, compel the absorption or promote the transmission of particular rays? The supposition appears by no means improbable, especially if we call to mind the hydrogen volcanoes which have been discovered on the photosphere of the sun. Indeed, there are a few small stars which afford a spectrum of bright lines instead of dark ones, and this we know denotes a gaseous or vaporized state of things, from which it may be inferred that such orbs are in a different condition from most of their relations.

And as, if for the very purpose of throwing light upon this interesting question, an event of the most striking character occurred in the heavens, almost as soon as the spectroscopists were prepared to interpret it correctly.

On the 12th of May, 1866, a great conflagration, infinitely larger than that of London or Moscow, was announced. To use the expression of a distinguished astronomer, a world was found to be on fire! A star, which till then had shone weakly and unobtrusively in the *corona borealis*, suddenly blazed up into a luminary of the second magnitude. In the course of three days from its discovery in this new character, by Birmingham, at Tuam, it had declined to the third or fourth order of brilliancy. In twelve days, dating from its first apparition in the Irish heavens, it had sunk to the eighth rank, and it went on waning until the 26th of June, when it ceased to be discernible except through the medium of the telescope. This was a remarkable, though certainly not an unprecedented proceeding on the part of a star; but one singular circumstance in its behavior was that, after the lapse of nearly two months, it began to blaze up again, though not with equal ardor, and after maintaining its glow for a few weeks, and passing through sundry phases of color, it gradually paled its fires, and returned to its former insignificance. How many years had elapsed since this awful conflagration actually took place, it would be presumptuous to guess; but it must be remembered that news from the heavens, though carried by the fleetest of messengers, light, reaches us long after the event has transpired, and that the same celestial carrier is still dropping the tidings at each station it reaches in space, until it sinks exhausted by the length of its flight.

As the star had suddenly flamed up, was it not a natural supposition that it had become inwrapped in burning hydrogen, which in consequence of some great convulsion had been liberated in prodigious quantities, and then combining with other elements, had set this hapless world on fire? In such a fierce conflagration, the combustible gas would soon be consumed, and the glow would therefore begin to decline, subject, as in this case, to a second eruption, which occasioned the renewed outburst of light on the 20th of August.

By such a catastrophe, it is not wholly impossible that our own globe may some time be ravaged; for if a word from the

Almighty were to unloose for a few moments the bonds of affinity which unite the elements of water, a single spark would bring them together with a fury that would kindle the funeral pyre of the human race, and be fatal to the planet and all the works that are thereon.

"Your argument," he then instantly added, "is by no means a good one. What do we know of the Supreme Architect of the Universe, or of his designs? He builds up worlds, and he pulls them down; he kindles suns and he extinguishes them. He inflames the comet, in one portion of its orbit, with a heat that no human imagination can conceive of; and in another, subjects the same blazing orb to a cold intenser than that which invests forever the antarctic pole. All that we know of Him we gather through His works. I have shown you that He burns other worlds, why not this? The habitable parts of our globe are surrounded by water, and water you know is fire in possibility."

"But all this," I rejoined, "is pure, baseless, profitless speculation."

"Not so fast," he answered. And then rising, he seized the small vial, and handing it to me, requested me to open it.

I confess I did so with some trepidation.

"Now smell it."

I did so.

"What odor do you perceive?"

"Potassium," I replied.

"Of course," he added, "you are familiar with the chief characteristic of that substance. It ignites instantly when brought in contact with water. Within that little globule of potassium, I have imbedded a pill of my own composition and discovery. The moment it is liberated from the potassium, it commences the work of decomposing the fluid on which it floats. The potassium at once ignites the liberated oxygen, and the conflagration of this mighty globe is begun."

"Yes," said I, "begun, if you please, but your little pill soon evaporates or sinks, or melts in the surrounding seas, and your conflagration ends just where it began."

"My reply to that suggestion could be made at once by simply testing the experiment on a small scale, or a large one, either. But I prefer at present to refute your proposition by an argument drawn from nature herself. If you correctly remember, the first time I had the pleasure of seeing you was on the island of Galveston, many years ago. Do you remember relating to me at that time an incident concerning the effects of a prairie on fire, that you had yourself witnessed but a few days previously, near the town of Matagorde? If I recollect correctly, you stated that on your return journey from that place, you passed on the way the charred remains of two wagon-loads of cotton, and three human beings, that the night before had perished in the flames; that three slaves, the property of a Mr. Horton, had started a few days before to carry to market a shipment of cotton; that a norther overtook them on the treeless prairie, and a few minutes afterwards they were surprised by beholding a line of rushing fire, surging, roaring and advancing like the resistless billows of an ocean swept by a gale; that there was no time for escape, and they perished terribly in fighting the devouring element?"

"Yes; I recollect the event."

"Now, then, I wish a reply to the simple question: Did the single spark, that kindled the conflagration, consume the negroes and their charge? No? But what did? You reply, of course, that the spark set the entire prairie on fire; that each spear of grass added fuel to the flame, and kindled by degrees a conflagration that continued to burn so long as it could feed on fresh material. The pillule in that vial is the little spark, the oceans are the prairies, and the oxygen the fuel upon which the fire is to feed until the globe perishes in inextinguishable flames. The elementary substances in that small vial recreate themselves; they are self-generating, and when once fairly under way must necessarily sweep onward, until the waters in all the seas are exhausted. There is, however, one great difference between the burning of a prairie and the combustion of an ocean: the fire in the first spreads slowly, for the fuel is difficult to ignite; in the last, it flies with the rapidity of the wind, for the substance consumed is oxygen, the most inflammable agent in nature."

Rising from my seat, I went to the washstand in the corner of the apartment, and drawing a bowl half full of Spring Valley water, I turned to Summerfield, and remarked, "Words are empty, theories are ideal—but facts are things."

"I take you at your word." So saying, he approached the bowl, emptied it of nine-tenths of its contents, and silently dropped the potassium-coated pill into the liquid. The potassium danced around the edges of the vessel, fuming, hissing, and blazing, as it always does, and seemed on the point of expiring—when, to my astonishment and alarm, a sharp explosion took place, and in a second of time the water was blazing in a red, lurid column, half way to the ceiling.

"For God's sake," I cried, "extinguish the flames, or we shall set the building on fire!"

"Had I dropped the potassium into the bowl as you prepared it," he quietly remarked, "the building would indeed have been consumed."

Lower and lower fell the flickering flames, paler and paler grew the blaze, until finally the fire went out, and I rushed up to see the effects of the combustion.

Not a drop of water remained in the vessel! Astonished beyond measure at what I had witnessed, and terrified almost to the verge of insanity, I approached Summerfield, and tremblingly inquired, "To whom, sir, is this tremendous secret known?" "To myself alone," he responded; "and now answer me a question: is it worth the money?"

* * * * * * *

It is entirely unnecessary to relate in detail the subsequent events connected with this transaction. I will only add a general statement, showing the results of my negotiations. Having fully satisfied myself that Summerfield actually held in his hands the fate of the whole world, with its millions of human beings, and by experiment having tested the combustion of sea-water, with equal facility as fresh, I next deemed it my duty to call the attention of a few of the principal men in San Francisco to the extreme importance of Summerfield's discovery.

A leading banker, a bishop, a chemist, two State university professors, a physician, a judge, and two Protestant divines, were selected by me to witness the experiment on a large scale. This was done at a small sand-hill lake, near the sea-shore, but separated from it by a ridge of lofty mountains, distant not more than ten miles from San Francisco. Every single drop of water in the pool was burnt up in less than fifteen minutes. We next did all that we could to pacify Summerfield, and endeavored to induce him to lower his price and bring it within the bounds of a reasonable possibility. But without avail. He began to grow urgent in his demands, and his brow would cloud like a tempest-ridden sky whenever we approached him on the subject. Finally, ascertaining that no persuasion could soften his heart or touch his feelings, a sub-committee was appointed, to endeavor, if possible, to raise the money by subscription. Before taking that step, however, we ascertained beyond all question that Summerfield was the sole custodian of his dread secret, and that he kept no written memorial of the formula of his prescription. He even went so far as to offer us a penal bond that his secret should perish with him in case we complied with his demands.

The sub-committee soon commenced work amongst the wealthiest citizens of San Francisco, and by appealing to the terrors of a few, and the sympathies of all, succeeded in raising one half the amount within the prescribed period. I shall never forget the woe-begone faces of California Street during the month of October. The outside world and the newspapers spoke most learnedly of a money panic—a pressure in business, and the disturbances in the New York gold-room. But to the initiated, there was an easier solution of the enigma. The pale spectre of Death looked down upon them all, and pointed with its bony finger to the fiery tomb of the whole race, already looming up in the distance before them. Day after day, I could see the dreadful ravages of this secret horror; doubly terrible, since they dared not divulge it. Still, do all that we could, the money could not be obtained. The day preceding the last one given, Summerfield was summoned before the committee, and full information given him of the state of affairs. Obdurate, hard and cruel, he still continued. Finally, a proposition was started, that an attempt should be made to raise the other half of the money in the city of New York. To this proposal Summerfield ultimately yielded, but with extreme reluctance. It was agreed in committee, that I should accompany him thither, and take with me, in my own possession, evidences of the sums subscribed here; that a proper appeal should be made to the leading capitalists, scholars and clergymen of that metropolis, and that, when the whole amount was raised, it should be paid over to Summerfield, and a bond taken from him never to divulge his awful secret to any human being.

With this, he seemed to be satisfied, and left us to prepare for his going the next morning.

As soon as he left the apartment, the bishop arose, and "deprecated the action that had been taken, and characterized it as childish and absurd. He declared that no man was safe one moment whilst "that diabolical wretch" still lived; that the only security for us all, was in his immediate extirpation from the face of the earth, and that no amount of money could seal his lips, or close his hands. It would be no crime, he said, to deprive him of the means of assassinating the whole human family, and that as for himself he was for dooming him to immediate death.

With a unanimity that was extraordinary, the entire committee coincided.

A great many plans were proposed, discussed and rejected, having in view the extermination of Summerfield. In them all there was the want of that proper caution which would lull the apprehensions of an enemy; for should he for an instant suspect treachery, we knew his nature well enough to be satisfied, that he would waive all ceremonies and carry his threats into immediate execution.

It was finally resolved that the trip to New York

should not be abandoned, apparently. But that we were to start out in accordance with the original programme; that during the journey, some proper means should be resorted to by me to carry out the final intentions of the committee, and that whatever I did would be sanctioned by them all, and full protection, both in law and conscience, afforded me in any stage of the proceeding.

Nothing was wanting but my own consent; but this was difficult to secure.

At the first view, it seemed to be a most horrible and unwarrantable crime to deprive a fellow-being of life, under any circumstances; but especially so where, in meeting his fate, no opportunity was to be afforded him for preparation or repentance. It was a long time before I could disassociate, in my mind, the two ideas of act and intent. My studies had long ago made me perfectly familiar with the doctrine of the civil law, that in order to constitute guilt, there must be a union of action and intention. Taking the property of another is not theft, unless, as the lawyers term it, there is the *animus furandi*. So, in homicide, life may be lawfully taken in some instances, whilst the deed may be excused in others. The sheriff hangs the felon, and deprives him of existence; yet nobody thinks of accusing the officer of murder. The soldier slays his enemy, still the act is considered heroical. It does not therefore follow that human life is too sacred to be taken away under all circumstances. The point to be considered was thus narrowed down into one grand inquiry, whether Summerfield was properly to be regarded as *hostis humani generis* the enemy of the human race or not. If he should justly be so considered, then it would not only be not a crime to kill him, but an act worthy of the highest commendation. Who blamed McKenzie for hanging Spencer to the yard-arm? Yet in his case, the lives of only a small ship's crew were in jeopardy. Who condemned Pompey for exterminating the pirates from the Adriatic? Yet, in his case, only a small portion of the Roman Republic was liable to devastation. Who accuses Charlotte Corday of assassination for stabbing Murat in his bath? Still, her arm only saved the lives of a few thousands of revolutionary Frenchmen. And to come down to our own times, who heaps accusation upon the heads of Lincoln, Thomas or Sheridan, or even Grant, though in marching to victory over a crushed rebellion, they deemed it necessary to wade through seas of human gore? If society has the right to defend itself from the assaults of criminals, who, at best, can only destroy a few of its members, why should I hesitate when it was apparent that the destiny of the globe itself hung in the balance? If Summerfield should live and carry out his threats, the whole world would feel the shock; his death was the only path to perfect safety.

I asked the privilege of meditation for one hour, at the hands of the committee, before I would render a decision either way. During that recess the above argumentation occupied my thoughts. The time expired, and I again presented myself before them. I did not deem it requisite to state the grounds of my decision; I briefly signified my assent, and made instant preparation to carry the plan into execution.

Having passed on the line of the Pacific Railway more than once, I was perfectly familiar with all of its windings, gorges and precipices.

I selected Cape Horn as the best adapted to the purpose, and . . . the public knows the rest.

Having been fully acquitted by two tribunals of the law, I make this final appeal to my fellow-men throughout the State, and ask them confidently not to reverse the judgments already pronounced.

I am conscious of no guilt; I feel no remorse; I need no repentance. For me justice has no terrors, and conscience no sting. Let me be judged solely by the motives which actuated me, and the importance of the end accomplished, and I shall pass, unscathed, both temporal and eternal tribunals.

LEONIDAS PARKER.

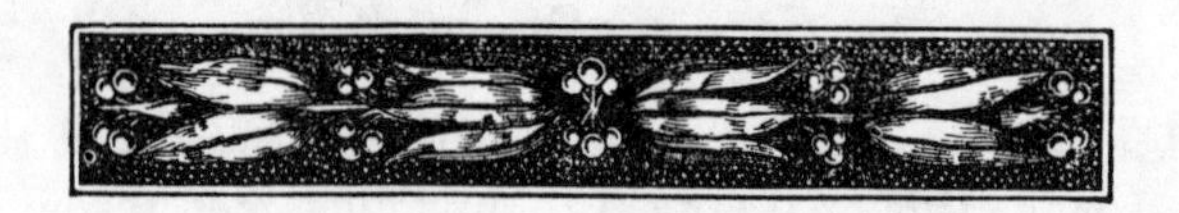

II.

THE MERCHANT'S EXCHANGE.

ONE summer eve, as homeward saunt'ring slowly,
  My toils and tasks for that day's business done;
With thoughts composed, and aspirations holy,
  That heavenward rose, as downward sank the sun,
I heard a throng, whose multitudinous voices
  Proclaimed some act of public weal begun.

The glad acclaim invited close inspection;
  And through the crowd I gently made my way,
Till, standing firm upon a light projection,
  That spanned a chasm dug deep into the clay,
I heard above the din of city noises,
  An honored voice, in solemn accents say:

" In presence of Creation's awful Builder,
  I lay for you this polished corner-stone;
God grant no ills your architect bewilder
  Till into strength and beauty shall have grown
The MERCHANT'S 'CHANGE that shall adorn your Guilder
  When ye have mouldered into dust and bone!"

Day after day, whilst passing to my labor,
  I saw that gorgeous edifice arise;
Until its dome, like crest of sacred Tabor,
  Sprang from the earth, and arching in the skies,
O'ertopp'd the peak of each aspiring neighbor
  That wooed a tribute from the upturned eyes.

There was no pomp of pious dedication,
  Boasting this Temple sanctified to God;

And yet my soul, in prayerful meditation,
 Believed no less it might be His abode:
For when His arm from bondage led a nation,
 He heard their cry, though kneeling on the sod!

Around this mart the world's great trade shall centre;
 Within these walls a Babel tumult sound,
Not that which made doomed Shinar a memento
 Of human pride laid level to the ground,
But blended music of all tongues shall enter,
 And in trade's peaceful symphonies resound!

Above this portal shall no monarch thunder,
 No grand patrician lord it o'er a slave;
Here shall the pagan's bonds be snapt asunder,
 And creed and race no proud distinction crave;
Here shall mankind their shackles trample under,
 And freedom's banner over freemen wave!

Here shall Confucius braid his ebon tresses,
 Perfume the cup with aromatic teas,
Supply gay beauty with her gaudiest dresses,—
 The worm's fine fabric, and the Bactrian fleece;
And in exchange shall quaff a balm that blesses,
 Freedom and truth, in every passing breeze!

Here Kamehameha realize the splendor
 Foretold by sirens, singing 'round his isles,
How cane and pulu be the realm's defender,
 And roof his palaces with golden tiles;—
When sturdy Saxons should their hearts surrender
 In captive bonds to coy Kanaka wiles!

Here Petropaulowski store her richest sables,
 Tahiti waft her oranges and limes,
The Lascar weave his stout manila cables,
 The Malay chafler midst his porcelain chimes,
Ceylon with spices scent our groaning tables,
 Pariah bring Golconda's gems, not crimes;

Beneath this dome the Tycoon's gory dragon
  Shall fold his wings, and close his fiery eyes;
Here quaffing from the same enchanted flagon,
  Fraternal incense shall to Heaven arise;
Whilst Vishnu, Thor, Jehovah, Bhudd, and Dagon,
  Shall cease all strife, and struggle for the prize!

Oh! tell me not the Christian's God will thunder,
  And rock these hills, with unforgiving ire;
By storm or earthquake rend the globe asunder,
  And quench His wrath in everliving fire—
When He beholds on earth so strange a wonder,
  All peoples kneeling to a common Sire!

Prophets and priests have from primeval ages
  Drenched all mankind in seas of human gore;
Jurists and statesmen, orators and sages,
  Have deepened gulfs, which boundless were before;
The merchant sails, where'er an ocean rages,
  Bridges its depths, and throws the Rainbow o'er!

All hail! ye founders of Pacific's glory,
  Who serve bold Commerce at his mightiest shrine:
Your names shall live in endless song and story,
  When black Oblivion flings her pall o'er mine;
And when these walls shall totter, quaint and hoary,
  Bards still shall sing, your mission was Divine!

III.

THE DESERTED SCHOOLHOUSE.

"Oh! never may a son of thine,
Where'er his wand'ring steps incline,
Forget the sky which bent above
His childhood, like a dream of love."

—WHITTIER.

THERE is no silence like that sombre gloom which sometimes settles down upon the deserted playgrounds, the unoccupied benches, and the voiceless halls of an old schoolhouse. But if, in addition to abandonment, the fingers of decay have been busy with their work; if the moss has been permitted to grow, and the mould to gather; if the cobwebs cluster, like clouds, in all the corners, and the damp dust incrusts the windowpanes like the frosts of a northern winter; if the old well has caved in, and the little paths through the brushwood been smothered, and the fences rotted down, and the stile gone to ruin, then a feeling of utter desolation seizes upon the soul, which no philosophy can master, no recollections soothe, and no lapse of time dissipate.

Perchance a lonely wanderer may be observed, traversing the same scenes which many years ago were trodden by his ungrown feet, looking pensively at each tree which sheltered his boyhood, peeping curiously under the broken benches on which he once sat, and turning over most carefully with his cane every scrap of old paper, that strangely enough had survived the winds and the rains of many winters.

Such a schoolhouse now stands near the little village of Woodville, in the State of North Carolina, and such a wanderer was I in the autumn of 1852.

Woodville was the scene of my first studies, my earliest adventures, and my nascent loves. There I was taught to read and write, to swim and skate, to wrestle and box, to play marbles and make love. There I fought my first fight, had the mumps and the measles, stole my first watermelon, and received my first flogging. And I can never forget, that within that tattered schoolroom my young heart first swelled with those budding passions, whose full development in others has so often changed the fortunes of the world. There eloquence produced its first throb, ambition struck its first spark, pride mounted its first stilts, love felt its first glow. There the eternal ideas of God and heaven, of patriotism and country, of love and woman, germinated in my bosom; and there, too, Poesy sang her first song in my enchanted ear, lured me far off into the "grand old woods" alone, sported with the unlanguaged longings of my boyish heart, and subdued me for the first time with that mysterious sorrow, whose depths the loftiest intellect cannot sound, and yet whose wailings mournfully agitate many a schoolboy's breast.

I reached the village of Woodville one afternoon in November, after an absence of twenty-two years. Strange faces greeted me, instead of old, familiar ones; huge dwellings stood where once I had rambled through cornfields, groves of young pines covered the old common in which I had once played at ball, and everything around presented such an aspect of change, that I almost doubted my personal identity. Nor was my astonishment diminished in the slightest degree when the landlord of the inn announced his name, and I recognized it as once belonging to a playmate famous for mischief and fleetness. Now he appeared bloated, languid, and prematurely old. Bushy whiskers nearly covered his face, a horrid gash almost closed up one of his eyes, and an ominous limp told that he would run no more foot-races forever.

Unwilling to provoke inquiries by mentioning my own name, and doubly anxious to see the old schoolhouse, which I had traveled many miles out of my way to visit, I took my cane and strolled leisurely along the road that my feet had hurried over so often in boyhood.

The schoolhouse was situated in a small grove of oaks and hickories, about half a mile from the village, so as to be more retired, but at the same time more convenient for those who resided in the country. My imagination flew faster than my steps, and under its influence the half mile dwindled to a mere rod. Passing a turn in the road, which concealed it until within a few paces, it suddenly burst upon my vision in all the horrors of its desolation. A fearful awe took possession of me, and as I stood beneath the trees I had so often climbed in years gone by, I could not refrain from looking uneasily behind me, and treading more softly upon the sacred leaves, just commencing to wither and fall.

I approached the door with as much reverence as ever crept Jew or Mussulman, on bended knee and with downcast eye, to the portals of the Kabbala or Holy of Holies, and as I reached forth my hand to turn the latch, I involuntarily paused to listen before I crossed the threshold.

Ah, manhood! what are all thy triumphs compared to a schoolboy's palms! What are thy infamies compared to his disgraces! As head of his class, he carries a front which a monarch might emulate in vain; as master of the playground, he wields a sceptre more indisputable than Czar or Cæsar ever bore! As a favorite, he provokes a bitterer hostility than ever greeted a Bute or a Buckingham; as a coward or traitor, he is loaded with a contumely beneath which Arnold or Hull would have sunk forever!

I listened. The pleasant hum of busy voices, the sharp tones of the master, the mumbled accents of hurried recitations, all were gone. The gathering shadows of evening corresponded most fittingly with the deepening gloom of my recollections, and I abandoned myself to their guidance, without an effort to control or direct them.

I stood *alone* upon the step. Where was he, whose younger hand always locked in mine, entered that room and left it so often by my side; that bright-eyed boy, whose quick wit and genial temper won for him the affections both of master and scholar; that gentle spirit that kindled into love, or saddened into tears, as easily as sunshine dallies with a flower or raindrops fall from a summer cloud; that brother, whose genius was my pride, whose courage my admiration, whose soul my glory; he who faltered not before the walls of Camargo, when but seven men, out of as many hundred in his regiment, volunteered to go forward, under the command of Taylor, to endure all the hardships of a soldier's life, in a tropical clime, and to brave all the dangers of a three days' assault upon a fortified city; he who fought so heroically at Monterey, and escaped death in so many forms on the battle-field, only to meet it at last as a victim to contagion, contracted at the bedside of a friend? Where was he? The swift waters of the Rio Grande, as they hurry past his unsculptured grave, sing his requiem, and carry along proudly to the everlasting sea the memory of his noble self sacrifice, as the purest tribute they bear upon their tide!

Such were my thoughts, as I stood pensively upon the block that served as a step when I was boy, and which still occupied its ancient position. I noticed that a large crack extended its whole length, and several shrubs, of no insignificant size, were growing out of the aperture. This prepared me for the wreck and ruin of the interior. The door had been torn from its hinge, and was sustained in an upright position by a bar or prop on the inside. This readily gave way on a slight pressure, and as the old door tumbled headlong upon the floor, it awoke a thousand confused and muffled echoes, more startling to me than a clap of the loudest thunder. But the moment I passed the threshold, the gloom and terror instantly vanished. I noticed that the back door was open, and in casting my glance to the upper end of the room, where the Rev. Mr. Craig once presided in state, my eyes were greeted by an apparition, that had evidently become domiciliated in the premises, and whose appearance revolutionized the whole tenor of my thoughts. Before me stood one of those venerable-looking billy-goats, of sedate eye, fantastic beard, and crumpled horn, the detestation of perfumed belle, and the dread of mischievous urchin. I had seen a *fac-simile* of him many years before, not exactly in the same place, but hard by in a thicket of pines. I could almost fancy it to be the ghost of the murdered ancestor, or some phantom sent to haunt me near the spot of his execution. I shed no tear, I heaved no sigh, as I trod the dust-covered floor of the "Woodville Academy," but greeted my *Alma Mater* with a shout of almost boyish laughter as I approached the spot where the pedagogue once sat upon his throne.

To explain why it was that my feelings underwent a revulsion so sudden, I must relate the Story of the Murdered Billy-goat.

Colonel Averitt, a brave soldier in the war of 1812, retired from the army at the termination of hostilities, and settled upon a farm adjoining the village of Woodville. He was rather a queer old gentleman; had a high Roman nose, and, on muster days, was the general admiration of all Bertie County. He then officiated as colonel commandant of militia, and dressed in full uniform, with a tall, white feather waving most belligerently from his three-cornered cocked hat. He wore a sash and sword, and always reviewed the troops on horseback.

One day, after a statutory review of the militia of the county, a proposition was started to form a volunteer company of mounted hussars. A nucleus was soon obtained, and in less than a week a sufficient number had enrolled themselves to authorize the Colonel to order a drill. It happened on a Saturday; the place selected was an old field near the schoolhouse, and I need not add that the entire battalion of boys was out in full force, as spectators of the warlike exercises. How they got through with the parade, I have forgotten; but I do remember that the mania for soldiering, from that day forward, took possession of the school.

The enrollment at first consisted entirely of infantry, and several weeks elapsed before anybody ventured to suggest a mounted corps. Late one afternoon, however, as we were returning homeward, with drums beating and colors flying, we disturbed a flock of lazy goats, browsing upon dry grass, and evincing no great dread for the doughty warriors advancing. Our captain, whose dignity was highly offended at this utter want of respect, gave the order to "form column!" "present arms!" and "charge!" Austrian nor Spaniard, Italian nor Prussian, before the resistless squadrons of Murat or Macdonald, ever displayed finer qualities of light infantry or flying artillery, than did the vanquished enemy of the "Woodville Cadets" on this memorable occasion. They were taken entirely by surprise, and, without offering the least resistance, right-about-faced, and fled precipitously from the field. Their terrified bleating mingled fearfully with our shouts of victory; and when, at the command of our captain, I blew the signal to halt and rendezvous, our brave fellows magnanimously gave up the pursuit, and returned from the chase, bringing with them no less than five full-grown prisoners, as trophies of victory!

A council of war was immediately called, to determine in what way we should dispose of our booty. After much learned discussion, and some warm disputes, the propositions were narrowed down to two:

Plan the first was, to cut off all the beard of each prisoner, flog, and release him.

Plan the second, on the contrary, was, to conduct the prisoners to the playground, treat them kindly, and endeavor to train them to the bit and saddle, so as to furnish the officers with what they needed so much,—war-steeds for battle, fiery chargers for review.

The vote was finally taken, and plan number two was adopted by a considerable majority.

Obstacles are never insurmountable to boys and Bonapartes! Our *coup d'etat* succeeded quite as well as that of the 2d of December, and before a week elapsed the chief officers were all splendidly mounted and fully equipped.

At this stage of the war against the "bearded races,"

the cavalry question was propounded by one of the privates in Company A. For his part, he declared candidly that he was tired of marching and countermarching afoot, and that he saw no good reason why an invasion of the enemy's country should not at once be undertaken, to secure animals enough to mount the whole regiment.

Another council was held, and the resolve unanimously adopted, to cross the border in full force, on the next Saturday afternoon.

In the meantime, the clouds of war began to thicken in another quarter. Colonel Averitt had been informed of the *coup d'etat* related above, and determined to prevent any further depredations on his flock by a stroke of masterly generalship, worthy of his prowess in the late war with Great Britain.

And now it becomes proper to introduce upon the scene the most important personage in this history, and the hero of the whole story. I allude, of course, to the bold, calm, dignified, undaunted and imperturbable natural guardian of the Colonel's fold—Billy Goat!

He boasted of a beard longer, whiter, and more venerable than a high-priest in Masonry; his mane emulated that of the king of beasts; his horns were as crooked, and almost as long, as the Cashie River, on whose banks he was born; his tail might have been selected by some Spanish hidalgo, as a coat of arms, emblematic of the pride and hauteur of his family; whilst his *tout ensemble* presented that dignity of demeanor, majesty of carriage, consciousness of superior fortune, and defiance of all danger, which we may imagine characterized the elder Napoleon previous to the battle of Waterloo. But our hero possessed moral qualities quite equal to his personal traits. He was brave to a fault, combative to a miracle, and as invincible in battle as he was belligerent in mood. The sight of a coat-tail invariably excited his anger, and a red handkerchief nearly distracted him with rage. Indeed, he had recently grown so irascible that Colonel Averitt was compelled to keep him shut up in the fowl-yard, a close prisoner, to protect him from a justly indignant neighborhood.

Such was the champion that the Colonel now released and placed at the head of the opposing forces. Saturday came at last, and the entire morning was devoted to the construction of the proper number of wooden bits, twine bridle-reins, leather stirrups and pasteboard saddles. By twelve o'clock everything was ready, and the order given to march. We were disappointed in not finding the enemy at his accustomed haunt, and had to prolong our march nearly half a mile before we came up with him. Our scouts, however, soon discovered him in an old field, lying encamped beneath some young persimmon bushes, and entirely unconscious of impending danger. We approached stealthily, according to our usual plan, and then at a concerted signal rushed headlong upon the foe. But we had no sooner given the alarm than our enemies sprang to their feet, and clustered about a central object, which we immediately recognized, to our chagrin and terror, as none other than Billy Goat himself.

The captain, however, was not to be daunted or foiled; he boldly made a plunge at the champion of our adversaries, and would have succeeded in seizing him by the horns, if he had not been unfortunately butted over before he could reach them. Two or three of our bravest comrades flew to his assistance, but met with the same fate before they could rescue him from danger. The remainder of us drew off a short but prudent distance from the field of battle, to hold a council of war, and determine upon a plan of operations. In a few moments our wounded companions joined us, and entreated us to close at once upon the foe and surround him. They declared they were not afraid to beard the lion in his den, and that being butted heels over head two or three times but whetted their courage, and incited them to deeds of loftier daring. Their eloquence, however, was more admired than their prudence, and a large majority of the council decided that "it was inopportune, without other munitions of war than those we had upon the field, to risk a general engagement." It was agreed, however, *nem. con.*, that on the next Saturday we would provide ourselves with ropes and fishing-poles, and such other arms as might prove advantageous, and proceed to surround and noose our most formidable enemy, overpower him by the force of numbers, and take him prisoner at all hazards. Having fully determined upon this plan of attack, we hoisted our flag once more, ordered the drum to beat Yankee Doodle, and retreated in most excellent order from the field—our foe not venturing to pursue us.

The week wore slowly and uneasily away. The clouds of war were gathering rapidly, and the low roll of distant thunder announced that a battle storm of no ordinary importance was near at hand. Colonel Averitt, by some traitorous trick of war, had heard of our former defeat, and publicly taunted our commander with his failure. Indeed, more than one of the villagers had heard of the disastrous result of the campaign, and sent impertinent messages to those who had been wounded in the encounter. Two or three of the young ladies, also, in the girls' department, had been inoculated with the *fun* (as it was absurdly denominated), and a leather medal was pinned most provokingly to the short jacket of the captain by one of those hoydenish Amazons.

All these events served to whet the courage of our men, and strange as it may appear, to embitter our hostility to our victorious foe. Some of the officers proceeded so far as to threaten Colonel Averitt himself, and at one time, I am confident, he stood in almost as much danger as the protector of his flock.

Saturday came at last, and at the first blast of the bugle, we formed into line, and advanced with great alacrity into the enemy's country. After marching half an hour, our scouts hastily returned, with the information that the enemy was drawn up, in full force, near the scene of the Persimmon bush battle. We advanced courageously to within speaking distance, and then halted to breathe the troops and prepare for the engagement. We surveyed our enemies with attention, but without alarm. There they stood right before us!

> "Firm paced and slow, a horrid front they form;
> Still as the breeze, but dreadful as the storm!"

Our preparations were soon made, and at the command of the captain, we separated into single files, one half making a *detour* to the right, and the other to the left, so as to encircle the foe. Our instructions were to spare all non-combatants, to pass by as unworthy of notice all minor foes, and to make a simultaneous rush upon the proud champion of our adversaries.

By this masterly manœuvre it was supposed we should be enabled to escape unharmed, or at any rate without many serious casualties. But as it afterward appeared, we did not sufficiently estimate the strength and activity of our enemy.

After this preparatory manœuvre had been successfully accomplished, our captain gave the order to "charge!" in a stentorian voice, and at the same time rushed forward most gallantly at the head of the squadron. The post of honor is generally the post of danger also, and so it proved on this occasion; for before the captain could grapple with the foe, Billy Goat rose suddenly on his hinder legs, and uttering a loud note of defiance, dashed with lightning speed at the breast of our commander, and at a single blow laid him prostrate on the field. Then wheeling quickly, ere any of his assailants could attack his rear flank, he performed the same exploit upon the first and second lieutenants, and made an unsuccessful pass at the standard bearer, who eluded the danger by a scientific retreat. At this moment, when the fortunes of the day hung, as it were, on a single hair, our drummer, who enjoyed the *sobriquet* of "Weasel," advanced slowly but chivalrously upon the foe.

As the hosts of Israel and Gath paused upon the field of Elah, and awaited with fear and trembling the issue of the single-handed contest between David and Goliah; as Roman and Sabine stood back and reposed on their arms, whilst Horatio and Curiatii fought for the destiny of Rome and the mastery of the world, so the "Woodville Cadets" halted in their tracks on this memorable day, and all aghast with awe and admiration, watched the prŏgress of the terrible duello between "Weasel," the drummer boy, and Billy Goat, the hero of the battle of the Persimmon bush.

The drummer first disengaged himself from the incumbrance of his martial music, then threw his hat fiercely upon the ground, and warily and circumspectly approached his foe. Nor was that foe unprepared, for rearing as usual on his nether extremities, he bleated out a long note of contempt and defiance, and dashed suddenly upon the "Weasel."

Instead of waiting to receive the force of the blow upon

his breast or brow, the drummer wheeled right-about face, and falling suddenly upon all fours with most surprising dexterity, presented a less vulnerable part of his body to his antagonist, who, being under full headway, was compelled to accept the substituted buttress, and immediately planted there a herculean thump. I need not say that the drummer was hurled many feet heels over head, by this disastrous blow; but he had obtained the very advantage he desired to secure, and springing upon his feet he leaped quicker than lightning upon the back of his foe, and in spite of every effort to dislodge him, sat there in security and triumph!

With a loud huzza, the main body of the "Cadets" now rushed forward, and after a feeble resistance, succeeded in overpowering the champion of our foes.

As a matter of precaution, we blindfolded him with several handkerchiefs, and led him away in as much state as the Emperor Aurelian displayed when he carried Zenobia to Rome, a prisoner at his chariot-wheels.

The fate of the vanquished Billy Goat is soon related. A council of war decided that he should be taken into a dense pine thicket, there suspended head downwards, and thrashed *ad libitum*, by the whole army.

The sentence was carried into execution immediately; and though he was cut down and released after our vengeance was satisfied, I yet owe it to truth and history to declare, that before a week elapsed, he died of a broken heart, and was buried by Colonel Averitt with all the honors of war.

If it be any satisfaction to the curious inquirer, I may add in conclusion, that the Rev. Mr. Craig avenged his *manes*, by wearing out a chinquapin apiece on the backs of "Weasel," the captain and officers, and immediately afterward disbanded the whole army.

IV.

FOR AN ALBUM.

WHEN first our father, Adam, sinned
  Against the will of Heaven,
And forth from Eden's happy gates
  A wanderer was driven,
He paused beside a limpid brook,
  That through the garden ran,
And, gazing in its mirrored wave,
  Beheld himself—*a man!*

God's holy peace no longer beamed
  In brightness from his eye;
But in its depths dark passions blazed,
  Like lightnings in the sky.
Young Innocence no longer wreathed
  His features with her smile;
But Sin sat there in scorched dismay,
  Like some volcanic isle.

No longer radiant beauty shone
  Upon his manly brow;
But care had traced deep furrows there,
  With stern misfortune's plow.
Joy beamed no longer from his face;
  His step was sad and slow;
His heart was heavy with its grief;
  His bosom with its woe.

Whilst gazing at his altered form
  Within the mirrored brook,
He spied an angel leaning o'er,
  With pity in her look.

He turned, distrustful of his sight,
  Unwilling to believe,
When, lo! in Heaven's own radiance smiled,
  His sweet companion, Eve!

Fondly he clasped her to his heart,
  And blissfully he cried,
"What tho' I've lost a Paradise,
  I've gained an angel bride!
No flowers in Eden ever bloomed,
  No! not in heaven above,
Sweeter than woman brings to man—
  Her friendship, truth, and love!"

These buds were brought by Adam's bride,
  Outside of Eden's gate,
And scattered o'er the world; *to them*
  This book I dedicate.

V.

PHASES IN THE LIFE OF JOHN POLLEXFEN.

PHASE THE FIRST.

THERE are but three persons now living who can truthfully answer the question, "How did John Pollexfen, the photographer, make his fortune?"

No confidence will be violated, now that he is dead, and his heirs residents of a foreign country, if I relate the story of that singular man, whose rapid accumulation of wealth astonished the whole circle of his acquaintance.

Returning from the old man's funeral a few days since, the subject of Pollexfen's discoveries became the topic of conversation; and my companions in the same carriage, aware that, as his attorney and confidential friend, I knew more of the details of his business than any one else, extorted from me a promise that at the first leisure moment I would relate, in print, the secret of that curious invention by which the photographic art was so largely enriched, and himself elevated at once to the acme of opulence and renown.

Few persons who were residents of the city of San Francisco at an early day, will fail to remember the site of the humble gallery in which Pollexfen laid the foundations of his fame. It was situated on Merchant Street, about midway between Kearny and Montgomery Streets, in an old wooden building; the ground being occupied at present by the solid brick structure of Thomas R. Bolton. It fed the flames of the great May fire of 1851, was rebuilt, but again consumed in December, 1853. It was during the fall of the latter year that the principal event took place which is to constitute the most prominent feature of my narrative.

I am aware that the facts will be discredited by many, and doubted at first by all; but I beg to premise, at the outset, that because they are uncommon, by no means proves that they are untrue. Besides, should the question ever become a judicial one, I hold in my hands such *written proofs*, signed by the parties most deeply implicated, as will at once terminate both doubt and litigation. Of this, however, I have at present no apprehensions; for Lucile and her husband are both too honorable to assail the reputation of the dead, and too rich themselves to attempt to pillage the living.

As it is my wish to be distinctly understood, and at the same time to be exculpated from all blame for the part I myself acted in the drama, the story must commence with my first acquaintance with Mademoiselle Lucile Marmont.

In the spring of 1851, I embarked at New York for Panama, or rather Chagres, on board the steamship "Ohio," Captain Schenck, on my way to the then distant coast of California, attracted hither by the universal desire to accumulate a rapid fortune, and return at the earliest practicable period to my home, on the Atlantic seaboard.

There were many hundred such passengers on the same ship. But little sociability prevailed, until after the steamer left Havana, where it was then the custom to touch on the "outward bound," to obtain a fresh supply of fuel and provisions. We were detained longer than customary at Havana, and most of the passengers embraced the opportunity to visit the Bishop's Garden and the tomb of Columbus.

One morning, somewhat earlier than usual, I was standing outside the railing which incloses the monument of the great discoverer, and had just transcribed in my note-book the following epitaph:

> "O! Restos y Imagen
> Del Grande Colon:
> Mil siglos durad guardados
> En lare Urna,
> Y en la Remembranza
> De Nuestra Nacion,"

when I was suddenly interrupted by a loud scream directly behind me. On turning, I beheld a young lady whom I had seen but once before on the steamer, leaning over the prostrate form of an elderly female, and applying such restoratives as were at hand to resuscitate her, for she had fainted. Seeing me, the daughter exclaimed, "*Oh, Monsieur! y-a-t-il un medecin ici?*" I hastened to the side of the mother, and was about to lift her from the pavement, when M. Marmont himself entered the cathedral. I assisted him in placing his wife in a *volante* then passing, and she was safely conveyed to the hotel.

Having myself some knowledge of both French and Spanish, and able to converse in either tongue, Lucile Marmont, then sixteen years of age, and I, from that time forward, became close and confidential friends.

The steamer sailed the next day, and in due time anchored off the roadstead of Chagres. But Mme. Marmont, in the last stages of consumption when she embarked at New York, continued extremely ill until we passed Point Concepcion, on this coast, when she suddenly expired from an attack of hemorrhage of the lungs.

She was buried at sea; and never can I forget the unutterable anguish of poor Lucile, as her mother's body splashed into the cold blue waters of the Pacific. There she stood, holding on to the railing, paler than monumental marble, motionless as a statue, rigid as a corpse. The whole scene around her seemed unperceived. Her eyes gazed upon vacancy; her head was thrust slightly forward, and her disheveled tresses, black as Plutonian night, fell neglected about her shoulders.

Captain Watkins, then commanding the "Panama" —whom, may God bless—wept like a child; and his manly voice, that never quailed in the dread presence of the lightning or the hurricane, broke, chokingly, as he attempted to finish the burial rite, and died away in agitated sobs.

One by one the passengers left the spot, consecrated to the grief of that only child—now more than orphaned by her irreparable loss. Lifting my eyes, at last, none save the daughter and her father stood before me. Charmed to the spot was I, by a spell that seemed irresistible. Scarcely able to move a muscle, there I remained, speechless and overpowered. Finally the father spoke, and then Lucile fell headlong into his arms. He bore her into his state-room, where the ship's surgeon was summoned, and where he continued his ministrations until we reached this port.

It is scarcely necessary to add, that I attended them ashore, and saw them safely and commodiously lodged at the old Parker House, before I once thought of my own accommodations.

Weeks passed, and months, too, stole gradually away, before I saw anything more of the bereaved and mourning child. One day, however, as I was lolling carelessly in my office, after business hours (and that meant just at dark in those early times), Lucile hastily entered. I was startled to see her; for upon her visage I thought I beheld the same stolid spell of agony that some months before had transfixed my very soul. Before I had time to recover myself, or ask her to be seated, she approached closer, and said in a half whisper, "Oh, sir, come with me home."

On our way she explained that her father was lying dangerously ill, and that she knew no physician to whom she could apply, and in whose skill she could place confidence. I at once recommended Dr. H. M. White (since dead), well knowing not only his great success, but equally cognizant of that universal charity that rendered him afterwards no less beloved than illustrious. Without a moment's hesitation, the Doctor seized his hat, and hastened along with us, to the wretched abode of the sick, and, as it afterwards proved, the palsied father. The disease was pronounced apoplexy, and recovery doubtful. Still, there was hope. Whilst we were seated around the bedside, a tall, emaciated, feeble, but very handsome young man entered, and staggered to a seat. He was coarsely and meanly clad; but there was something about him that not only betokened the gentleman, but the well-bred and accomplished scholar. As he seated himself, he exchanged a glance with Lucile, and in that silent look I read the future history of both their lives. On lifting my eyes toward hers, the pallor fled for an instant from her cheek, and a traitor blush flashed its crimson confession across her features.

The patient was copiously bled from an artery in the temple, and gradually recovered his consciousness, but on attempting to speak we ascertained that partial paralysis had resulted from the fit.

As I rose, with the Doctor, to leave, Lucile beckoned

me to remain, and approaching me more closely, whispered in French, "Stay, and I will tell you all." The main points of her story, though deeply interesting to me, at that time, were so greatly eclipsed by subsequent events, that they are scarcely worthy of narration. Indeed, I shall not attempt to detail them here fully, but will content myself with stating, in few words, only such events as bear directly upon the fortunes of John Pollexfen.

As intimated above, Lucile was an only child. She was born in Dauphiny, a province of France, and immigrated to America during the disastrous year 1848. Her father was exiled, and his estates seized by the officers of the government, on account of his political tenets. The family embarked at Marseilles, with just sufficient ready money to pay their passage to New York, and support them for a few months after their arrival. It soon became apparent that want, and perhaps starvation, were in store, unless some means of obtaining a livelihood could be devised. The sole expedient was music, of which M. Marmont was a proficient, and to this resource he at once applied himself most industriously. He had accumulated a sufficient sum to pay his expenses to this coast, up to the beginning of 1851, and took passage for San Francisco, as we have already seen, in the spring of that year.

Reaching here, he became more embarrassed every day, unacquainted as he was with the language, and still less with the wild life into which he was so suddenly plunged. Whilst poverty was pinching his body, grief for the loss of his wife was torturing his soul. Silent, sad, almost morose to others, his only delight was in his child. Apprehensions for her fate, in case of accident to himself, embittered his existence, and hastened the catastrophe above related. Desirous of placing her in a situation in which she could earn a livelihood, independent of his own precarious exertions, he taught her drawing and painting, and had just succeeded in obtaining for her the employment of coloring photographs at Pollexfen's gallery the very day he was seized with his fatal disorder.

Some weeks previous to this, Charles Courtland, the young man before mentioned, became an inmate of his house under the following circumstances:

One evening, after the performances at the Jenny Lind Theatre (where M. Marmont was employed) were over, and consequently very late, whilst he was pursuing his lonely way homewards he accidentally stumbled over an impediment in his path. He at once recognized it as a human body, and being near home, he lifted the senseless form into his house. A severe contusion behind the ear had been the cause of the young man's misfortune, and his robbery had been successfully accomplished whilst lying in a state of insensibility.

His recovery was extremely slow, and though watched by the brightest pair of eyes that ever shot their dangerous glances into a human soul, Courtland had not fully recovered his strength up to the time that I made his acquaintance.

He was a Virginian by birth; had spent two years in the mines on Feather River, and having accumulated a considerable sum of money, came to San Francisco to purchase a small stock of goods, with which he intended to open a store at Bidwell's Bar. His robbery frustrated all these golden dreams, and his capture by Lucile Marmont completed his financial ruin.

Here terminates the first phase in the history of John Pollexfen.

PHASE THE SECOND.

"Useless! useless! all useless!" exclaimed John Pollexfen, as he dashed a glass negative, which he had most elaborately prepared, into the slop-bucket. "Go, sleep with your predecessors." After a moment's silence, he again spoke: "But I know *it exists.* Nature has the secret locked up securely, as she thinks, but I'll tear it from her. Doesn't the eye see? Is not the retina impressible to the faintest gleam of light? What telegraphs to my soul the colors of the rainbow? Nothing but the eye, the human eye. And shall John Pollexfen be told, after he has lived half a century, that the compacted humors of this little organ can do more than his whole laboratory? By heaven! I'll wrest the secret from the labyrinth of nature, or pluck my own eyes from their sockets."

Thus soliloquized John Pollexfen, a few days after the events narrated in the last chapter.

He was seated at a table, in a darkened chamber, with a light burning, though in the middle of the day, and his countenance bore an unmistakable expression of disappointment, mingled with disgust, at the failure of his last experiment. He was evidently in an ill-humor, and seemed puzzled what to do next. Just then a light tap came at the door, and in reply to an invitation to enter, the pale, delicate features of Lucile Marmont appeared at the threshold.

"Oh! is it you, my child?" said the photographer, rising. "Let me see your touches." After surveying the painted photographs a moment, he broke out into a sort of artistic glee: "Beautiful! beautiful! an adept, quite an adept! Who taught you? Come, have no secrets from me; I'm an old man, and may be of service to you yet. What city artist gave you the cue?"

Before relating any more of the conversation, it becomes necessary to paint John Pollexfen as he was. Methinks I can see his tall, rawboned, angular form before me, even now, as I write these lines. There he stands, Scotch all over, from head to foot. It was whispered about in early times—for really no one knew much about his previous career—that John Pollexfen had been a famous sea captain; that he had sailed around the world many times; had visited the coast of Africa under suspicious circumstances, and finally found his way to California from the then unpopular region of Australia. Without pausing to trace these rumors further, it must be admitted that there was something in the appearance of the man sufficiently repulsive, at first sight, to give them currency. He had a large bushy head, profusely furnished with hair almost brickdust in color, and growing down upon a broad, low forehead, indicative of great mathematical and constructive power. His brows were long and shaggy, and overhung a restless, deep-set, cold, gray eye, that met the fiercest glance unquailingly, and seemed possessed of that magnetic power which dazzles, reads and confounds whatsoever it looks upon. There was no escape from its inquisitive glitter. It sounded the very depths of the soul it thought proper to search. Whilst gazing at you, instinct felt the glance before your own eye was lifted so as to encounter his. There was no human weakness in its expression. It was as pitiless as the gleam of the lightning. But you felt no less that high intelligence flashed from its depths. Courage, you knew, was there; and true bravery is akin to all the nobler virtues. This man, you at once said, may be cold, but it is impossible for him to be unjust, deceitful or ungenerous. He might, like Shylock, insist on a *right*, no matter how vindictive, but he would never forge a claim, no matter how insignificant. He might crush, like Cæsar, but he could never plot like Catiline. In addition to all this, it required but slight knowledge of physiognomy to perceive that his stern nature was tinctured with genuine enthusiasm. Earnestness beamed forth in every feature. His soul was as sincere as it was unbending. He could not trifle, even with the most inconsiderable subject. Laughter he abhorred. He could smile, but there was little contagion in his pleasantry. It surprised more than it pleased you. Blended with this deep, scrutinizing, earnest and enthusiastic nature, there was an indefinable something, shading the whole character—it might have been early sorrow, or loss of fortune, or baffled ambition, or unrequited love. Still, it shone forth patent to the experienced eye, enigmatical, mysterious, sombre. There was danger, also, in it, and many, who knew him best, attributed his eccentricity to a softened phase of insanity.

But the most marked practical trait of Pollexfen's character was his enthusiasm for his art. He studied its history, from the humble hints of Niépce to the glorious triumphs of Farquer, Bingham, and Bradley, with all the soul-engrossing fidelity of a child, and spent many a midnight hour in striving to rival or surpass them. It was always a subject of astonishment with me, until after his death, how it happened that a rough, athletic seaman, as people declared he was originally, should become so intensely absorbed in a science requiring delicacy of taste, and skill in manipulation rather than power of muscle, in its practical application. But after carefully examining the papers tied up in the same package with his last will and testament, I ceased to wonder, and sought no further for an explanation.

Most prominent amongst these carefully preserved documents was an old diploma, granted by the University of Edinburgh, in the year 1821, to "John Pollexfen, Gent., of Hallicardin, Perthshire," constituting him Doctor of Medicine. On the back of the diploma, written in a round, clear hand, I found indorsed as follows:

> Fifteen years of my life have I lost by professing modern quackery. Medicine is not a science, properly so called. It is at most but an art. He best succeeds who creates his own system. Each generation adopts its peculiar manual: Sangrado to-day; Thomson to-morrow; Hahnemann the day after. Surgery advances; physic is stationary. But chemistry, glorious chemistry, *is* a science. Born amid dissolving ruins, and cradled upon rollers of fire, her step is onward. At her side, as an humble menial, henceforth shall be found
>
> JOHN POLLEXFEN.

The indorsement bore no date, but it must have been written long before his immigration to California.

Let us now proceed with the interview between the photographer and his employee. Repeating the question quickly, "Who gave you the cue?" demanded Pollexfen.

"My father taught me drawing and painting, but my own taste suggested the coloring."

"Do you mean to tell me, really, that you taught yourself, Mlle. Marmont?" and as he said this, the cold, gray eye lit up with unwonted brilliancy.

"What I say is true," replied the girl, and elevating her own lustrous eyes,. they encountered his own, with a glance quite as steady.

"Let us go into the sunlight, and examine the tints more fully;" and leading the way they emerged into the sitting-room where customers were in the habit of awaiting the artist's pleasure.

Here the pictures were again closely scrutinized, but

far more accurately than before; and after fully satisfying his curiosity on the score of the originality of the penciling, approached Lucile very closely, and darting his wonderful glance into the depths of her own eyes, said, after a moment's pause, "You have glorious eyes."

Lucile was about to protest, in a hurried way, against such adulation, when he continued: "Nay, nay, do not deny it. Your eyes are the most fathomless orbs that ever I beheld—large, too, and lustrous—the very eyes I have been searching for these five years past. A judge of color; a rare judge of color! How is your father to-day, my child?"

The tone of voice in which this last remark was made had in it more of the curious than the tender. It seemed to have been propounded more as a matter of business than of feeling. Still, Lucile replied respectfully, "Oh! worse, sir; a great deal worse. Doctor White declares that it is impossible for him to recover, and that he cannot live much longer."

"Not live?" replied Pollexfen, "not live?" Then, as if musing, he solemnly added, "When your father is dead, Lucile, come to me, and I will make your fortune. That is, if you follow my advice, and place yourself exclusively under my instructions. Nay, but you shall earn it yourself. See!" he exclaimed, and producing a bank deposit-book from his pocket, "See! here have I seven thousand five hundred dollars in bank, and I would gladly exchange it for one of your eyes."

Astonishment overwhelmed the girl, and she could make no immediate reply; and before she had sufficiently recovered her self-possession to speak, the photographer hastily added, "Don't wonder; farewell, now. Remember what I have said—seven thousand five hundred dollars just for one eye!"

Lucile was glad to escape, without uttering a syllable. Pursuing her way homewards, she pondered deeply over the singular remark with which Pollexfen closed the conversation, and half muttering, said to herself, "Can he be in earnest? or is it simply the odd way in which an eccentric man pays a compliment?" But long before she could solve the enigma, other thoughts, far more engrossing, took sole possession of her mind.

She fully realized her situation—a dying father, and a sick lover, both dependent in a great measure upon her exertions, and she herself not yet past her seventeenth year.

On reaching home she found the door wide open, and Courtland standing in the entrance, evidently awaiting her arrival. As she approached, their eyes met, and a glance told her that all was over.

"Dead!" softly whispered Courtland.

A stifled sob was all that broke from the lips of the child, as she fell lifeless into the arms of her lover.

I pass over the mournful circumstances attending the funeral of the exiled Frenchman. He was borne to his grave by a select few of his countrymen, whose acquaintance he had made during his short residence in this city. Like thousands of others, who have perished in our midst, he died, and "left no sign." The newspapers published the item the next morning, and before the sun had set upon his funeral rites the poor man was forgotten by all except the immediate persons connected with this narrative.

To one of them, at least, his death was not only an important event, but it formed a great epoch in her history.

Lucile was transformed, in a moment of time, from a helpless, confiding, affectionate girl, into a full-grown, self-dependent, imperious woman. Such revolutions, I know, are rare in everyday life, and but seldom occur; in fact, they never happen except in those rare instances where nature has stamped a character with the elements of inborn originality and force, which accident, or sudden revulsion, develops at once into full maturity. To such a soul, death of an only parent operates like the summer solstice upon the winter snow of Siberia. It melts away the weakness and credulity of childhood almost miraculously, and exhibits, with the suddenness of an apparition, the secret and hitherto unknown traits that will forever afterwards distinguish the individual. The explanation of this curious moral phenomenon consists simply in bringing to the surface what already was in existence below; not in the instantaneous creation of new elements of character. The tissues were already there; circumstance hardens them into bone. Thus we sometimes behold the same marvel produced by the marriage of some characterless girl, whom we perhaps had known from infancy, and whose individuality we had associated with cake, or crinoline—a gay humming-bird of social life, so light and frivolous and unstable, that, as she flitted across our pathway, we scarcely deigned her the compliment of a thought. Yet a week or a month after her nuptials, we meet the self-same warbler, not as of old, beneath the paternal roof, but under her own "vine and fig-tree," and in astonishment we ask ourselves, "Can this be the bread-and-butter Miss we passed by with the insolence of a sneer, a short time ago?" Behold her now! On her brow sits womanhood. Upon her features beam out palpably traits of great force and originality. She moves with the majesty of a queen, and astounds us by taking a leading part in the discussion of questions of which we did not deem she ever dreamed. What a transformation is here! Has nature proven false to herself? Is this a miracle? Are all her laws suspended, that she might transform, in an instant, a puling trifler into a perfect woman? Not so, oh! doubter. Not nature is false, but you are yourself ignorant of her laws. Study Shakspeare; see Gloster woo, and win, the defiant, revengeful and embittered Lady Anne, and confess in your humility that it is far more probable that you should err, than that Shakspeare should be mistaken.

Not many days after the death of M. Marmont, it was agreed by all the friends of Lucile, that the kind offer extended to her by Pollexfen should be accepted, and that she should become domiciliated in his household. He was unmarried, it is true, but still he kept up an establishment. His housekeeper was a dear old lady, Scotch, like her master, but a direct contrast in every trait of her character. Her duties were not many, nor burdensome. Her time was chiefly occupied in family matters—cooking, washing, and feeding the pets—so that it was but seldom she made her appearance in any other apartment than those entirely beneath her own supervision.

The photographer had an assistant in his business, a Chinaman; and upon him devolved the task of caring for the outer offices.

Courtland, with a small stock of money, and still smaller modicum of health, left at once for Bidwell's Bar, where he thought of trying his fortune once more at mining, and where he was well and most cordially known.

It now only remained to accompany Lucile to her new home, to see her safely ensconced in her new quarters, to speak a flattering word in her favor to Pollexfen, and then, to bid her farewell, perhaps forever. All this was duly accomplished, and with good-bye on my lips, and a sorrowful sympathy in my heart, I turned away from the closing door of the photographer, and wended my way homewards.

Mademoiselle Marmont was met at the threshold by Martha McClintock, the housekeeper, and ushered at once into the inner apartment, situated in the rear of the gallery.

After removing her veil and cloak, she threw herself into an arm-chair, and shading her eyes with both her hands, fell into a deep reverie. She had been in that attitude but a few moments, when a large Maltese cat leaped boldly into her lap, and began to court familiarity by purring and playing, as with an old acquaintance. Lucile cast a casual glance at the animal, and noticed immediately that it had but *one eye!* Expressing no astonishment, but feeling a great deal, she cast her eyes cautiously around the apartment.

Near the window hung a large tin cage, containing a blue African parrot, with crimson-tipped shoulders and tail. At the foot of the sofa, a silken-haired spaniel was quietly sleeping, whilst, outside the window, a bright little canary was making the air melodious with its happy warbling. A noise in an adjoining room aroused the dog, and set it barking. As it lifted its glossy ears and turned its graceful head toward Lucile, her surprise was enhanced in the greatest degree, by perceiving that it, too, had lost an eye. Rising, she approached the window, impelled by a curiosity that seemed irresistible. Peering into the cage, she coaxed the lazy parrot to look at her, and her amazement was boundless when she observed that the poor bird was marred in the same mournful manner. Martha witnessed her astonishment, and indulged in a low laugh, but said nothing. At this moment Pollexfen himself entered the apartment, and with his appearance must terminate the second phase of his history.

PHASE THE THIRD.

"Come and sit by me, Mademoiselle Marmont," said Pollexfen, advancing at the same time to the sofa, and politely making way for the young lady, who followed almost mechanically. "You must not believe me as bad as I may seem at first sight, for we all have redeeming qualities, if the world would do us the justice to seek for them as industriously as for our faults."

"I am very well able to believe that," replied Lucile, "for my dear father instructed me to act upon the maxim, that good predominates over evil, even in this life; and I feel sure that I need fear no harm beneath the roof of the only real benefactor——"

"Pshaw! we will not bandy compliments at our first sitting; they are the prelude amongst men, to hypocrisy first, and wrong afterwards. May I so far transgress the rules of common politeness as to ask your age? Not from idle curiosity, I can assure you."

"At my next birthday," said Lucile, "I shall attain the age of seventeen years."

"And when may that be?" pursued her interlocutor. "I had hoped you were older, by a year."

"My birthday is the 18th of November, and really, sir, I am curious to know why you feel any disappointment that I am not older."

"Oh! nothing of any great consequence; only this, that by the laws of California, on reaching the age of eighteen you become the sole mistress of yourself."

"I greatly fear," timidly added the girl, "that I shall have to anticipate the law, and assume that responsibility at once.

"But you can only contract through a guardian before that era in your life; and in the agreement *between us, that is to be*, no third person shall intermeddle. But we will not now speak of that. You must consider yourself my equal here; there must be no secrets to hide from each other; no suspicions engendered. We are both artists. Confidence is the only path to mutual improvement. My business is large, but my ambition to excel greater, far. Listen to me, child!" and suddenly rising, so as to confront Lucile, he darted one of those magnetic glances into the very fortress of her soul, which we have before attempted to describe, and added, in an altered tone of voice, "The sun's raybrush paints the rainbow upon the evanescent cloud, and photographs an iris in the skies. The human eye catches the picture ere it fades, and transfers it with all its beauteous tints to that prepared albumen, the retina. The soul sees it there, and rejoices at the splendid spectacle. Shall insenate nature outpaint the godlike mind? Can she leave her brightest colors on the dark *collodion* of a thunder-cloud, and I not transfer the blush of a rose, or the vermilion of a dahlia, to my *Rivi* or *Saxe?* No! no! I'll not believe it. Let us work together, girl; we'll lead the age we live in. My name shall rival Titian's, and you shall yet see me snatch the colors of the dying dolphin from decay, and bid them live forever."

And so saying, he turned with a suddenness that startled his pupil, and strode hastily out of the apartment.

Unaccustomed, as Lucile had been from her very birth, to brusque manners, like those of the photographer, their grotesqueness impressed her with an indefinable relish for such awkward sincerity, and whetted her appetite to see more of the man whose enthusiasm always got the better of his politeness.

"He is no Frenchman," thought the girl, "but I like him none the less. He has been very, very kind to me, and I am at this moment dependent upon him for my daily bread." Then, changing the direction of her thoughts, they recurred to the subject-matter of Pollexfen's discourse. "Here," thought she, "lies the clue to the labyrinth. If insane, his madness is a noble one; for he would link his name with the progress of his art. He seeks to do away with the necessity of such poor creatures as myself, as adjuncts to photography. Nature, he thinks, should lay on the coloring, not man—the Sun himself should paint, not the human hand." And with these, and kindred thoughts, she opened her escritoire, and taking out her pencils sat down to the performance of her daily labor.

Oh, blessed curse of Adam's posterity, healthful toil, all hail! Offspring of sin and shame—still heaven's best gift to man. Oh, wondrous miracle of Providence! divinest alchemy of celestial science! by which the chastisement of the progenitor transforms itself into a priceless blessing upon the offspring! None but God himself could transmute the sweat of the face into a panacea for the soul. How many myriads have been cured by toil of the heart's sickness and the body's infirmities! The clink of the hammer drowns, in its music, the lamentations of pain and the sighs of sorrow. Even the distinctions of rank and wealth and talents are all forgotten, and the inequalities of stepdame Fortune all forgiven, whilst the busy whirls of industry are bearing us onward to our goal. No condition in life is so much to be envied as his who is too busy to indulge in reverie. Health is his companion, happiness his friend. Ills flee from his presence as night-birds from the streaking of the dawn. Pale Melancholy, and her sister Insanity, never invade his dominions; for Mirth stands sentinel at the border, and Innocence commands the garrison of his soul.

Henceforth let no man war against fate whose lot has been cast in that happy medium, equidistant from the lethargic indolence of superabundant wealth, and the abject paralysis of straitened poverty. Let them toil on, and remember that God is a worker, and strews infinity with revolving worlds! Should he forget, in a moment of grief or triumph, of gladness or desolation, that being born to toil, in labor only shall he find contentment, let him ask of the rivers why they never rest, of the sunbeams why they never pause. Yea, of the great globe itself, why it travels on forever in the golden pathway of the ecliptic, and nature, from her thousand voices, will respond: Motion is life, inertia is death; action is health, stagnation is sickness; toil is glory, torpor is disgrace!

I cannot say that thoughts as profound as these found their way into the mind of Lucile, as she plied her task, but nature vindicated her own laws in her case, as she will always do, if left entirely to herself.

As day after day and week after week rolled by, a softened sorrow, akin only to grief—

"As the mist resembles the rain"—

took the place of the poignant woe which had overwhelmed her at first, and time laid a gentle hand upon her afflictions. Gradually, too, she became attached to her art, and made such rapid strides towards proficiency that Pollexfen ceased, finally, to give any instruction, or offer any hints as to the manner in which she ought to paint. Thus her own taste became her only guide; and before six months had elapsed after the death of her father, the pictures of Pollexfen became celebrated throughout the city and state, for the correctness of their coloring and the extraordinary delicacy of their finish. His gallery was daily thronged with the wealth, beauty and fashion of the great metropolis, and the hue of his business assumed the coloring of success.

But his soul was the slave of a single thought. Turmoil brooded there, like darkness over chaos ere the light pierced the deep profound.

During the six months which we have just said had elapsed since the domiciliation of Mlle. Marmont beneath his roof, he had had many long and perfectly frank conversations with her, upon the subject which most deeply interested him. She had completely fathomed his secret, and by degrees had learned to sympathize with him, in his search into the hidden mysteries of photographic science. She even became the frequent companion of his chemical experiments, and night after night attended him in his laboratory, when the lazy world around them was buried in the profoundest repose.

Still, there was one subject which, hitherto, he had not broached, and that was the one in which she felt all a woman's curiosity—*the offer to purchase an eye.* She had long since ascertained the story of the one-eyed pets in the parlor, and had not only ceased to wonder, but was mentally conscious of having forgiven Pollexfen, in her own enthusiasm for art.

Finally, a whole year elapsed since the death of her

father, and no extraordinary change took place in the relations of the master and his pupil. True, each day their intercourse became more unrestrained, and their art-association more intimate. But this intimacy was not the tie of personal friendship or individual esteem. It began in the laboratory, and there it ended. Pollexfen had no soul except for his art; no love outside of his profession. Money he seemed to care for but little, except as a means of supplying his acids, salts and plates. He rigorously tested every metal, in its iodides and bromides; industriously coated his plates with every substance that could be albumenized, and plunged his negatives into baths of every mineral that could be reduced to the form of a vapor. His activity was prodigious; his ingenuity exhaustless, his industry absolutely boundless. He was as familiar with chemistry as he was with the outlines of the geography of Scotland. Every headland, spring and promontory of that science he knew by heart. The most delicate experiments he performed with ease, and the greatest rapidity. Nature seemed to have endowed him with a native aptitude for analysis. His love was as profound as it was ready; in fact, if there was anything he detested more than loud laughter, it was superficiality. He instinctively pierced at once to the roots and sources of things; and never rested, after seeing an effect, until he groped his way back to the cause. "Never stand still," he would often say to his pupil, "where the ground is boggy. Reach the rock before you rest." This maxim was the great index to his character; the key to all his researches.

Time fled so rapidly, and to Lucile so pleasantly, too, that she had reached the very verge of her legal maturity before she once deigned to bestow a thought upon what change, if any, her eighteenth birthday would bring about. A few days preceding her accession to majority, a large package of letters from France, *via* New York, arrived, directed to M. Marmont himself, and evidently written without a knowledge of his death. The bundle came to my care, and I hastened at once to deliver it, personally, to the blooming and really beautiful Lucile. I had not seen her for many months, and was surprised to find so great an improvement in her health and appearance. Her manners were more marked, her conversation more rapid and decided, and the general contour of her form far more womanly. It required only a moment's interview to convince me that she possessed unquestioned talent of a high order, and a spirit as imperious as a queen's. Those famous eyes of hers, that had, nearly two years before, attracted in such a remarkable manner the attention of Pollexfen, had not failed in the least; on the contrary, time had intensified their power, and given them a depth of meaning and a dazzling brilliancy that rendered them almost insufferably bright. It seemed to me that contact with the magnetic gaze of the photographer had lent them something of his own expression, and I confess that when my eye met hers fully and steadily, mine was always the first to droop.

Knowing that she was in full correspondence with her lover, I asked after Courtland, and she finally told me all she knew. He was still suffering from the effect of the assassin's blow, and very recently had been attacked by inflammatory rheumatism. His health seemed permanently impaired, and Lucile wept bitterly as she spoke of the poverty in which they were both plunged, and which prevented him from essaying the only remedy that promised a radical cure.

"Oh!" exclaimed she, "were it only in our power to visit *La belle France*, to bask in the sunshine of Dauphiny, to sport amid the lakes of the Alps, to repose beneath the elms of Chálons!"

"Perhaps," said I, "the very letters now unopened in your hands may invite you back to the scenes of your childhood."

"Alas! no," she rejoined, "I recognize the handwriting of my widowed aunt, and I tremble to break the seal."

Rising shortly afterwards, I bade her a sorrowful farewell.

Lucile sought her private apartment before she ventured to unseal the dispatches. Many of the letters were old, and had been floating between New York and Havre for more than a twelvemonth. One was of recent date, and that was the first one perused by the niece. Below is a free translation of its contents. It bore date at "Bordeaux, July 12, 1853," and ran thus:

Ever dear and beloved Brother:

Why have we never heard from you since the beginning of 1851? Alas! I fear some terrible misfortune has overtaken you, and overwhelmed your whole family. Many times have I written during that long period, and prayed, oh! so promptly, that God would take you, and yours, in His holy keeping. And then our dear Lucile! Ah! what a life must be in store for her, in that wild and distant land! Beg of her to return to France; and do not fail, also, to come yourself. We have a new Emperor, as you must long since have learned, in the person of Louis Bonaparte, nephew of the great Napoleon. Your reactionist principles against Cavaignac and his colleagues, can be of no disservice to you at present. Napoleon is lenient. He has even recalled Louis Blanc. Come, and apply for restitution of the old estates; come, and be a protector of my seven orphans, now, alas! suffering even for the common necessaries of life. Need a fond sister say more to her only living brother?

Thine, as in childhood,

ANNETTE.

"Misfortunes pour like a pitiless winter storm upon my devoted head," thought Lucile, as she replaced the letter in its envelope. "Parents dead; aunt broken-hearted; cousins starving, and I not able to afford relief. I cannot even moisten their sorrows with a tear. I would weep, but rebellion against fate rises in my soul, and dries up the fountain of tears. Had Heaven made me a man it would not have been thus. I have something here," she exclaimed, rising from her seat and placing her hand upon her forehead, "that tells me I could do and dare, and endure."

Her further soliloquy was here interrupted by a distinct rap at her door, and on pronouncing the word "enter," Pollexfen, for the first time since she became a member of his family, strode heavily into her chamber. Lucile did not scream, or protest, or manifest either surprise or displeasure at this unwonted and uninvited visit. She politely pointed to a seat, and the photographer, without apology or hesitation, seized the chair, and moving it so closely to her own that they came in contact, seated himself without uttering a syllable. Then, drawing a document from his breast pocket, which was folded formally, and sealed with two seals, but subscribed only with one name, he proceeded to read it from beginning to end, in a slow, distinct, and unfaltering tone.

I have the document before me, as I write, and I here insert a full and correct copy. It bore date just one month subsequent to the time of the interview, and was intended, doubtless, to afford his pupil full opportunity for consultation before requesting her signature:

This Indenture, Made this nineteenth day of November, A. D. 1853, by John Pollexfen, photographer, of the first part, and Lucile Marmont, artiste, of the second part, both of the city of San Francisco, and State of California, WITNESSETH:

WHEREAS, the party of the first part is desirous of obtaining a living, sentient, human eye, of perfect organism, and unquestioned strength, for the sole purpose of chemical analysis and experiment in the lawful prosecution of his studies as photograph chemist. AND WHEREAS, the party of the second part can supply the desideratum aforesaid. AND WHEREAS FURTHER, the first party is willing to purchase, and the second party willing to sell the same:

NOW, THEREFORE, the said John Pollexfen, for and in consideration of such eye, to be by him safely and instantaneously removed from its left socket, at the rooms of said Pollexfen, on Monday, November 19, at the hour of eleven o'clock P. M., hereby undertakes, promises and agrees, to pay unto the said Lucile Marmont, in current coin of the United States, in advance, the full and just sum of seven thousand five hundred dollars. AND the said Lucile Marmont, on her part, hereby agrees and covenants to sell, and for and in consideration of the said sum of seven thousand and five hundred dollars, does hereby sell, unto the said Pollexfen, her left eye, as aforesaid, to be by him extracted, in time, place and manner above set forth; only stipulating on her part, further, that said money shall be deposited in the Bank of Page, Bacon & Co. on the morning of that day, in the name of her attorney and agent, Thomas J. Falconer, Esq., for her sole and separate use.

As witness our hands and seals, this nineteenth day of November, A. D. 1853.

(Signed) JOHN POLLEXFEN, [L. S.]
.... [L. S.]

Having finished the perusal, the photographer looked up, and the eyes of his pupil encountered his own.

And here terminates the third phase in the history of John Pollexfen.

PHASE THE FOURTH.

The confronting glance of the master and his pupil was not one of those casual encounters of the eye which lasts but for a second, and terminates in the almost instantaneous withdrawal of the vanquished orb. On the contrary, the scrutiny was long and painful. Each seemed determined to conquer, and both knew that flight was defeat, and quailing ruin. The photographer felt a consciousness of superiority in himself, in his cause and his intentions. These being pure and commendable, he experienced no sentiment akin to the weakness of guilt. The girl, on the other hand, struggled with the emotions of terror, curiosity and defiance. He thought, "Will she yield?" She, "Is this man in earnest?" Neither seemed inclined to speak, yet both grew impatient.

Nature finally vindicated her own law, that the most powerful intellect must magnetize the weaker, and Lucile, dropping her eye, said, with a sickened smile, "Sir, are you jesting?"

"I am incapable of trickery," dryly responded Pollexfen.

"But not of delusion?" suggested the girl.

"A fool may be deceived, a chemist never."

"And you would have the fiendish cruelty to tear out one of my eyes before I am dead? Why, even the vulture waits till his prey is carrion."

"I am not cruel," he responded; "I labor under no delusion. I pursue no phantom. Where I now stand experiment forced me. With the rigor of a mathematical demonstration I have been driven to the proposition set forth in this agreement. Nature cannot lie. The earth revolves because it *must*. Causation controls the universe. Men speak of *accidents*, but a fortuitous circumstance never happened since matter moved at the fiat of the Almighty. Is it chance that the prism decomposes a ray of light?. Is it chance, that by mixing hydrogen and oxygen in the proportion of two to one in volume, water should be the result? How can Nature err?"

"She cannot," Lucile responded, "but man may."

"That argues that I, too, am but human, and may fall into the common category."

"Such was my thought."

"Then banish the idea forever. I deny not that I am but mortal, but man was made in the image of God. Truth is as clear to the perception of the creature, *when seen at all*, as it is to that of the Creator. What is man but a finite God? He moves about his little universe its sole monarch, and with all the absoluteness of a deity, controls its motions and settles its destiny. He may not be able to number the sands on the seashore, but he can count his flocks and herds. He may not create a comet, or overturn a world, but he can construct the springs of a watch, or the wheels of a mill, and they obey him as submissively as globes revolve about their centres, or galaxies tread in majesty the measureless fields of space!

"For years," exclaimed he, rising to his feet, and fixing his eagle glance upon his pupil, "for long and weary years, I have studied the laws of light, color, and motion. Why are my pictures sharper in outline, and truer to nature, than those of rival artists around me? Poor fools! whilst they slavishly copied what nobler natures taught, I boldly trod in unfamiliar paths. I invented, whilst they traveled on the beaten highway. Look at my lenses! They use glass—yes, common glass

—with a spectral power of 10, because they catch up the childish notion of Dawson, and Harwick, that it is impossible to prepare the most beautiful substance in nature, next to the diamond—crystalized quartz—for the purposes of art. Yet quartz has a power of refraction equal to 74! Could John Pollexfen sleep quietly in his bed whilst such an outrage was being perpetrated daily against God and His universe? No! Lucile; never! Yon snowy hills conceal in their bosoms treasures far richer than the sheen of gold. With a single blast I tore away a ton of crystal. How I cut and polished it is my secret, not the world's. The result crowds my gallery daily, whilst theirs are half deserted."

"And are you not satisfied with your success?" demanded the girl, whose own eye began to dilate, and gleam, as it caught the kindred spark of enthusiasm from the flaming orbs of Pollexfen.

"Satisfied!" cried he; "satisfied! Not until my *camera* flashes back the silver sheen of the planets, and the golden twinkle of the stars. Not until earth and all her daughters can behold themselves in yon mirror, clad in their radiant robes. Not until each hue of the rainbow, each tint of the flower, and the fitful glow of roseate beauty, changeful as the tinge of summer sunsets, have all been captured, copied, and embalmed forever by the triumphs of the human mind! Least of all, could I be satisfied now at the very advent of a nobler era in my art."

"And do you really believe," inquired Lucile, "that color can be photographed as faithfully as light and shade?"

"Believe, girl? *I know it.* Does not your own beautiful eye print upon its retina tints, dyes and hues innumerable? And what is the eye but a lens? God was the first photographer. Give me but a living, sentient, perfect human eye to dissect and analyze, and I swear by the holy book of science that I will detect the secret, though hidden deep down in the primal particles of matter."

"And why a human eye? Why not an eagle's or a lion's?"

"A question I once propounded to myself, and never rested till it was solved," replied Pollexfen. "Go into my parlor, and ask my pets if I have not been diligent, faithful, and honest. I have tested every eye but the human. From the dull shark's to the imperial condor's, I have tried them all. Months elapsed ere I discovered the error in my reasoning. Finally, a little boy explained it all. 'Mother,' said a child, in my hearing, 'when the pigeons mate, do they choose the prettiest birds?' 'No,' said his mother. 'And why not?' pursued the boy. Because, responded I, waking as from a dream, *they have no perception of color!* The animal world sports in light and shade; the human only rejoices in the apprehension of color. Does the horse admire the rainbow? or does the ox spare the buttercup and the violet, because they are beautiful? The secret lies in the human eye alone. An eye! an eye! give me but one, Lucile!"

As the girl was about to answer, the photographer again interposed, "Not now; I want no answer now; I give you a month for reflection." And so saying, he left the room as unceremoniously as he had entered.

The struggle in the mind of Lucile was sharp and decisive. Dependent herself upon her daily labor, her lover an invalid, and her nearest kindred starving, were facts that spoke in deeper tones than the thunder to her soul. Besides, was not one eye to be spared her, and was not a single eye quite as good as two? She thought, too, how glorious it would be if Pollexfen should not be mistaken, and she herself should conduce so essentially to the noblest triumph of the photographic art.

A shade, however, soon overspread her glowing face, as the unbidden idea came forward: "And will my lover still be faithful to a mutilated bride? Will not my beauty be marred forever? But," thought she, "is not this sacrifice for him? Oh, yes! we shall cling still more closely in consequence of the very misfortune that renders our union possible." One other doubt suggested itself to her mind: "Is this contract legal? Can it be enforced? If so," and here her compressed lips, her dilated nostril, and her clenched hand betokened her decision, "*if so, I yield!*"

Three weeks passed quickly away, and served but to strengthen the determination of Lucile. At the expiration of that period, and just one week before the time fixed for the accomplishment of this cruel scheme, I was interrupted, during the trial of a cause, by the entry of my clerk, with a short note from Mademoiselle Marmont, requesting my immediate presence at the office. Apologizing to the judge, and to my associate counsel, I hastily left the court-room.

On entering, I found Lucile completely veiled. Nor was it possible, during our interview, to catch a single glimpse of her features. She rose, and advancing toward me, extended her hand; whilst pressing it I felt it tremble.

"Read this document, Mr. Falconer, and advise me as to its legality. I seek no counsel as to my duty. My mind is unalterably fixed on that subject, and I beg of you, as a favor, in advance, to spare yourself the trouble, and me the pain, of reopening it."

If the speech, and the tone in which it was spoken, surprised me, I need not state how overwhelming was my astonishment at the contents of the document. I was absolutely stunned. The paper fell from my hands as though they were paralyzed. Seeing my embarrassment, Lucile rose and paced the room in an excited manner. Finally pausing, opposite my desk, she inquired, "Do you require time to investigate the law?"

"Not an instant," said I, recovering my self-possession. "This paper is not only illegal, but the execution of it an offense. It provides for the perpetration of the crime of *mayhem*, and it is my duty, as a good citizen, to arrest the wretch who can contemplate so heinous and inhuman an act, without delay. See! he has even had the insolence to insert my own name as paymaster for his villainy."

"I did not visit your office to hear my benefactor and friend insulted," ejaculated the girl, in a bitter and defiant tone. "I only came to get an opinion on a matter of law."

"But this monster is insane, utterly crazy," retorted I. "He ought, this moment, to be in a madhouse."

"Where they did put Tasso, and tried to put Galileo," she rejoined.

"In the name of the good God!" said I, solemnly, "are you in earnest?"

"Were I not, I should not be here."

"Then our conversation must terminate just where it began."

Lucile deliberately took her seat at my desk, and seizing a pen hastily affixed her signature to the agreement, and rising, left the office without uttering another syllable.

"I have, at least, the paper," thought I, "and that I intend to keep."

My plans were soon laid. I sat down and addressed a most pressing letter to Mr. Courtland, informing him fully of the plot of the lunatic, for so I then regarded him, and urged him to hasten to San Francisco without a moment's delay. Then, seizing my hat, I made a most informal call on Dr. White, and consulted him as to the best means of breaking through the conspiracy. We agreed at once that, as Pollexfen had committed no overt act in violation of law, he could not be legally arrested, but that information must be lodged with the chief of police, requesting him to detail a trustworthy officer, whose duty it should be to obey us implicitly, and be ready to act at a moment's notice.

All this was done, and the officer duly assigned for duty. His name was Cloudsdale. We explained to him fully the nature of the business intrusted to his keeping, and took great pains to impress upon him the necessity of vigilance and fidelity. He entered into the scheme with alacrity, and was most profuse in his promises.

Our settled plan was to meet at the outer door of the photographer's gallery, at half-past ten o'clock P.M., on the 19th of November, 1853, and shortly afterwards to make our way, by stratagem or force, into the presence of Pollexfen, and arrest him on the spot. We hoped to find such preparations on hand as would justify the arrest, and secure his punishment. If not, Lucile was to be removed, at all events, and conducted to a place of safety. Such was the general outline. During the week we had frequent conferences, and Cloudsdale effected an entrance, on two occasions, upon some slight pretext, into the room of the artist. But he could discover nothing to arouse suspicion; so, at least, he informed us. During the morning of the 19th, a warrant of arrest was duly issued, and lodged in the hands of Cloudsdale for execution. He then bade us good morning, and urged us to be promptly on the ground at half-past ten. He told us that he had another arrest to make on the Sacramento boat, when she arrived, but would not be detained five minutes at the police office. This was annoying, but we submitted with the best grace possible.

During the afternoon, I got another glimpse at our "trusty." The steamer left for Panama at one P.M., and I went on board to bid adieu to a friend who was a passenger.

Cloudsdale was also there, and seemed anxious and restive. He told me that he was on the lookout for a highway robber, who had been tracked to the city, and it might be possible that he was stowed away secretly on the ship. Having business up town, I soon left, and went away with a heavy heart.

As night approached I grew more and more nervous, for the party most deeply interested in preventing this crime had not made his appearance. Mr. Courtland had not reached the city. Sickness, or the miscarriage of my letter, was doubtless the cause.

The Doctor and myself supped together, and then proceeded to my chambers, where we armed ourselves as heavily as though we were about to fight a battle. We were both silent. The enormity of Pollexfen's contemplated crime struck us dumb. The evening, however, wore painfully away, and finally our watches pointed to the time when we should take our position, as before agreed upon.

We were the first on the ground. This we did not specially notice then; but when five, then ten, and next, fifteen minutes elapsed, and the officer still neglected to make his appearance, our uneasiness became extreme. Twenty—*twenty-five* minutes passed; still Cloudsdale was unaccountably detained. "Can he be already in the rooms above?" we eagerly asked one another. "Are we not betrayed ?" exclaimed I, almost frantically.

"We have no time to spare in discussion," replied the Doctor, and, advancing, we tried the door. It was locked. We had brought a step-ladder, to enter by the window, if necessary. Next, we endeavored to hoist the window; it was nailed down securely. Leaping to the ground we made an impetuous, united onset against the door; but it resisted all our efforts to burst it in. Acting now with all the promptitude demanded by the occasion, we mounted the ladder, and by a simultaneous movement broke the sash, and leaped into the room. Groping our way hurriedly to the stairs, we had placed our feet upon the first step, when our ears were saluted with one long, loud, agonizing shriek. The next instant we rushed into the apartment of Lucile, and beheld a sight that seared our own eyeballs with horror, and baffles any attempt at description.

Before our faces stood the ferocious demon, holding in his arms the fainting girl, and hurriedly clipping, with a pair of shears, the last muscles and integuments which held the organ in its place.

"Hold! for God's sake, hold!" shouted Dr. White, and instantly grappled with the giant. Alas! alas! it was too late, forever! The work had been done; the eye torn, bleeding, from its socket, and just as the Doctor laid his arm upon Pollexfen, the ball fell, dripping with gore, into his left hand.

This is the end of the fourth phase.

PHASE THE FIFTH, AND LAST.

"Monster," cried I, "we arrest you for the crime of mayhem."

"Perhaps, gentlemen," said the photographer, "you will be kind enough to exhibit your warrant." As he said this, he drew from his pocket with his right hand, the writ of arrest which had been intrusted to Cloudsdale, and deliberately lighting it in the candle, burned it to ashes before we could arrest his movement. Lucile had fallen upon a ready prepared bed, in a fit of pain, and fainting. The Doctor took his place at her side, his own eyes streaming with tears, and his very soul heaving with agitation.

As for me, my heart was beating as audibly as a drum. With one hand I grappled the collar of Pollexfen, and with the other held a cocked pistol at his head.

He stood as motionless as a statue. Not a nerve trembled nor a tone faltered, as he spoke these words: "I am most happy to see you, gentlemen; especially the Doctor, for he can relieve me of the duties of surgeon. You, sir, can assist him as nurse." And shaking off my hold as though it had been a child's, he sprang into the laboratory adjoining, and locked the door as quick as thought.

The insensibility of Lucile did not last long. Consciousness returned gradually, and with it pain of the most intense description. Still she maintained a rigidness of feature, and an intrepidity of soul that excited both sorrow and admiration. "Poor child! poor child!" was all we could utter, and even that spoken in whispers. Suddenly a noise in the laboratory attracted attention. Rising, I went close to the door.

"Two to one in measure; eight to one in weight;

water, only water," soliloquized the photographer. Then silence. "Phosphorus; yellow in color; burns in oxygen." Silence again.

"Good God!" cried I, "Doctor, he is analyzing her eye! The fiend is actually performing his incantations!"

A moment elapsed. A sudden, sharp explosion; then a fall, as if a chair had been upset, and——

"Carbon in combustion! Carbon in combustion!" in a wild, excited tone, broke from the lips of Pollexfen, and the instant afterwards he stood at the bedside of his pupil. "Lucile! Lucile! the secret is ours; ours only!"

At the sound of his voice the girl lifted herself from her pillow, whilst he proceeded: "Carbon in combustion; I saw it ere the light died from the eyeball."

A smile lighted the pale face of the girl as she faintly responded, "Regulus gave both eyes for his country; I have given but one for my art."

Pressing both hands to my throbbing brow, I asked myself, "Can this be real? Do I dream? If real, why do I not assassinate the fiend? Doctor," said I, "we must move Lucile. I will seek assistance."

"Not so," responded Pollexfen; the excitement of motion might bring on erysipelas, or still worse, *tetanus*.

A motion from Lucile brought me to her bedside. Taking from beneath her pillow a bank deposit-book, and placing it in my hands, she requested me to hand it to Courtland the moment of his arrival, which she declared would be the 20th, and desire him to read the billet attached to the banker's note of the deposit. "Tell him," she whispered, "not to love me less in my mutilation;" and again she relapsed into unconsciousness.

The photographer now bent over the senseless form of his victim, and muttering, "Yes, carbon in combustion," added, in a softened tone, "Poor girl!" As he lifted his face, I detected a solitary tear course down his impressive features. "The first I have shed," said he, sternly, "since my daughter's death."

Saying nothing, I could only think—"And this wretch once had a child!"

The long night through we stood around her bed. With the dawn, Martha, the housekeeper, returned, and we then learned, for the first time, with what consummate skill Pollexfen had laid all his plans. For even the housekeeper had been sent out of the way, and on a fictitious pretense that she was needed at the bedside of a friend, whose illness was feigned for the occasion. Nor was the day over before we learned with certainty, but no longer with surprise, that Cloudsdale was on his way to Panama, with a bribe in his pocket.

As soon as it was safe to remove Lucile, she was borne on a litter to the hospital of Dr. Peter Smith, where she received every attention that her friends could bestow.

Knowing full well, from what Lucile had told me, that Courtland would be down in the Sacramento boat, I awaited his arrival with the greatest impatience. I could only surmise what would be his course. But judging from my own feelings, I could not doubt that it would be both desperate and decisive.

Finally, the steamer rounded to, and the next moment the pale, emaciated form of the youth sank, sobbing, into my arms. Other tears mingled with his own.

The story was soon told. Eagerly, most eagerly, Courtland read the little note accompanying the bank-book. It was very simple, and ran thus:

My own life's Life: Forgive the first, and only act, that you will ever disapprove of in the conduct of your mutilated but loving Lucile. Ah! can I still hope for your love, in the future, as in the past? Give me but that assurance, and death itself would be welcome.

L. M.

We parted very late; he going to a hotel, I to the bedside of the wounded girl. Our destinies would have been reversed, but the surgeon's order was imperative, that she should see no one whose presence might conduce still further to bring on inflammation of the brain.

The next day, Courtland was confined to his bed until late in the afternoon, when he dressed, and left the hotel. I saw him no more until the subsequent day. Why, it now becomes important to relate.

About eight o'clock in the evening of the 21st, the day after his arrival, Courtland staggered into the gallery, or rather the den of John Pollexfen. He had no other arms than a short double-edged dagger, and this he concealed in his sleeve.

They had met before; as he sometimes went there, anterior to the death of M. Marmont, to obtain the photographs upon which Lucile was experimenting, previous to her engagement by the artist.

Pollexfen manifested no surprise at his visit; indeed, his manner indicated that it had been anticipated.

"You have come into my house, young man," slowly enunciated the photographer, "to take my life."

"I do not deny it," replied Courtland.

As he said this, he took a step forward. Pollexfen threw open his vest, raised himself to his loftiest height, and solemnly said: "Fire! or strike! as the case may be; I shall offer no resistance. I only beg of you, as a gentleman, to hear me through before you play the part of assassin."

Their eyes met. The struck lamb gazing at the eagle! Vengeance encountering Faith! The pause was but momentary. "I will hear you," said Courtland, sinking into a chair, already exhausted by his passion.

Pollexfen did not move. Confronting the lover, he

told his story truthfully to the end. He plead for his life; for he felt the proud consciousness of having performed an act of duty that bordered upon the heroic.

Still, there was no relenting in the eye of Courtland. It had that expression in it that betokens blood. Cæsar saw it as Brutus lifted his dagger. Henry of Navarre recognized it as the blade of Ravillac sank into his heart. Joaquin beheld it gleaming in the vengeful orbs of Harry Love! Pollexfen, too, understood the language that it spoke.

Dropping his hands, and taking one stride toward the young man, he sorrowfully said: "I have but one word more to utter. Your affianced bride has joyfully sacrificed one of her lustrous eyes to science. In doing so, she expressed but one regret, that you, whom she loved better than vision, or even life, might, as the years roll away, forget to love her in her mutilation as you did in her beauty. Perfect yourself, she feared mating with imperfection might possibly estrange your heart. Your superiority in personal appearance might constantly disturb the perfect equilibrium of love."

He ceased. The covert meaning was seized with lightning rapidity by Courtland. Springing to his feet, he exclaimed joyfully: "The sacrifice must be mutual. God never created a soul that could outdo Charles Courtland's in generosity."

Flinging his useless dagger upon the floor, he threw himself into the already extended arms of the photographer, and begged him "to be quick with the operation." The artist required no second invitation, and ere the last words died upon his lips, the sightless ball of his left eye swung from its socket.

There was no cry of pain; no distortion of the young man's features with agony; no moan, or sob, or sigh.

As he closed firmly his right eye, and compressed his pallid lips, a joyous smile lit up his whole countenance that told the spectator how superior even human love is to the body's anguish; how willingly the severest sacrifice falls at the beck of honor!

I shall attempt no description of the manner in which I received the astounding news from the lips of the imperturbable Pollexfen; nor prolong this narrative by detailing the meeting of the lovers, their gradual recovery, their marriage, and their departure for the vales of Dauphiny. It is but just to add, however, that Pollexfen added two thousand five hundred dollars to the bank account of Mademoiselle Marmont, on the day of her nuptials, as a bridal present, given, no doubt, partially as a compensation to the heroic husband for his voluntary mutilation.

Long months elapsed after the departure of Lucile and her lover before the world heard anything more of the photographer.

One day, however, in the early spring of the next season, it was observed that Pollexfen had opened a new and most magnificent gallery upon Montgomery Street, and had painted prominently upon his sign, these words:

JOHN POLLEXFEN, PHOTOGRAPHER.

Discoverer of the Carbon Process,
By which Colored Pictures are Painted by the Sun.

The news of this invention spread, in a short time, over the whole civilized world; and the Emperor Napoleon the Third, with the liberality characteristic of great princes, on hearing from the lips of Lucile a full account of this wonderful discovery, revived, in favor of

John Pollexfen, the pension which had been bestowed upon Niépce, and which had lapsed by his death, in 1839; and with a magnanimity that would have rendered still more illustrious his celebrated uncle, revoked the decree of forfeiture against the estates of M. Marmont, and bestowed them, with a corresponding title of nobility, upon Lucile and her issue.

This ends my story. I trust the patient reader will excuse its length, for it was all necessary, in order to explain how John Pollexfen made his fortune.

VI.

THE LOVE KNOT.

UPON my bosom lies
  A knot of blue and gray;
You ask me why tears fill my eyes
  As low to you I say:

"I had two brothers once,
  Warmhearted, bold and gay;
They left my side—one wore the blue,
  The other wore the gray.

One rode with "Stonewall" and his men,
  And joined his fate with Lee;
The other followed Sherman's march,
  Triumphant to the sea.

Both fought for what they deemed the right,
  And died with sword in hand;
One sleeps amid Virginia's hills,
  And one in Georgia's land.

Why should one's dust be consecrate,
  The other's spurned with scorn—
Both victims of a common fate,
  Twins cradled, bred and born?

Oh! tell me not—a patriot one,
  A traitor vile the other;
John was my mother's favorite son,
  But Eddie was my brother.

The same sun shines above their graves,
  My love unchanged must stay—
And so upon my bosom lies
  Love's knot of blue and gray."

VII.

THE AZTEC PRINCESS.

"Speaking marble."—BYRON.

CHAPTER I.

IN common with many of our countrymen, my attention has been powerfully drawn to the subject of American antiquities, ever since the publication of the wonderful discoveries made by Stephens and Norman among the ruins of Uxmal and Palenque.

Yucatan and Chiapas have always spoken to my imagination more forcibly than Egypt or Babylon; and in my early dreams of ambition I aspired to emulate the fame of Champollion *le Jeune*, and transmit my name to posterity on the same page with that of the decipherer of the hieroglyphics on the pyramids of Ghizeh.

The fame of warriors and statesmen is transient and mean, when compared to that of those literary colossii whose herculean labors have turned back upon itself the tide of oblivion, snatched the scythe from the hands of Death, and, reversing the duties of the fabled Charon, are now busily engaged in ferrying back again across the Styx the shades of the illustrious dead, and landing them securely upon the shores of true immortality, the ever-living Present! Even the laurels of the poet and orator, the historian and philosopher, wither, and

"Pale their ineffectual fires"

in the presence of that superiority—truly godlike in its attributes—which, with one wave of its matchless wand, conjures up whole realms, reconstructs majestic empires, peoples desolate wastes—voiceless but yesterday, save with the shrill cry of the bittern—and, contemplating the midnight darkness shrouding Thebes and Nineveh, cries aloud, "Let there be light!" and suddenly Thotmes starts from his tomb, the dumb pyramids become vocal, Nimroud wakes from his sleep of four thousand years, and, springing upon his battle-horse, once more leads forth his armies to conquest and glory. The unfamiliar air learns to repeat accents, forgotten ere the foundations of Troy were laid, and resounds once more with the echoes of a tongue in which old Menes wooed his bride, long before Noah was commanded to build the Ark, or the first rainbow smiled upon the cloud.

All honor, then, to the shades of Young and Champollion, Lepsius and De Lacy, Figeac and Layard. Alexander and Napoleon conquered kingdoms, but they were ruled by the living. On the contrary, the heroes I have mentioned vanquished mighty realms, governed alone by the

"Monarch of the Scythe and Glass,"

that unsubstantial king, who erects his thrones on broken columns and fallen domes, waves his sceptre over dispeopled wastes, and builds his capitals amid the rocks of Petræa and the catacombs of Egypt.

Such being the object of my ambition, it will not appear surprising that I embraced every opportunity to enlarge my knowledge of my favorite subject—American Antiquities — and eagerly perused every new volume purporting to throw any light upon it. I was perfectly familiar with the works of Lord Kingsborough and Dr. Robertson before I was fifteen years of age, and had studied the explorations of Bernal Diaz, Waldeck, and Dupaix, before I was twenty. My delight, therefore, was boundless when a copy of Stephens's travels in Yucatan and Chiapas fell into my hands, and I devoured his subsequent publications on the same subject with all the avidity of an enthusiast. Nor did my labors stop here. Very early I saw the importance of an acquaintance with aboriginal tongues, and immediately set about mastering the researches of Humboldt and Schoolcraft. This was easily done; for I discovered, much to my chagrin and disappointment, that but little is known of the languages of the Indian tribes, and that little is soon acquired. Dissatisfied with such information as could be gleaned from books only, I applied for and obtained an agency for dispensing Indian rations among the Cherokees and Ouchitaws, and set out for Fort Towson in the spring of 1848.

Soon after my arrival I left the fort, and took up my residence at the wigwam of Sac-a-ra-sa, one of the principal chiefs of the Cherokees. My intention to make myself familiar with the Indian tongues was noised abroad, and every facility was afforded me by my hospitable friends. I took long voyages into the interior of the continent, encountered delegations from most of the western tribes, and familiarized myself with almost every dialect spoken by the Indians dwelling west of the Rocky Mountains. I devoted four years to this labor, and at the end of that period, with my mind enriched by a species of knowledge unattainable by a mere acquaintance with books, I determined to visit Central America in person, and inspect the monuments of Uxmal and Palenque with my own eyes.

Full of this intention, I took passage on the steamship "Prometheus," in December, 1852, bound from

New York to Greytown, situated in the State of Nicaragua; a point from which I could easily reach Chiapas or Yucatan.

And at this point of my narrative, it becomes necessary to digress for a moment, and relate an incident which occurred on the voyage, and which, in its consequences, changed my whole mode of investigation, and introduced a new element of knowledge to my attention.

It so happened that Judge E——, formerly on the Bench of the Supreme Court of the State of New York, was a fellow-passenger. He had been employed by the Nicaragua Transit Company to visit Leon, the capital of Nicaragua, and perfect some treaty stipulations with regard to the project of an interoceanic canal. Fellow-passengers, we of course became acquainted almost immediately, and at an early day I made respectful inquiries concerning that science to which he had of late years consecrated his life—I mean the "Theory of Spiritual Communion between the Two Worlds of Matter and Spirit." The judge was as communicative as I could desire, and with the aid of two large manuscript volumes (which were subsequently given to the public), he introduced me at once into the profoundest arcana of the science. I read his books through with the deepest interest, and though not by any means convinced, I was startled and bewildered. The most powerful instincts of my nature were aroused, and I frankly acknowledged to my instructor, that an irresistible curiosity had seized me to witness some of those strange phenomena with which his volumes superabounded. Finally, I extorted a promise from him, that on our arrival at Greytown, if a favorable opportunity presented, he would endeavor to form the mystical circle, and afford me the privilege I so much coveted—*to see for myself.* The anticipated experiments formed the staple of our conversation for the six weary days and nights that our trip occupied. Finally, on the morning of the seventh day, the low and wooded coast of Nicaragua gently rose in the western horizon, and before twelve o'clock we were safely riding at anchor within the mouth of the San Juan River. But here a new vexation was in store for us. The river boats commenced firing up, and before dark we were transferred from our ocean steamer to the lighter crafts, and were soon afterwards leisurely puffing our way up the river.

The next day we arrived at the upper rapids, where the little village of Castillo is situated, and where we had the pleasure of being detained five or six days, awaiting the arrival of the California passengers. This delay was exactly what I most desired, as it presented the opportunity long waited for with the utmost impatience. But the weather soon became most unfavorable, and the rain commenced falling in torrents. The Judge declared that it was useless to attempt anything so long as it continued to rain. But on the third evening he consented to make the experiment, provided the materials of a circle could be found. We were not long in suspense, for two young ladies from Indiana, a young doctor from the old North State (now a practicing physician in Stockton, California), and several others, whose names I have long since forgotten, volunteered to take part in the mysterious proceedings.

But the next difficulty was to find a place to meet in. The doctor and I started off on a tour through the village to prepare a suitable spot. The rain was still falling, and the night as dark as Erebus. Hoisting our umbrellas, we defied night and storm. Finally, we succeeded in hiring a room in the second story of a building in process of erection, procured one or two lanterns, and illuminated it to the best of our ability. Soon afterwards we congregated there, but as the doors and windows were not put in, and there were no chairs or tables, we were once more on the point of giving up in despair. Luckily there were fifteen or twenty baskets of claret wine unopened in the room, and these we arranged for seats, substituting an unhinged door, balanced on a pile of boxes, for the leaf of a table. Our rude contrivance worked admirably, and before an hour had rolled by we had received a mass of communications from all kinds of people in the spirit world, and fully satisfied ourselves that the Judge was either a wizard or what he professed to be—a *medium* of communication with departed spirits.

It is unnecessary to detail all the messages we received; one only do I deem it important to notice. A spirit, purporting to be that of Horatio Nelson, rapped out his name, and stated that he had led the assault on the Spaniards in the attack of the old Fort of Castillo frowning above us, and there first distinguished himself in life. He declared that these mouldering ruins were one of his favorite haunts, and that he prided himself more on the assault and capture of *Castillo Viejo* than on the victory of the Nile or triumph of Trafalgar.

The circle soon afterwards dispersed, and most of those who had participated in it were, in a few minutes, slumbering in their cots. As for myself, I was astounded with all that I had witnessed, but at the same time delighted beyond measure at the new field opening before me. I tossed from side to side, unable to close my eyes or to calm down the excitement, until, finding that sleep was impossible, I hastily rose, threw on my coat, and went to the door, which was slightly ajar. On looking out, I observed a person passing toward the foot of the hill upon which stood the Fort of Castillo Viejo. The shower had passed off, and the full moon was riding majestically in mid heavens. I thought I recognized the figure, and I ventured to accost him. It was the Judge. He also had been unable to sleep, and declared that a sudden impulse drove him forth into the open air.

Gradually he had approached the foot of the hill, which shot up, like a sugar-loaf, two or three hundred feet above the level of the stream, and had just made up his mind to ascend it when I spoke to him. I readily consented to accompany him, and we immediately commenced climbing upwards.

The ascent was toilsome, as well as dangerous, and more than once we were on the point of descending without reaching the summit. Still, however, we clambered on, and at half-past one o'clock A.M., we succeeded in our effort, and stood upon the old stone rampart that had for more than half a century been slowly yielding to the remorseless tooth of Time. Abandoned for many years, the ruins presented the very picture of desolation. Rank vines clung upon every stone, and half filled up with their green tendrils the yawning crevices everywhere gaping at us, and whispering of the flight of years.

We sat down on a broken fragment that once served as the floor of a port-hole, and many minutes elapsed before either of us spoke a word. We were busy with the past. Our thoughts recalled the terrible scenes which this same old fort witnessed on that glorious day when the youthful Nelson planted with his own hand the flag of St. George upon the very ramparts where we were sitting.

How long we had been musing I know not; but suddenly we heard a low, long-drawn sigh at our very ears. Each sprang to his feet, looked wildly around, but seeing nothing, gazed at the other in blank astonishment. We resumed our seats, but had hardly done so, when a deep and most anguishing groan was heard, that pierced our very hearts. This time we retained our position. I had unclosed my lips, preparatory to speaking to my companion, when I felt myself distinctly touched upon the shoulder. My voice died away inarticulately, and I shuddered with ill-concealed terror. But my companion was perfectly calm, and moved not a nerve or a muscle. Able at length to speak, I said, "Judge, let us leave this haunted sepulchre."

"Not for the world," he coolly replied. "You have been anxious for spiritual phenomena; now you can witness them unobserved and without interruption."

As he said this, my right arm was seized with great force, and I was compelled to resign myself to the control of the presence that possessed me. My right hand was then placed on the Judge's left breast, and his left hand laid gently on my right shoulder. At the same time he took a pencil and paper from his pocket, and wrote very rapidly the following communication, addressed to me:

The Grave hath its secrets, but the Past has none. Time may crumble pyramids in the dust, but the genius of man can despoil him of his booty, and rescue the story of buried empires from oblivion. Even now the tombs of Egypt are unrolling their recorded epitaphs. Even now the sculptured mounds of Nineveh are surrendering the history of Nebuchadnezzar's line. Before another generation shall pass away, the columns of Palenque shall find a tongue, and the *bas-reliefs* of Uxmal wake the dead from their sleep of two thousand years. Young man! open your eyes; we shall meet again amid the ruins of the *Casa Grande!*

At this moment the Judge's hand fell palsied at his side, and the paper was thrust violently into my left hand. I held it up so as to permit the rays of the moon to fall full upon it, and read it carefully from beginning to end. But no sooner had I finished reading it than a shock something like electricity struck us simultaneously, and seemed to rock the old fort to its very foundation. Everything near us was apparently affected by it, and several large bowlders started from their ticklish beds and rolled away down the mountain. Our surprise at this was hardly over, ere one still greater took possession of us. On raising our eyes to the moss-grown parapet, we beheld a figure sitting upon it that bore a very striking resemblance to the pictures in the Spanish Museum at Madrid of the early Aztec princes. It was a female, and she bore upon her head a most gorgeous headdress of feathers, called a *Panache*. Her face was calm, clear, and exceedingly beautiful. The nose was prominent—more so than the Mexican or Tezcucan—and the complexion much lighter. Indeed, by the gleam of the moonlight, it appeared as white as that of a Caucasian princess, and wore an expression full of benignity and love.

Our eyes were riveted upon this beautiful apparition, and our lips silent. She seemed desirous of speaking, and once or twice I beheld her lips faintly moving. Finally, raising her white, uncovered arm, she pointed to the north, and softly murmured, "*Palenque!*"

Before we could resolve in our minds what to say in reply, the fairy princess folded her arms across her breast, and disappeared as suddenly and mysteriously as she had been evoked from night. We spoke not a word to each other, but gazed long and thoughtfully at the spot where the bright vision had gladdened and bewildered our sight. By a common impulse, we turned to leave, and descended the mountain in silence as deep as that which brooded over chaos ere God spoke creation into being. We soon reached the foot of the hill, and parted, with no word upon our lips, though with the wealth of untold worlds gathered up in our hearts.

Never, since that bright and glorious tropical night, have I mentioned the mysterious scene we witnessed on the ramparts of Fort Castillo; and I have every reason to believe that my companion has been as discreet.

This, perhaps, will be the only record that shall transmit it to the future; but well I know that its fame will render me immortal.

Through me and me alone, the sculptured marbles of Central America have found a tongue. By my efforts, Palenque speaks of her buried glories, and Uxmal wakes from oblivion's repose. Even the old pyramid of Cholula yields up its bloody secrets, and *Casa Grande* reveals the dread history of its royalties.

The means by which a key to the monumental hieroglyphics of Central America was furnished me, as well as a full account of the discoveries made at Palenque, will be narrated in the subsequent chapters of this history.

CHAPTER II.

"Amid all the wreck of empires, nothing ever spoke so forcibly the world's mutations, as this immense forest, shrouding what was once a great city."—STEPHENS.

AT daylight on the next morning after the singular adventure recorded in the preceding chapter, the California passengers bound eastward arrived, and those of us bound to the westward were transshipped to the same steamer which they had just abandoned. In less than an hour we were all aboard, and the little river-craft was busily puffing her way toward the fairy shores of Lake Nicaragua.

For me, however, the evergreen scenery of the tropics possessed no charms, and its balmy air no enchantments. Sometimes, as the steamer approached the ivy-clad banks, laden as they were with flowers of every hue, and alive with ten thousand songsters of the richest and most variegated plumage, my attention would be momentarily aroused, and I enjoyed the sweet fragrance of the flowers, and the gay singing of the birds. But my memory was busy with the past, and my imagination with the future. With the Judge, even, I could not converse for any length of time, without falling into a reverie by no means flattering to his powers of conversation. About noon, however, I was fully aroused to the beauty and sublimity of the surrounding scenery. We had just passed Fort San Carlos, at the junction of the San Juan River with the lake, and before us was spread out like an ocean that magnificent sheet of water. It was dotted all over with green islands, and reminded me of the picture drawn by Addison of the Vision of Mirza.

Here, said I to myself, is the home of the blest. These emerald islets, fed by vernal skies, never grow sere and yellow in the autumn; never bleak and desolate in the winter. Perpetual summer smiles above them, and wavelets dimpled by gentle breezes forever lave their shores. Rude storms never howl across these sleeping billows, and the azure heavens whisper eternal peace to the lacerated heart.

Hardly had these words escaped my lips, when a loud report, like a whole park of artillery, suddenly shook the air. It seemed to proceed from the westward, and on turning our eyes in that direction, we beheld the true cause of the phenomenon. Ometepe was in active eruption. It had given no admonitory notice of the storm which had been gathering in its bosom, but like the wrath of those dangerous men we sometimes encounter in life, it had hidden its vengeance beneath flowery smiles, and covered over its terrors with deceitful calm.

In a moment the whole face of nature was changed. The skies became dark and lurid, the atmosphere heavy and sultry, and the joyous waters across which we had been careering only a moment before with animation and laughter, rose in tumultuous swells, like the cross-seas in the Mexican Gulf after a tornado. Terror seized all on board the steamer, and the passengers were clamorous to return to Fort San Carlos. But the captain was inexorable, and seizing the wheel himself, he defied the war of the elements, and steered the vessel on her ordinary course. This lay directly to the south of Ometepe, and within a quarter of a mile of the foot of the volcano.

As we approached the region of the eruption, the waters of the lake became more and more troubled, and the air still more difficult to respire. Pumice-stone, seemingly as light as cork, covered the surface of the lake, and soon a terrific shower of hot ashes darkened the very sun. Our danger at this moment was imminent in the extreme, for, laying aside all consideration of peril from the volcano itself, it was with great difficulty that the ashes could be swept from the deck fast enough to prevent the woodwork from ignition. But our chief danger was still in store for us; for just as we had arrived directly under the impending summit, as it were, a fearful explosion took place, and threatened to ingulf us all in ruin. The crater of the volcano, which previously had only belched forth ashes and lava, now sent up high into the heavens a sheet of lurid fire. It did not resemble gases in combustion, which we denominate flame, flickering for a moment in transitory splendor, and then dying out forever. On the contrary, it looked more like *frozen fire,* if the expression may be allowed. It presented an appearance of solidity that seemed to defy abrasion or demolition, and rose into the blue sky like a marble column of lightning. It was far brighter than ordinary flame, and cast a gloomy and peculiar shadow upon the deck of the steamer. At the same instant the earth itself shook like a summer reed when swept by a storm, and the water struck the sides of the vessel like some rocky substance. Every atom of timber in her trembled and quivered for a moment, then grew into senseless wood once more. At this instant, the terrific cry of "Fire!" burst from a hundred tongues, and I had but to cast my eyes toward the stern of the ship to realize the new peril at hand. The attention of the passengers was now equally divided between the burning ship and the belching volcano. The alternative of a death by flame, or by burial in the lake was presented to each of us.

In a few moments more the captain, crew, and passengers, including seventeen ladies, were engaged hand to hand with the enemy nearest to us. Buckets, pumps, and even hats, were used to draw up water from the lake and pass to those hardy spirits that dared to press closest to the flames. But I perceived at once that all would prove unavailing. The fire gained upon the combatants every moment, and a general retreat took place toward the stem of the steamer. Fully satisfied what would be the fate of those who remained upon the ship, I commenced preparing to throw myself into the water, and for that purpose was about tearing one of the cabin doors from its hinges, when the Judge came up, and accosted me.

He was perfectly calm; nor could I, after the closest scrutiny of his features, detect either excitement, impatience, or alarm. In astonishment I exclaimed:

"Sir, death is at the doors! Prepare to escape from the burning ship."

"There is no danger," he replied calmly; "and even if there were, what is this thing that we call *death*, that we should fear it? Compose yourself, young man; there is as yet no danger. I have been forewarned of this scene, and not a soul of us shall perish."

Regarding him as a madman, I tore the door from its hinges with the strength of despair, and rushing to the side of the ship, was in the very act of plunging overboard, when a united shriek of all the passengers rose upon my ear, and I paused involuntarily to ascertain the new cause of alarm. Scarcely did I have time to cast one look at the mountain, ere I discovered that the flames had all been extinguished at its crater, and that the air was darkened by a mass of vapor, rendering the sunlight a mockery and a shadow. But this eclipse was our redemption. The next moment a sheet of cool water fell upon the ship, and in such incredible masses, that many articles were washed overboard, and the door I held closely in my hands was borne away by the flood. The fire was completely extinguished, and, ere we knew it, the danger over.

Greatly puzzled how to account for the strange turn in our affairs, I was ready at the moment to attribute it to Judge E——, and I had almost settled the question that he was a necromancer, when he approached me, and putting an open volume in my hand, which I ascertained was a "History of the Republic of Guatemala," I read the following incident:

> Nor is it true that volcanoes discharge only fire and molten lava from their craters. On the contrary, they frequently shower down water in almost incredible quantities, and cause oftentimes as much mischief by floods as they do by flames. An instance of this kind occurred in the year 1542, which completely demolished one half the buildings in the city of Guatemala. It was chiefly owing to this cause that the site of the city was changed; the ancient site being abandoned, and the present locality selected for the capital.*

Six months after the events recorded above, I dismounted from my mule near the old *cabilda* in the modern village of Palenque. During that interval I had met with the usual fortune of those who travel alone in the interior of the Spanish-American States. The war of castes was at its height, and the cry of *Carrera* and *Morazan* greeted the ear of the stranger at almost every turn of the road. Morazan represented the aristocratic idea, still prevalent amongst the better classes in Central America; whilst Carrera, on the other hand, professed the wildest liberty and the extremest democracy. The first carried in his train the wealth, official power, and refinement of the country; the latter drew after him that huge old giant, *Plebs.*, who in days gone by has pulled down so many thrones, built the groundwork of so many republics, and then, by fire and sword and barbarian ignorance, laid their trophies in the dust. My sense and sympathy took different directions. Reason led me to the side of Morazan; but early prejudices carried me over to Carrera. Very soon, however, I was taught the lesson, that power in the hands of the

* Thompson's History of Guatemala, p. 238.

rabble is the greatest curse with which a country can be afflicted, and that a *paper constitution* never yet made men free. I found out, too, that the entire population was a rabble and that it made but little difference which hero was in the ascendant. The plunder of the laboring-classes was equally the object of both, and anarchy the fate of the country, no matter who held the reins. Civil wars have corrupted the whole population. The men are all *bravos*, and the women coquettes. The fireside virtues are unknown. It will be generations before these pseudo-republicans will learn that there can be no true patriotism where there is no country; there can be no country where there are no homes; there can be no home where woman rules not from the throne of Virtue with the sceptre of Love!

I had been robbed eighteen times in six months; taken prisoner four times by each party; sent in chains to the city of Guatemala, twice by Carrera, and once by Morazan as a spy; and condemned to be shot as a traitor by both chieftains. In each instance I owed my liberation to the American Consul-General, who, having heard the object with which I visited the country, determined that it should not be thwarted by these intestine broils.

Finally, as announced above, I reached the present termination of my journey, and immediately commenced preparations to explore the famous ruins in the neighborhood. The first want of a traveler, no matter whither he roams, is a guide; and I immediately called at the redstone residence of the Alcalde, and mentioned to him my name, the purport of my visit to Central America, and the object of my present call upon him. Eying me closely from head to foot, he asked me if I had any money ("Tiene V. dinero ?")

"Si, senor."

"Cuanto?"

"Poco mas de quinientos pesos."

"Bien; sientase."

So I took a seat upon a shuck-bottom stool, and awaited the next move of the high dignitary. Without responding directly to my application for a guide, he suddenly turned the conversation, and demanded if I was acquainted with Senor Catherwood or *el gobernador*. (I afterwards learned that Mr. Stephens was always called Governor by the native population in the vicinity of Palenque.) I responded in the negative. He then informed me that these gentlemen had sent him a copy of their work on Chiapas, and at the same time a large volume, that had been recently translated into Spanish by a member of the Spanish Academy, named Don Donoso Cortes, which he placed in my hands.

My astonishment can be better imagined than described, when, on turning to the title-page, I ascertained that the book was called "*Nature's Divine Revelations*. By A. J. DAVIS. *Traducido, etc.*"

Observing my surprise, the Alcalde demanded if I knew the author.

"Most assuredly," said I; "he is my——" But I must not anticipate.

After assuring me that he regarded the work as the greatest book in the world, next to the Bible and Don Quixote, and that he fully believed every line in it, *including the preface*, he abruptly left the room, and went into the court-yard behind the house.

I had scarcely time to take a survey of the ill-furnished apartment, when he returned, leading in by a rope, made of horsehair, called a "larriete," a youth whose arms were pinioned behind him, and whose features wore the most remarkable expression I ever beheld.

Amazed, I demanded who this young man was, and why he had been introduced to my notice. He replied, without noticing in the slightest degree my surprise, that *Pio*—for that was his name—was the best guide to the ruins that the village afforded; that he was taken prisoner a few months before from a marauding party of *Caribs* (here the young man gave a low, peculiar whistle and a negative shake of the head), and that if his escape could be prevented by me, he would be found to be invaluable.

I then asked Pio if he understood the Spanish language, but he evinced no comprehension of what I said. The Alcalde remarked that the *mozo* was very cunning, and understood a great deal more than he pretended; that he was by law his (the Alcalde's) slave, being a Carib by birth, and uninstructed totally in religious exercises; in fact, that he was a neophyte, and had been placed in his hands by the Padre to teach the rudiments of Christianity.

I next demanded of Pio if he was willing to conduct me to the ruins. A gleam of joy at once illuminated his features, and, throwing himself at my feet, he gazed upward into my face with all the simplicity of a child.

But I did not fail to notice the peculiar posture he assumed whilst sitting. It was not that of the American Indian, who carelessly lolls upon the ground, nor that of the Hottentot, who sits flatly, with his knees upraised. On the contrary, the attitude was precisely the same as that sculptured on the *basso-rilievos*, at Uxmal, Palenque, and throughout the region of Central American ruins. I had first observed it in the Aztec children exhibited a few years ago throughout the United States. The weight of the body seemed to be thrown on the inside of the thighs, and the feet turned outward, but drawn up closely to the body. No sooner did I notice this circumstance than I requested Pio to rise, which he did. Then, pretending suddenly to change my mind, I requested him to be seated again. This I did to ascertain if the first attitude was accidental. But on resuming his seat, he settled down with great ease and celerity into the self-same position, and I felt assured that I was not mistaken. It would have required the united certificates of all the population in the village, after that, to convince me that Pio was a Carib. But aside from this circumstance, which might by possibility have been accidental, neither the color, expression, nor structure of his face indicated Caribbean descent. On the contrary, the head was smaller, the hair finer, the complexion several shades lighter, and the facial angle totally different. There was a much closer resemblance to Jew than to Gentile; indeed, the peculiar curve of the nose, and the Syrian leer of the eye, disclosed an Israelitish ancestry rather than an American.

Having settled these points in my own mind very rapidly, the Alcalde and I next chaffered a few moments over the price to be paid for Pio's services. This was soon satisfactorily arranged, and the boy was delivered into my charge. But before doing so formally, the Alcalde declared that I must never release him whilst in the woods or amongst the ruins, or else he would escape, and fly back to his barbarian friends, and the Holy Apostolic Church would lose a convert. He also added, by way of epilogue, that if I permitted him to get away, his price was *cien pesos* (one hundred dollars).

The next two hours were devoted to preparations for a life in the forest. I obtained the services of two additional persons; one to cook and the other to assist in clearing away rubbish and stones from the ruins.

Mounting my mule, already heavily laden with provisions, mosquito bars, bedding, cooking utensils, etc., we turned our faces toward the southeast, and left the modern village of Palenque. For the first mile I obeyed strictly the injunctions of the Alcalde, and held Pio tightly by the rope. But shortly afterwards we crossed a rapid stream, and on mounting the opposite bank, we entered a dense forest. The trees were of a gigantic size, very lofty, and covered from trunk to top with parasites of every conceivable kind. The undergrowth was luxuriant, and in a few moments we found ourselves buried in a tomb of tropical vegetation. The light of the sun never penetrates those realms of perpetual shadow, and the atmosphere seems to take a shade from the pervading gloom. Occasionally a bright-plumed songster would start up and dart through the inaccessible foliage, but more frequently we disturbed snakes and lizards in our journey.

After traversing several hundred yards of this primeval forest I called a halt, and drew Pio close up to the side of my mule. Then, taking him by the shoulder, I wheeled him round quickly, and drawing a large knife which I had purchased to cut away the thick foliage in my exploration, I deliberately severed the cords from his hands, and set him free. Instead of bounding off like a startled deer, as my attendants expected to see him do, he seized my hand, pressed it respectfully between his own, raised the back of it to his forehead, and then imprinted a kiss betwixt the thumb and forefinger. Immediately afterward, he began to whistle in a sweet low tone, and taking the lead of the party, conducted us rapidly into the heart of the forest.

We had proceeded about seven or eight miles, crossing two or three small rivers in our way, when the guide suddenly threw up his hands, and pointing to a huge pile of rubbish and ruins in the distance, exclaimed "*El Palacio!*"

This was the first indication he had as yet given of his ability to speak or to understand the Spanish, or, indeed, any tongue, and I was congratulating myself upon the discovery, when he subsided into a painful silence, interrupted only by an occasional whistle, nor would he make any intelligible reply to the simplest question.

We pushed on rapidly, and in a few moments more I stood upon the summit of the pyramidal structure, upon which, as a base, the ruins known as *El Palacio* are situated.

These ruins have been so frequently described, that I deem it unnecessary to enter into any detailed account of them; especially as by doing so but little progress would be made with the more important portions of this narrative. If, therefore, the reader be curious to get a more particular insight into the form, size, and appearance of these curious remains, let him consult the splendidly illuminated pages of Del Rio, Waldeck, and Dupaix. Nor should Stephens and Catherwood be neglected; for though their explorations are less scientific and thorough than either of the others, yet being more modern, they will prove not less interesting.

Several months had now elapsed since I swung my hammock in one of the corridors of the old palace. The rainy season had vanished, and the hot weather once more set in for the summer. Still I worked on. I took accurate and correct drawings of every engraved entablature I could discover. With the assistance of my taciturn guide, nothing seemed to escape me. Certain am I that I was enabled to copy *basso-rilievos* never seen by any of the great travelers whose works I had read; for Pio seemed to know by intuition exactly where they were to be found. My collection was far more complete than Mr. Catherwood's, and more faithful to the original than Lord Kingsborough's. Pio leaned over my shoulder whilst I was engaged in drawing, and if I committed the slightest error his quick glance detected it at once, and a short, rough whistle recalled my pencil back to its duty.

Finally, I completed the last drawing I intended to make, and commenced preparations to leave my quarters, and select others affording greater facilities for the study of the various problems connected with these mysterious hieroglyphics. I felt fully sensible of the immense toil before me, but having determined long since to devote my whole life to the task of interpreting these silent historians of buried realms, hope gave me strength to venture upon the work, and the first step toward it had just been successfully accomplished.

But what were paintings, and drawings, and sketches, without some key to the system of hieroglyphs, or some clue to the labyrinth, into which I had entered? For hours I sat and gazed at the voiceless signs before me, dreaming of Champollion, and the *Rosetta Stone*, and vainly hoping that some unheard-of miracle would be wrought in my favor, by which a single letter might be interpreted. But the longer I gazed, the darker became the enigma, and the more difficult seemed its solution.

I had not even the foundation, upon which Dr. Young, and Lepsius, and De Lacy, and Champollion commenced. There were no living Copts, who spoke a dialect of the dead tongue in which the historian had engraved his annals. There were no descendants of the extinct nations, whose sole memorials were the crumbling ruins before me. Time had left no teacher whose lessons might result in success. Tradition even, with her uncertain light, threw no flickering glare around, by which the groping archæologist might weave an imaginary tale of the past.

> "Chaos of ruins, who shall trace the void,
> O'er the dim fragments cast a lunar light,
> And say, '*Here was, or is,*' where all is doubly night?"

CHAPTER III.

> "I must except, however, the attempt to explore an aqueduct, which we made together. Within, it was perfectly dark, and we could not move without candles. The sides were of smooth stones, about four feet high, and the roof was made by stones lapping over like the corridors of the buildings. At a short distance from the entrance, the passage turned to the left, and at a distance of one hundred and sixty feet it was completely blocked up by the ruins of the roof which had fallen down."—Incidents of Travel in Chiapas.

One day I had been unusually busy in arranging my drawings and forming them into something like system, and toward evening, had taken my seat, as I always did, just in front of the large *basso-rilievo* ornamenting the main entrance into the corridor of the palace, when Pio approached me from behind and laid his hand upon my shoulder.

Not having observed his approach, I was startled by the suddenness of the contact, and sprang to my feet, half in surprise and half in alarm. He had never before been guilty of such an act of impoliteness, and I was on the eve of rebuking him for his conduct, when I caught the kind and intelligent expression of his eye, which at once disarmed me, and attracted most strongly my attention. Slowly raising his arm, he pointed with the forefinger of his right hand to the entablature before us and began to whistle most distinctly, yet most musically, a low monody, which resembled the cadencial rise and fall of the voice in reading poetry. Occasionally, his tones would almost die entirely away, then rise very high, and then modulate themselves with the strictest regard to rhythmical measure. His finger ran rapidly over the hieroglyphics, first from left to right, and then from right to left.

In the utmost amazement I turned toward Pio, and demanded what he meant. Is this a musical composition, exclaimed I, that you seem to be reading? My companion uttered no reply, but proceeded rapidly with his task. For more than half an hour he was engaged in whistling down the double column of hieroglyphics engraved upon the entablature before me. So soon as his task was accomplished, and without offering the slightest explanation, he seized my hand and made a signal for me to follow.

Having provided himself with a box of lucifer matches and a fresh candle, he placed the same implements in my possession, and started in advance. I obeyed almost instinctively.

We passed into the innermost apartments of *El Palacio*, and approached a cavernous opening into which Mr. Stephens had descended, and which he supposed had been used as a tomb.

It was scarcely high enough in the pitch to enable me to stand erect, and I felt a cool damp breeze pass over my brow, such as we sometimes encounter upon entering a vault.

Pio stopped and deliberately lighted his candle and beckoned me to do the same. As soon as this was effected, he advanced into the darkest corner of the dungeon, and stooping with his mouth to the floor, gave a long, shrill whistle. The next moment, one of the paving-stones was raised *from within*, and I beheld an almost perpendicular stone staircase leading down still deeper under ground. Calling me to his side, he pointed to the entrance and made a gesture for me to descend. My feelings at this moment may be better imagined than described. My memory ran back to the information given me by the Alcalde, that Pio was a Carib, and I felt confident that he had confederates close at hand. The Caribs, I well knew, had never been christianized nor subdued, but roved about the adjacent swamps and fastnesses in their aboriginal state. I had frequently read of terrible massacres perpetrated by them, and the dreadful fate of William Beanham, so thrillingly told by Mr. Stephens in his second volume, uprose in my mind at this instant, with fearful distinctness. But then, thought I, what motive can this poor boy have in alluring me to ruin? What harm have I done him? Plunder surely cannot be his object, for he was present when I intrusted all I possessed to the care of the Alcalde of the village. These considerations left my mind in equal balance, and I turned around to confront my companion, and draw a decision from the expression of his countenance.

One look reassured me at once. A playful smile wreathed his lips, and lightened over his face a gleam of real benevolence, not unmixed, as I thought, with pity. Hesitating no longer, I preceded him into those realms of subterranean night. Down, down, down, I trod, until there seemed no bottom to the echoing cavern. Each moment the air grew heavier, and our candles began to flicker and grow dimmer, as the impurities of the confined atmosphere became more and more perceptible. My head felt lighter, and began to swim. My lungs respired with greater difficulty, and my knees knocked and jostled, as though faint from weakness.

Still there seemed no end to the descent. Tramp, tramp, tramp, I heard the footsteps of my guide behind me, and I vainly explored the darkness before. At length we reached a broad even platform, covered over with the peculiar tiling found among these ruins. As soon as Pio reached the landing-place, he beckoned me to be seated on the stone steps, which I was but too glad to do. He at once followed my example, and seemed no less rejoiced than I that the descent had been safely accomplished.

I once descended from the summit of Bunker Hill Monument, and counted the steps, from the top to the bottom. That number I made 465. The estimate of the depth of this cavern, made at the time, led me to believe that it was nearly equal to the height of that column. But there was no railing by which to cling, and no friend to interrupt my fall, in case of accident. *Pio was behind me!*

After I became somewhat rested from the fatigue, my curiosity returned with tenfold force, and I surveyed the apartment with real pleasure. It was perfectly circular, and was about fifteen feet in diameter, and ten feet high. The walls seemed to be smooth, except a close, damp coating of moss, that age and humidity had fastened upon them.

I could perceive no exit, except the one by which we had reached it.

But I was not permitted to remain long in doubt on this point; for Pio soon rose, walked to the side of the chamber exactly opposite the stairs, whistled shrilly, as before, and an aperture immediately manifested itself, large enough to admit the body of a man! Through this he crawled, and beckoned me to follow. No sooner had I crept through the wall, than the stone dropped from above, and closed the orifice completely. I now found myself standing erect in what appeared to be a subterranean aqueduct. It was precisely of the same size, with a flat, cemented floor, shelving sides, and circular, or rather *Aztec-arched* roof. The passage was not straight, but wound about with frequent turnings as far as we pursued it.

Why these curves were made, I never ascertained, although afterward I gave the subject much attention. We started down the aqueduct at a brisk pace, our candles being frequently extinguished by fresh drafts of air, that struck us at almost every turn. Whenever they occurred, we paused a moment, to reillume them, and then hastened on, as silently and swiftly as before.

After traversing at least five or six miles of this passage, occasionally passing arched chambers like that at the foot of the staircase, we suddenly reached the termination of the aqueduct, which was an apartment the *fac-simile* of the one at the other end of it. Here also we observed a stone stairway, and my companion at once began the ascent. During our journey through the long arched way behind us, we frequently passed through rents, made possibly by earthquakes, and more than once were compelled to crawl through openings half filled with rubbish, sand and stones. Nor was the road dry in all places. Indeed, generally, the floor was wet, and twice we forded small brooks that ran directly across the path. Behind us, and before, we could distinctly hear the water dripping from the ceiling, and long before we reached the end of the passage, our clothing had been completely saturated. It was, therefore, with great and necessary caution, that I followed my guide up the slippery stairs. Our ascent was not so tedious as our descent had been, nor was the distance apparently more than half so great to the surface. Pio paused a moment at the head of the stairway, extinguished his candle, and then requested me by a gesture to do likewise. When this was accomplished, he touched a spring and the trap-door flew open, *upwards*. The next instant I found myself standing in a chamber but dimly lighted from above. We soon emerged into open daylight, and there, for the first time since the conquest of Mexico by Cortes, the eyes of a white man rested upon the gigantic ruins of *La Casa Grande*.

These ruins are far more extensive than any yet explored by travelers in Central America. Hitherto, they have entirely escaped observation. The natives of the country are not even aware of their existence, and it will be many years before they are visited by the curious.

But here they were, a solid reality! Frowning on the surrounding gloom of the forest, and the shadows of approaching night, they stretched out on every side, like the bodies of dead giants slain in battle with the Titans.

Daylight was nearly gone, and it soon became impossible to see anything with distinctness. For the first time, the peculiarity of my lonely situation forced itself upon my attention. I was alone with the Carib boy. I had not even brought my side-arms with me, and I knew that it was now too late to make any attempt to escape through the forest. The idea of returning by the subterranean aqueduct never crossed my mind as a possibility; for my nerves flinched at the bare thought of the shrill whistle of Pio, and the mysterious obedience of the stones.

Whilst revolving these unpleasant ideas through my

brain, the boy approached me respectfully, opened a small knapsack that I had not before observed he carried, and offered me some food. Hungry and fatigued as I was, I could not eat; the same peculiar smile passed over his features; he rose and left me for a moment, returned, and offered me a gourd of water. After drinking, I felt greatly refreshed, and endeavored to draw my companion into a conversation. But all to no purpose. He soon fell asleep, and I too, ere long, was quietly reposing in the depths of the forest.

It may seem remarkable that the ruins of *Casa Grande* have never been discovered, as yet, by professional travelers. But it requires only a slight acquaintance with the characteristics of the surrounding country, and a peep into the intricacies of a tropical forest, to dispel at once all wonder on this subject. These ruins are situated about five miles in a westerly direction from those known as *El Palacio*, and originally constituted a part of the same city. They are as much more grand and extensive than those of *El Palacio* as those are than the remains at Uxmal, or Copan. In fact, they are gigantic, and reminded me forcibly of the great Temple of Karnak, on the banks of the Nile. But they lie buried in the fastnesses of a tropical forest. One half of them is entombed in a sea of vegetation, and it would require a thousand men more than a whole year to clear away the majestic groves that shoot up like sleepless sentinels from court-yard and corridor, send their fantastic roots into the bedchamber of royalty, and drop their annual foliage upon pavements where princes once played in their infancy, and courtiers knelt in their pride. A thousand vines and parasites are climbing in every direction, over portal and pillar, over corridor and sacrificial shrine. So deeply shrouded in vegetation are these awful memorials of dead dynasties, that a traveler might approach within a few steps of the pyramidal mound, upon which they are built, and yet be totally unaware of their existence. I cannot convey a better idea of the difficulties attending a discovery and explanation of these ruins than to quote what Mr. Stephens has said of *El Palacio*. "The whole country for miles around is covered by a dense forest of gigantic trees, with a growth of brush and underwood unknown in the wooded deserts of our own country, and impenetrable in any direction, except by cutting away with a machete. What lies buried in that forest it is impossible to say of my own knowledge. Without a guide we might have gone within a hundred feet of all the buildings without discovering one of them.

I awoke with a start and a shudder. Something cold and damp seemed to have touched my forehead, and left a chill that penetrated into my brain. How long I had been asleep, I have no means of ascertaining; but judging from natural instinct, I presume it was near midnight when I awoke. I turned my head toward my companion, and felt some relief on beholding him just where he had fallen asleep. He was breathing heavily, and was completely buried in unconsciousness. When I was fully aroused I felt most strangely. I had never experienced the same sensation but once before in my whole life, and that was whilst in company with Judge E—— on the stone ramparts of *Castillo Viejo*.

I was lying flat upon my back, with my left hand resting gently on my naked right breast, and my right hand raised perpendicularly from my body. The arm rested on the elbow and was completely paralyzed, or in common parlance, asleep.

On opening my eyes, I observed that the full moon was in mid-heavens, and the night almost as bright as day. I could distinctly see the features of Pio, and even noticed the regular rise and fall of his bosom, as the tides of life ebbed and flowed into his lungs. The huge old forest trees, that had been standing amid the ruins for unnumbered centuries, loomed up into the moonshine, hundreds of feet above me, and cast their deep black shadows upon the pale marbles, on whose fragments I was reposing.

All at once, I perceived that my hand and arm were in rapid motion. It rested on the elbow as a fulcrum, and swayed back and forth, round and round, with great ease and celerity. Perfectly satisfied that it moved without any effort of my own will, I was greatly puzzled to arrive at any satisfactory solution of the phenomenon. The idea crossed my mind that the effect was of *spiritual* origin, and that I had become self-magnetized. I had read and believed that the two sides of the human frame are differently electrified, and the curious phases of the disease called *paralysis* sufficiently established the dogma, that one half the body may die, and yet the other half live on. I had many times experimented on the human hand, and the philosophical fact had long been demonstrated, to my own satisfaction, that the inside of the hand is totally different from the outside. If we desire to ascertain the temperature of any object, we instinctively touch it with the inside of the fingers; on the contrary, if we desire to ascertain our own temperature, we do so by laying the back of the hand upon some isolated and indifferent object. Convinced, therefore, that the right and left sides of the human body are differently magnetized, I was not long in finding a solution of the peculiar phenomenon, which at first astonished me so greatly. In fact, my body had become an electrical machine, and by bringing the two poles into contact, as was affected by linking my right and left sides together, by means of my left hand, a battery had been formed, and the result was, the paralysis or magnetization of my right arm and hand, such being precisely the effect caused by a *spiritual circle*,—as it has been denominated. My arm and hand represented, in all respects, a table duly charged, and the same phenomenon could be produced, if I was right in my conjectures.

Immediately, therefore, I set about testing the truth of this hypothesis. I asked, half aloud, if there were any spirits present. My hand instantly closed, except the forefinger, and gave three distinctive jerks that almost elevated my elbow from its position. A negative reply was soon given to a subsequent question by a single jerk of the hand; and thus I was enabled to hold a conversation in monosyllables with my invisible companions.

It is unnecessary to detail the whole of the interview which followed. I will only add that portion of it which is intimately connected with this narrative. Strange as it may appear, I had until this moment forgotten all about the beautiful apparition that appeared and disappeared so mysteriously at *Castillo Viejo*. All at once, however, the recollection revived, and I remembered the promise contained in the single word she murmured, "Palenque!"

Overmastering my excitement, I whispered:

"Beautiful spirit, that once met me on the ramparts where Lord Nelson fought and conquered, art thou here?"

An affirmative reply.

"Will you appear and redeem your promise?"

Suddenly, the branches of the neighboring trees waved and nodded; the cold marbles about me seemed animated with life, and crashed and struck each other with great violence; the old pyramid trembled to its centre, as if shaken by an earthquake; and the forest around moaned as though a tempest was sweeping by. At the same instant, full in the bright moonlight, and standing within three paces of my feet, appeared the Aztec Princess, whose waving *panache,* flowing garments and benignant countenance had bewildered me many months before, on the moss-grown parapet of *Castillo Viejo.*

CHAPTER IV.

"Millions of spiritual creatures walk the earth
Unseen, both when we wake, and when we sleep."
—PARADISE LOST.

WAS I dreaming, or was the vision real, that my eyes beheld? This was the first calm thought that coursed through my brain, after the terror and amazement had subsided. Awe-struck I certainly was, when the beautiful phantom first rose upon my sight, at Castillo; awe-struck once more, when she again appeared, amid the gray old ruins of *Casa Grande.* I have listened very often to the surmises of others, as they detailed what *they* would do, were a supernatural being to rise up suddenly before them. Some have said, they would gaze deliberately into the face of the phantom, scan its every feature, and coolly note down, for the benefit of others, how long it "walked," and in what manner it faded from the sight. The nerves of these very men trembled while they spoke, and had an apparition burst at that instant into full view, these heroes in imagination would have crouched and hid their faces, their teeth chattering with terror, and their hearts beating their swelling sides, as audibly as the convict hears his own when the hangman draws the black-cap over his unrepentant head.

I blame no man for yielding to the dictates of Nature. He is but a fool who feels no fear, and hears not a warning in the wind, observes not a sign in the heavens, and perceives no admonition in the air, when hurricanes are brooding, clouds are gathering, or earthquakes muttering in his ears. The sane mind listens, and thwarts danger by its apprehensions.

The true hero is not the man who knows no fear—for that were idiotic—but he who sees it, and escapes it, or meets it bravely. Was it courage in the elder Pliny to venture so closely to the crater of Vesuvius, whilst in eruption, that he lost his life? How can man make war with the elements, or battle with his God?

There is, in the secret chambers of every human heart, one dark, weird cell, over whose portal is inscribed—MYSTERY. There Superstition sits upon her throne; there Idolatry shapes her monsters, and there Religion reveals her glories. Within that cell, the soul communes with itself most intimately, confesses its midnight cowardice, and in low whispers mutters its dread of the supernatural.

All races, all nations, and all times have felt its influences, oozing like imperceptible dews from the mouth of that dark cavern.

Vishnu heard its deep mutterings in the morning of our race, and they still sound hollow but indistinct, like clods upon a coffin-lid, along the wave of each generation, as it rises and rolls into the past. Plato and Numa and Cicero and Brutus listened to its prophetic cadences, as they fell upon their ears. Mohammed heard them in his cave, Samuel Johnson in his bed. Poets have caught them in the

> "Shivering whisper of startled leaves,"

martyrs in the crackling faggots, heroes amid the din of battle.

If you ask, what means this voice? I reply,

> "A solemn murmur in the soul
> *Tells of the world to be,*
> As travelers hear the billows roll
> Before they reach the sea."

Let no man, therefore, boast that he has no dread of the supernatural. When mortal can look spirit in the face, without blanching, man will be immortal.

To convince myself that I did not dream, I rose upon my elbow, and reclined for a moment in that attitude. Gradually I gained my feet, and then stood confronting the Aztec maiden. The midnight breeze of the tropics had set in, and by the clear moonlight I distinctly saw the *panache* of feathers that she wore upon her head swaying gracefully upon the air.

Convinced now, beyond all doubt, that the scene was real, the ruling desire of my life came back in full force upon me, and I spoke, in a hoarse whisper, the following words:

"Here lies a buried realm; I would be its historian!"

The apparition, without any reply in words, glided toward me, and approached so close that I could easily have touched her had I dared. But a sense of propriety subdued all unhallowed curiosity, and I determined to submit passively to all that my new friend should do. This state of mind seemed at once known to her, for she smiled approvingly, and came still nearer to where I stood.

Elevating her beautiful arm, she passed it gently over my face, her hand just touching my features, and imparting a cool sensation to my skin. I distinctly remember that the hand felt damp. No sooner was this done than my nervous system seemed to be restored to its usual tone, and every sensation of alarm vanished.

My brain began to feel light and swimmy, and my whole frame appeared to be losing its weight. This peculiar sensation gradually increased in intensity until full conviction flashed upon me that I could, by an effort of will, rise into the air, and fly with all the ease and rapidity of an eagle.

The idea was no sooner fully conceived, than I noticed a wavy, unsteady motion in the figure of the Aztec Princess, and almost immediately afterwards, I perceived that she was gradually rising from the broken pavement upon which she had been standing, and passing slowly upwards through the branches of the overshadowing trees. What was most remarkable, the relative distance between us did not seem to increase, and my amazement was inconceivable, when on casting my eyes toward my feet, I perceived that I was elevated more than twenty yards from the pavement where I had slept.

My ascent had been so gradual, that I was entirely unaware of moving, and now that I became sensible of it, the motion itself was still imperceptible. Upward, still upward, I was carried, until the tallest limbs of the loftiest trees had been left far below me. Still the ascent continued. A wide and beautiful panorama now opened before me. Above, all was flashing moonlight and starry radiance. The beams of the full moon grew more brilliant as we cleared the vapory atmosphere contiguous to the earth, until they shone with half the splendor of morn, and glanced upon the features of my companion with a mellow sheen, that heightened a thousandfold her supermundane beauty. Below, the gray old relics of a once populous capital glimmered spectrally in the distance, looking like tombs, shrouded by a weeping forest; whilst one by one, the mourners lost their individuality, and ere long presented but a dark mass of living green. After having risen several hundred feet perpendicularly, I was enabled to form an estimate of the extent of the forest, in the bosom of which sleep and moulder the monuments of the aboriginal Americans. There is no such forest existing elsewhere on the surface of this great globe. It has no parallel in nature. The Black Forest of Germany, the Thuringian Forest of Saxony, the Cross Timbers of Texas, the dense and inaccessible woods cloaking the headwaters of the Amazon and the La Plata, are mere parks in comparison. For miles and miles, leagues and leagues, it stretched out—north, south, east and west. It covers an area larger than the island of Great Britain; and throughout this immense extent of country there is but one mountain chain, and but one river. The summits of this range have been but seldom seen by white men, and have never been scaled. The river drains the whole territory, but loses itself in a terrific marsh before its tide reaches the Mexican gulf, toward which it runs. The current is exceedingly rapid; and, after passing for hundreds of miles under the land and under the sea, it unites its submarine torrent near the west end of Cuba, with that of the Orinoco and the Amazon, and thus forms that great oceanic river called the Gulf Stream. Professor Maury was right in his philosophic conjecture as to the origin of that mighty and resistless tide.

Having attained a great height perpendicularly above the spot of our departure, we suddenly dashed off with the speed of an express locomotive, toward the northeast.

Whither we were hastening, I knew not; nor did I trouble my mind with any useless conjectures. I felt secure in the power of my companion, and sure of her protection. I knew that by some unaccountable process she had neutralized the gravitating force of a material body, had elevated me hundreds, perhaps thousands, of feet in the atmosphere, and by some mysterious charm was attracting me toward a distant bourne. Years before, whilst a medical student at the University of Louisiana, the professor of *materia medica* had opened his course of lectures with an inquiry into the origin and essence of gravitation, and I had listened respectfully, but at that time doubtingly, to the theory he propounded. He stated that it was not unphilosophical to believe that the time would arrive when the gravitating power of dense bodies would be overcome, and balloons constructed to navigate the air with the same unerring certainty that ships traversed the ocean.

He declared that gravitation itself was not a *cause* but an *effect;* that it might be produced by the rotation of the earth upon its axis, or by some undiscovered current of electricity, or by some recondite and hitherto undetected agent or force in nature. Magnetism he thought a species of electricity, and subsequent investigations have convinced me that *sympathy* or *animal magnetism* was akin to the same parent power. By means of this latter agent I had seen the human body rendered so light that two persons could raise it with a single finger properly applied. More than this, I had but recently witnessed at Castillo, dead matter clothed with life and motion, and elevated several feet into the air without the aid of any human agency. This age I knew well to be an age of wonders. Nature was yielding up her secrets on every hand; the boundary between the natural and the spiritual had been broken down; new worlds were flashing upon the eyes of the followers of Galileo almost nightly from the ocean depths of space. Incalculable treasures had been discovered in the most distant ends of the earth, and I, unlettered hind that I was, did not presume to limit the power of the great Creator, and because an act seemed impossible to my narrow vision, and within my limited experience, to cry aloud, *imposture*, or to mutter sneeringly, *insanity*.

Before proceeding farther with the thread of this narrative, the attention of the reader is solicited to the careful perusal of the following extracts from Stephens's *Travels in Central America, Chiapas and Yucatan*, published at New York in 1841.

But the Padre told us more; something that increased our excitement to the highest pitch. On the other side of the great traversing range of Cordilleras lies the district of Vera Paz, once called Tierra de Guerra, or land of war, from the warlike character of its aboriginal inhabitants. Three times the Spaniards were driven back in their attempt to conquer it.*

The rest of the Tierra de Guerra never was conquered; and at this day the northeastern section bounded by the range of the Cordilleras and the State of Chiapa is occupied by Cadones, or unbaptized Indians, who live as their fathers did, acknowledging no submission to the Spaniards, and the government of Central America does not pretend to exercise any control over them. But the thing that roused us was the assertion by the Padre that four days on the road to Mexico, on the other side of the Great Sierra, was a Living City, large and populous, occupied by Indians, precisely in the same state as before the discovery of America. He had heard of it many years before, at the village of Chajal, and was told by the villagers that from the topmost

* Page 193, Vol. 2.

ridge of the Sierra this city was distinctly visible. He was then young, and with much labor climbed to the naked summit of the Sierra, from which, at a height of ten or twelve thousand feet, he looked over an immense plain extending to Yucatan and the Gulf of Mexico, and saw at a great distance a large city, spread over a great space, and with turrets white and glittering in the sun. The traditionary account of the Indians of Chajal is, that no white man has ever reached the city; that the inhabitants speak the Maya language; are aware that a race of strangers has conquered the whole country around, and murder any white man who attempts to enter their territory. They have no coin or other circulating medium; no horses, cattle, mules, or other domestic animals, except fowls, and the cocks they keep under ground to prevent their crowing being heard.*

Mr. Stephens then adds:

One look at that city is worth ten years of an every-day life. If he is right, a place is left where Indians and an Indian city exist as Cortez and Alvarado found them. There are living men who can solve the mystery that hangs over the ruined cities of America; perhaps, who can go to Copan and Palenque and read the inscriptions on their monuments.

* * * * * * * * * *

The moon, long past the meridian, was sinking slowly to her western goal, whilst the east was already beginning to blush and redden with the dawn. Before us rose high and clear three distinct mountain peaks, covered with a mantle of snow. I began to tremble with cold. But our pace did not slacken, nor our altitude diminish. On the contrary, we began to rise gradually, until we found ourselves nearly upon a level with the three peaks. Selecting an opening or gap betwixt the two westernmost, we glided through like the wind. I shivered and my teeth chattered as we skimmed along those everlasting snows. Here, thought I, the condor builds his nest in summer, and the ava-

* Ibid. Page 195.

lanches find a home. The eagle's wing has not strength enough to battle with this thin and freezing atmosphere, and no living thing but "the proud bird, the condor of the Andes," ever scaled these hoary summits. But our descent had already commenced. Gradually, as the morning broke, the region of ice and snow was left behind us, and just as the first ray of the rising sun shot over the peaks we had but a moment before surmounted, I beheld, glittering in the dim and shadowy distance, the white walls of a magnificent city. An exclamation of surprise and pleasure involuntarily escaped my lips; but one glance at my companion checked all further utterance. She raised her rounded forefinger to her lip, and made a gesture, whose purport I well understood.

We swept over forests and cornfields and vineyards, the city growing upon the vision every moment, and rising like the Mexican capital, when first beheld by Europeans from the bosom of a magnificent lake. Finally, we found ourselves immediately above it, and almost at the same moment, began to descend. In a few seconds I stood alone, in a large open space, surrounded upon all sides by lofty stone edifices, erected upon huge pyramidal structures, that resembled the forest-covered mounds at Palenque. The day had fully dawned, but I observed no inhabitants. Presently a single individual appeared upon one of the towers near me, and gave a loud, shrill whistle, such as we sometimes hear in crowded theatres. In an instant it was echoed and re-echoed a thousand times, upon every side, and immediately the immense city seemed to be awake, as if by magic. They poured by thousands into the open square, where I stood petrified with astonishment. Before me, like a vision of midnight, marched by, in almost countless throngs, battalion on battalion of a race of men deemed and recorded extinct by the wisest historians.

They presented the most picturesque appearance imaginable, dressed apparently in holiday attire, and keeping step to a low air, performed on instruments emitting a dull, confused sound, that seldom rose so as to be heard at any great distance.

They continued promenading the square, until the first level ray of sunshine fell upon the great Teocallis —as it was designated by the Spaniards—then with unanimous action they fell upon their faces, striking their foreheads three times upon the mosaic pavement. Just as they rose to their feet, I observed four persons, most gorgeously dressed, descending the steps of the Temple, bearing a palanquin, in which sat a single individual. My attention was at once arrested by her appearance, for she was a woman. She was arrayed in a *panache*, or head-dress, made entirely of the plumage of the *Quezale*, the royal bird of Quiche. It was by far the most tasteful and becoming ornament to the head I ever beheld, besides being the most magnificent. It is impossible to describe the graceful movement of those waving plumes, as they were stirred by the slightest inclination of the head, or the softest aspiration of the breeze. But the effect was greatly heightened by the constant change of color which they underwent. Blue and crimson, and orange and gold, were so blended that the eye was equally dazzled and delighted. But the utmost astonishment pervaded me, when, upon closely scrutinizing her features, I thought I recognized the beautiful face of the Aztec Princess. Little leisure, however, was afforded me for this purpose, for no sooner had her subjects, the assembled thousands, bowed with deferential respect to their sovereign, than a company of drilled guards marched up to where I stood, and unresistingly made me prisoner.

It is useless to attempt a full description of the imposing ceremony I had witnessed, or to portray the appearance of those who took the most prominent parts. Their costume corresponded precisely with that of the figures in *bas-relief* on the sculptured monuments at Palenque. Each wore a gorgeous head-dress, generally of feathers, carried an instrument decorated with ribbons, feathers and skins, which appeared to be a war-club, and wore huge sashes of yellow, green, or crimson cotton cloth, knotted before and behind, and falling in graceful folds almost to the ground.

Hitherto not a word had been spoken. The ceremony I had witnessed was a religious one, and was at once interpreted by me to be the worship of the sun. I remembered well that the ancient Peruvians were heliolaters, and my imagination had been dazzled when but a child by the gorgeous description given by the historian Robertson, of the great Temple of the Sun at Cuzco. There the Incas had worshiped the God of Day from the period when Manço Capac came from the distant Island of Oello, and taught the native Indians the rudiments of civilization, until the life of the last scion of royal blood was sacrificed to the perfidy of the Spanish invaders. These historical facts had long been familiar to my mind; but I did not recollect any facts going to show that the ancient Aztecs were likewise heliolaters; but further doubt was now impossible.

In perfect silence I was hurried up the stone steps of the great Teocallis, toward the palace erected upon its summit, into whose broad and lofty corridors we soon entered. These we traversed in several directions, leaving the more outward and gradually approaching the heart or central apartments.

Finally, I was ushered into one of the most magnificently decorated audience-chambers that the eye of man ever beheld.

We were surrounded by immense tablets of *bas-reliefs* sculptured in white and black marble, and presenting, evidently, a connected history of the ancient heroes of the race. Beside each tablet triple rows of hieroglyphics were carved in the solid stone, unquestionably giving in detail the history of the hero or chief whose likeness stood near them. Many of these appeared to be females, but, judging from the sceptre each carried, I was pursuaded that the old *Salique* law of France and other European nations never was acknowledged by the aboriginal Americans.

The roof was high, and decorated with the plumage of the Quezale and other tropical birds, whilst a throne was erected in the centre of the apartment, glittering in gold and silver ornaments, hung about with beautiful shells, and lined with the skins of the native leopard, prepared in the most exquisite style.

Seated upon a throne, I recognized the princess whose morning devotions I had just witnessed. At a gesture, I was carried up close to the foot of the throne.

After closely inspecting her features, I satisfied myself that she was not the companion of my mysterious journey, being several years older in appearance, and of a darker complexion. Still, there was a very striking resemblance between them, and it was evident that they not only belonged to the same race, but to the same family. I looked up at her with great respect, anticipating some encouraging word or sign. But instead of speaking, she commenced a low, melodious whistle, eying me intently during the whole time. Ceasing, she evidently anticipated some reply on my part, and I at once accosted her in the following terms:

"Most beautiful Princess, I am not voluntarily an invader of your realm. I was transported hither in a manner as mysterious as it was unexpected. Teach me but to read these hieroglyphics, and I will quit your territories forever."

A smile flitted across the features of the Princess as I uttered these words; and she gave an order, by a sharp whistle, to an officer that stood near, who immediately disappeared. In a few moments, he returned, bringing with him a native dressed very coarsely in white cotton cloth, and who carried an empty jar, or water tank, upon his head. He was evidently a laborer, and, judging from the low obeisances he constantly made, much to the amusement of the courtiers standing around, I am satisfied that he never before in his whole life had been admitted to the presence of his sovereign.

Making a gesture to the officer who had introduced him, he spoke a few low words to the native, who immediately turned toward me, and uttered, slowly and distinctly, the following sentence:

"Ix-itl hua-atl zi-petl poppicobatl."

I shook my head despairingly. Several other attempts to communicate with me were made, both by the Princess and the interpreter, but all to no purpose. I could neither understand the melodies nor the jargon. But I noticed throughout all these proceedings that there seemed to be two entirely distinct modes of expression; the first by whistling, and the second by utterance. The idea at once flashed across my mind, that there were two languages used in the country—one sacred to the blood royal and the nobility, and the other used by the common people. Impressed with this thought, I immediately set about verifying it by experiment.

It is unnecessary to detail the ingenious methods I devised to ascertain this fact. It is sufficient for the present purposes of this narrative to state, that, during the day, I was abundantly satisfied with the truth of my surmise; and that, before night, I learned another fact, equally important, that the hieroglyphics were written in the royal tongue, and could be read only by those connected by ties of blood with the reigning family.

There was at first something ludicrous in the idea of communicating thought by sound emitted in the way indicated above. In my wildest dreams, the notion of such a thing being possible had never occurred to my imagination. And when the naked fact was now demonstrated to me every moment, I could scarcely credit my senses. Still, when I reflected that night upon it, after I retired to rest, the system did not appear unnatural, nor even improbable. Birds, I knew, made use of the same musical tongue; and when but a boy, on the shores of the distant Albemarle, I had often listened, till long after midnight, to the wonderful loquacity of the common mocking-bird, as she poured forth her summer strains. Who has not heard the turtle dove wooing her mate in tones that were only not human, because they were more sadly beautiful? Many a belated traveler has placed his hand upon his sword-hilt, and looked suspiciously behind him, as the deep bass note of the owl has startled the dewy air. The cock's crow has become a synonym for a pæan of triumph.

Remembering all these varieties in sound that the air is capable of, when *cut,* as it were, by whistling, I no longer doubted that a language could easily be constructed by analyzing the several tones and giving value to their different modulations.

The ludicrousness of the idea soon gave place to admiration, and before I had been domiciliated in the palace of the Princess a month, I had become perfectly infatuated with her native language, and regarded it as the most beautiful and expressive ever spoken by man. And now, after several years have elapsed since its melodious accents have fallen upon my ears, I hesitate not to assert that for richness and variety of tone, for force and depth of expression, for harmony and sweetness—in short, for all those characteristics that give beauty and strength to spoken thought—the royal tongue of the aboriginal Americans is without a rival.

For many days after my mysterious appearance in the midst of the great city I have described, my fate still hung in the balance. I was examined and re-examined a hundred times as to the mode of my entrance into the valley; but I always persisted in making the same gestures, and pointed to the sky as the region whence I had descended. The guards stationed at every avenue of entrance and exit were summoned to the capital, and questioned closely as to the probability of my having passed them unawares; but they fully exculpated themselves from all blame, and were restored to their forfeited posts.

Gradually the excitement in the city subsided, and one by one the great nobles were won over to credit the story of my celestial arrival in their midst, and I believed the great object of my existence in a fair way to be accomplished.

Every facility was afforded me to learn the royal tongue, and after a little more than a year's residence in the palace, I spoke it with considerable fluency and accuracy.

But all my efforts hitherto were vain to obtain a key

to the hieroglyphics. Not only was the offense capital to teach their alphabet to a stranger, but equally so to natives themselves, unconnected with the blood royal. With all my ingenuity and industry, I had not advanced a single letter.

One night, as I lay tossing restlessly upon my bed, revolving this insoluble enigma in my mind, one of the mosaic paving-stones was suddenly lifted up in the middle of the room, and the figure of a young man with a lighted taper in his hand stood before me.

Raising my head hastily from the pillow, I almost sank back with astonishment when I recognized in the form and features of my midnight visitor, Pio the Carib boy.

CHAPTER V.

> "There are more things in heaven and earth, Horatio,
> Than are dreamt of in your philosophy."
> —SHAKSPEARE.

I SPRANG to my feet with all the eagerness of joy, and was about to rush into the arms of Pio, when he suddenly checked my enthusiasm by extinguishing the light. I stood still and erect, like one petrified into stone. That moment I felt a hand upon my arm, then around my waist, and ere I could collect my thoughts, was distinctly lifted from the ground. But I was carried only a few steps. On touching the floor with my feet, I was planted firmly, and the arms of my companion were tightly drawn around my own so as to prevent me from raising them. The next instant, and the stone upon which we stood suddenly slid from its position, and gradually sank perpendicularly,—we still retaining our position upon it.

Our descent was not rapid, nor did I deem it very

secure; for the trap-door trembled under us, and more than once seemed to touch the shaft into which we were descending. A few moments more and we landed securely upon a solid pavement. My companion then disengaged his hold, and stepping off a few paces, pronounced the words "*We are here!*" in the royal tongue, and immediately a panel slid from the side of the apartment, and a long passage-way, lighted at the further end by a single candle, displayed itself to view. Into that passage we at once entered, and without exchanging a single word, walked rapidly toward the light.

The light stood upon a stone stand about four feet high, at the intersection of these passages. We took the one to the left, and advanced twenty or thirty yards, when Pio halted. On coming up to him, he placed his mouth close to the wall, and exclaimed as before, "We are here." A huge block of granite swung inward, and we entered a small but well-lighted apartment, around which were hanging several costly and magnificent suits of Palenquin costume.

Hastily seizing two of them, Pio commenced arraying himself in one, and requested me by a gesture to don the other. With a little assistance, I soon found myself decked from head to foot in a complete suit of regal robes—*panache*, sash, and sandals inclusive.

When all was completed, Pio, for the first time, addressed me as follows: "Young stranger, whoever you may be, or to whatever nation you may belong, matters but little to me. The attendant guardian spirit of our race and country has conducted you hither, in the most mysterious manner, and now commands me to have you instructed in the most sacred lore of the Aztecs. Your long residence in this palace has fully convinced you of the danger to which we are both exposed; I in revealing and you in acquiring the key to the interpretation of the historical records of my country. I need not assure you that our lives are both forfeited, should the slightest suspicion be aroused in the breasts of the Princess or the nobility.

"You are now dressed in the appropriate costume of a student of our literature, and must attend me nightly at the gathering of the Queen's kindred to be instructed in the art. Express no surprise at anything you see or hear; keep your face concealed as much as possible, fear nothing, and follow me."

At a preconcerted signal given by Pio, a door flew open and we entered the vestibule of a large and brilliantly illuminated chamber.

As soon as we passed the entrance I saw before me not less than two hundred young persons of both sexes, habited in the peculiar garb of students, like our own. We advanced slowly and noiselessly, until we reached two vacant places, prepared evidently beforehand for us. Our entrance was not noticed by the classes, nor by those whom I afterwards recognized as teachers. All seemed intent upon the problem before them, and evinced no curiosity to observe the new comers. My own curiosity at this moment was intense, and had it not been for the prudent cautions constantly given me by Pio, by touching my robes or my feet, an exposure most probably would have occurred the first night of my initiation, and the narrative of these adventures never been written.

My presence of mind, however, soon came to my assistance, and before the evening was over, I had, by shrewdly noticing the conduct of others, shaped my own into perfect conformity with theirs, and rendered detection next to impossible.

It now becomes necessary to digress a moment from the thread of my story, and give an accurate description of the persons I beheld around me, the chamber in which we were gathered, and the peculiar mode of instruction pursued by the sages.

The scholars were mostly young men and women, averaging in age about twenty years. They all wore the emblem of royalty, which I at once recognized in the *panache* of Quezale plumes that graced their heads. They stood in semi-circular rows, the platform rising as they receded from the staging in front, like seats in an amphitheatre. Upon the stage were seated five individuals—two of the male, and three of the female sex. An old man was standing up, near the edge of the stage, holding in his hands two very cunningly-constructed instruments. At the back of the stage, a very large, smooth tablet of black marble was inserted in the wall, and a royal personage stood near it, upon one side, with a common piece of chalk in his right hand, and a cotton napkin in the left. This reminded me but too truthfully of the fourth book of Euclid and Nassau Hall; and I was again reminded of the great mathematician before the assembly broke up, and of his reply to that King of Sicily, who inquired if there were no easy way of acquiring mathematics. "None, your Highness," replied the philosopher; "there is no royal road to learning." Labor, I soon found, was the only price, even amongst the Aztecs, at which knowledge could be bought. Each student was furnished with the same species of instruments which the old man before-mentioned held in his hands.

The one held in the left hand resembled a white porcelain slate, only being much larger than those in common use. It was nearly twenty inches square, and was divided by mathematical lines into thirty-six compartments. It was covered over with a thin crystal, resembling glass, which is found in great quantities in the neighboring mountains, and is perfectly transparent. The crystal was raised about the one eighth of an inch from the surface of the slate, and allowed a very fine species of black sand to move at will between them. The instrument carried in the right hand resembled the bow of a common violin, more than anything else. The outer edge was constructed of a beautiful yellow wood, polished, and bent into the arc of a quarter circle; whilst a mass of small cords, made of the native hemp, united the two ends.

The method of using the bow was this: The slate was shaken violently once or twice, so as to distribute the black sand equally over the white surface, and then the bow was drawn perpendicularly down the edge of the slate, very rapidly, so as to produce a quick whistling sound. The effect produced upon the grains of sand was truly wonderful to the uninitiated in the laws of acoustics. They arranged themselves into peculiar figures, sometimes in the form of a semicircle, sometimes into that of a spiral, sometimes into a perfect circle, or a cone, or a rhomboid, or an oval, dependent entirely upon two things: first, the place where the slate was held by the left hand; and second, the point where the bow was drawn across the edge. As the slate was subdivided into thirty-six compartments, by either one of which it could be held, and as there was a corresponding point, across which the bow could be drawn, there were seventy-two primitive sounds that might be produced by means of this simple contrivance. Each of these sounds inherently and necessarily produced a different figure upon the slate, and there were consequently just seventy-two initial letters in the Aztec alphabet.

The mode of instruction was extremely simple. A word was pronounced by the aged teacher at the front of the stage, written upon his slate, exhibited to the scholar at the black tablet, and by him copied upon it. The whole class then drew down their bows, so as to produce the proper sound, and the word itself, or its initial letter, was immediately formed upon the slate.

After the seventy-two primitive letters or sounds had been learned, the next step was the art of combining them, so as not only to produce single words, but very often whole sentences. Thus the first hieroglyphic carved upon the tablet, on the back wall of the altar, in Casa No. 3 (forming the frontispiece of the second volume of Stephens's Travels in Central America), expresses, within itself, the name, date of birth, place of nativity, and parentage, of *Xixencotl*, the first king of the twenty-third dynasty of the Aztecs.

The hieroglyphics of the Aztecs are all of them both symbolical and phonetic. Hence, in almost every one we observe, first, the primitive sound or initial letter, and its various combinations; and, secondly, some symbolic drawing, as a human face, for instance, or an eagle's bill, or a fish, denoting some peculiar characteristic of the person or thing delineated.

But to return to the Hall of Students. The men and women on the stage were placed there as critics upon the pronunciation of each articulate sound. They were selected from the wisest men and best elocutionists in the kingdom, and never failed to detect the slightest error in the pronunciation of the tutor.

The royal tongue of the Aztecs is the only one now in existence that is based upon natural philosophy and the laws of sound. It appeals both to the eye and ear of the speaker, and thus the nicest shades of thought may be clearly expressed. There is no such thing as *stilted* language amongst them, and logomachy is unknown.

And here I may be permitted to observe that a wider field for research and discovery lies open in the domain of *sound* than in any other region of science. The laws of harmony, even, are but imperfectly understood, and the most accomplished musicians are mere tyros in the great science of acoustics. There is every reason to believe that there is an intimate but yet undiscovered link between *number, light,* and *sound,* whose solution will astonish and enlighten the generations that are to succeed our own. *When God spake the worlds into being, the globular form they assumed was not accidental, nor arbitrary, but depended essentially upon the tone of the great Architect, and the medium in which it resounded.*

Let the natural philosophers of the rising generation direct their especial attention toward the fields I have indicated, and the rewards awaiting their investigations will confer upon them immortality of fame.

There is a reason why the musical scale should not mount in whole tones up to the octave; why the mind grasps decimals easier than vulgar fractions, and why, by the laws of light, the blood-red tint should be heavier than the violet. Let Nature, in these departments, be studied with the same care that Cuvier explored the organization of insects, that Liebig deduced the property of acids, and that Leverier computed the orbit of that unseen world which his genius has half created, and all the wonderful and beautiful secrets now on the eve of bursting into being from the dark domain of sound, color, and shape, will at once march forth into view, and take their destined places in the ranks of human knowledge.

Then the science of computation will be intuitive, as it was in the mind of Zerah Colburn; the art of music creative, as in the plastic voices of Jehovah; and the great principles of light and shape and color divine, as in the genius of Swedenborg and the imagination of Milton.

I have now completed the outline of the sketch, which in the foregoing pages I proposed to lay before the world.

The peculiar circumstances which led me to explore the remains of the aboriginal Americans, the adventures attending me in carrying out that design, the mode of my introduction into the Living City, spoken of by Stephens, and believed in by so many thousands of enlightened men, and above all, the wonderful and almost incredible character of the people I there encountered, together with a rapid review of their language and literature, have been briefly but faithfully presented to the public.

It but remains for me now to present my readers with a few specimens of Aztec literature, translated from the hieroglyphics now mouldering amid the forests of Chiapa; to narrate the history of my escape from the Living City of the aborigines; to bespeak a friendly word for the forthcoming history of one of the earliest, most beautiful, and unfortunate of the Aztec queens, copied *verbatim* from the annals of her race, and to bid them one and all, for the present, a respectful adieu.

Before copying from the blurred and water-soaked manuscript before me, a single extract from the literary remains of the monumental race amongst whom I have spent three years and a half of my early manhood, it may not be deemed improper to remark that a large work upon this subject is now in course of publication, containing the minutest details of the domestic life, public institutions, language, and laws of that interesting people.

The extracts I present to the reader may be relied upon as exactly correct, since they are taken from the memoranda made upon the spot.

Directly in front of the throne, in the great audience-chamber described in the preceding chapter, and written in the most beautiful hieroglyphi extant, I found the following account of the origin of the land:

The Great Spirit, whose emblem is the sun, held the water-drops out of which the world was made, in the hollow of his hand, He breathed a tone, and they rounded into the great globe, and started forth on the errand of counting up the years.

Nothing existed but water and the great fishes of the sea. One eternity passed. The Great Spirit sent a solid star, round and beautiful, but dead and no longer burning, and plunged it into the depths of the oceans. Then the winds were born, and the rains began to fall. The animals next sprang into existence. They came up from the star-dust like wheat and maize. The round star floated upon the waters, and became the dry land; and the land was high, and its edges steep. It was circular, like a plate, and all connected together.

The marriage of the land and the sea produced man, but his spirit came from the beams of the sun.

Another eternity passed away, and the earth became too full of people. They were all white, because the star fell into the cold seas, and the sun could not darken their complexions.

Then the sea bubbled up in the middle of the land, and the country of the Aztecs floated off to the west. Wherever the star cracked open, there the waters rose up and made the deep sea.

When the east and the west come together again, they will fit like a garment that has been torn.

Then followed a rough outline of the western coasts of Europe and Africa, and directly opposite the coasts of North and South America. The projections of the one exactly fitted the indentations of the other, and gave a semblance of truth and reality to the wild dream of the Aztec philosopher. Let the geographer compare them, and he will be more disposed to wonder than to sneer.

I have not space enough left me to quote any further from the monumental inscriptions, but if the reader be curious upon this subject, I recommend to his attention the publication soon to come out, alluded to above.

Some unusual event certainly had occurred in the city. The great plaza in front of the palace was thronged with a countless multitude of men and women, all clamoring for a sacrifice! a sacrifice!

Whilst wondering what could be the cause of this commotion, I was suddenly summoned before the Princess in the audience-chamber, so often alluded to before.

My surprise was great when, upon presenting myself before her, I beheld, pinioned to a heavy log of mahogany, a young man, evidently of European descent.

The Princess requested me to interpret for her to the stranger, and the following colloquy took place. The conversation was in the French language.

Q. "Who are you, and why do you invade my dominions?"

A. "My name is Armand de L'Oreille. I am a Frenchman by birth. I was sent out by Lamartine, in 1848, as attaché to the expedition of M. de Bourbourg, whose duties were to explore the forests in the neighborhood of Palenque, to collate the language of the Central-American Indians, to copy the inscriptions on the monuments, and, if possible, to reach the LIVING

CITY mentioned by Waldeck, Dupaix, and the American traveler Stephens."

Q. "But why are you alone? Where is the party to which you belonged?"

A. "Most of them returned to Palenque, after wandering in the wilderness a few days. Five only determined to proceed; of that number I am the only survivor."

Here the interview closed.

The council and the queen were not long in determining the fate of M. de L'Oreille. It was unanimously resolved that he should surrender his life as a forfeit to his temerity.

The next morning, at sunrise, was fixed for his death. He was to be sacrificed upon the altar, on the summit of the great Teocallis—an offering to *Quetzalcohuatl*, the first great prince of the Aztecs. I at once determined to save the life of the stranger, if I could do so, even at the hazard of my own. But fate ordained it otherwise. I retired earlier than usual, and lay silent and moody, revolving on the best means to accomplish my end.

Midnight at length arrived; I crept stealthily from my bed, and opened the door of my chamber, as lightly as sleep creeps over the eyelids of children. But——

[Here the MS. is so blotted, and saturated with salt-water, as to be illegible for several pages. The next legible sentences are as follows.—ED.]

Here, for the first time, the woods looked familiar to me. Proceeding a few steps, I fell into the trail leading toward the modern village of Palenque, and, after an hour's walk, I halted in front of the *cabilda* of the town.

I was followed by a motley crowd to the office of the Alcalde, who did not recognize me, dressed as I was in skins, and half loaded down with rolls of MS., made from the bark of the mulberry. I related to him and M. de Bourbourg my adventures; and though the latter declared he had lost poor Armand and his five companions, yet I am persuaded that neither of them credited a single word of my story.

Not many days after my safe arrival at Palenque, I seized a favorable opportunity to visit the ruins of *Casa Grande*. I readily found the opening to the subterranean passage heretofore described, and after some troublesome delays at the various landing-places, I finally succeeded in reaching the very spot whence I had ascended on that eventful night, nearly three years before, in company with the Aztec Princess.

After exploring many of the mouldering and half-ruined apartments of this immense palace, I accidently entered a small room, that at first seemed to have been a place of sacrifice; but, upon closer inspection, I ascertained that, like many of those in the "Living City," it was a chapel dedicated to the memory of some one of the princes of the Aztec race.

In order to interpret the inscriptions with greater facility, I lit six or seven candles, and placed them in the best positions to illuminate the hieroglyphics. Then turning, to take a view of the grand tablet in the middle of the inscription, my astonishment was indescribable, when I beheld the exact features, dress and *panache* of the Aztec maiden, carved in the everlasting marble before me.

VIII.

THE MOTHER'S EPISTLE.

SWEET daughter, leave thy tasks and toys,
  Throw idle thoughts aside,
And hearken to a mother's voice,
  That would thy footsteps guide;
Though far across the rolling seas,
  Beyond the mountains blue,
She sends her counsels on the breeze,
  And wafts her blessings too.

To guard thy voyage o'er life's wave,
  To guide thy bark aright,
To snatch thee from an early grave,
  And gild thy way with light,
Thy mother calls thee to her side,
  And takes thee on her knee,
In spite of oceans that divide,
  And thus addresses thee:

I.

Learn first this lesson in thy youth,
  Which time cannot destroy,
To love and speak and act the truth—
  'Tis life's most holy joy;
Wert thou a queen upon a throne,
  Decked in each royal gem,
This little jewel would alone
  Outshine thy diadem.

II.

Next learn to conquer, as they rise,
Each wave of passion's sea;
Unchecked, 'twill sweep the vaulted skies,
And vanquish heaven and thee;
Lashed on by storms within thy breast,
These billows of the soul
Will wreck thy peace, destroy thy rest,
And ruin as they roll!

III.

But conquered passions were no gain,
Unless where once they grew
There falls the teardrop, like the rain,
And gleams the morning dew;
Sow flowers within thy virgin heart,
That spring from guileless love;
Extend to each a sister's part,
Take lessons of the dove.

IV.

But, daughter, empty were our lives,
And useless all our toils,
If that within us, which survives
Life's transient battle-broils,
Were all untaught in heavenly lore,
Unlearned in virtue's ways,
Ungifted with religion's store,
Unskilled our God to praise.

V.

Take for thy guide the Bible old,
Consult its pages fair
Within them glitter gems and gold,
Repentance, Faith, and Prayer;
Make these companions of thy soul;
Where e'er thy footsteps roam,
And safely shalt thou reach thy goal,
In heaven—the angel's home!

IX.

LEGENDS OF LAKE BIGLER.

I.—THE HAUNTED ROCK.

A GREAT many years ago, ere the first white man had trodden the soil of the American continent, and before the palaces of Uxmal and Palenque were masses of shapeless ruins—whilst the splendid structures, now lining the banks of the Gila with broken columns and fallen domes were inhabited by a nobler race than the cowardly Pimos or the Ishmaelitish Apaches, there lived and flourished on opposite shores of Lake Bigler two rival nations, disputing with each other for the supremacy of this inland sea, and making perpetual war in order to accomplish the object of their ambition.

The tribe dwelling upon the western shore was called the Ako-ni-tas, whilst those inhabiting what is now the State of Nevada were known by the name of Gra-so-po-itas. Each nation was subdivided into smaller principalities, over which subordinate sachems, or chiefs, presided. In number, physical appearance, and advance in the arts of civilization, both very much resembled, and neither could be said to have decidedly the pre-eminence.

At the time my story commences, Wan-ta-tay-to was principal chief or king of the Ako-ni-tas, or, as they were sometimes designated, O-kak-o-nitas, whilst Rhu-tog-au-di presided over the destinies of the Gra-so-po-itas. The language spoken by these tribes were dialects of the same original tongue, and could be easily understood the one by the other. Continued intercourse, even when at war, had assimilated their customs, laws and religion to such a degree that it often became a matter of grave doubt as to which tribe occasional deserters belonged. Intermarriage between the tribes was strictly forbidden, and punished with death in all cases, no matter what might be the rank, power or wealth of the violators of the law.

At this era the surface of the lake was about sixty feet higher than at the present time. Constant evaporation, or perhaps the wearing channel of the Truckee, has contributed to lower the level of the water, and the same causes still continue in operation, as is clearly perceptible by the watermarks of previous years. Thousands of splendid canoes everywhere dotted its surface; some of them engaged in the peaceful avocations of fishing and hunting, whilst the large majority were manned and armed for immediate and deadly hostilities.

The year preceding that in which the events occurred herein related, had been a very disastrous one to both tribes. A great many deaths had ensued from casualties in battle; but the chief source of disaster had been a most terrific hurricane, which had swept over the lake, upsetting, sinking, and destroying whole fleets of canoes, with all persons aboard at the time. Amongst the lost were both the royal barges, with the sons and daughters of the chiefs. The loss had been so overwhelming and general that the chief of the O-kak-o-nitas had but one solitary representative of the line royal left, and that was a beloved daughter named Ta-kem-ena. The rival chieftain was equally unfortunate, for his entire wigwam had perished with the exception of Mo-ca-ru-po, his youngest son. But these great misfortunes, instead of producing peace and good-will, as a universal calamity would be sure to do in an enlightened nation, tended only to embitter the passions of the hostile kings and lend new terrors to the war. At once made aware of what the other had suffered, each promulgated a sort of proclamation, offering an immense reward for the scalp of his rival's heir.

Wan-ta-tay-to declared that he would give one half his realm to whomsoever brought the body of Mo-ca-ru-po, dead or alive, within his lines; and Rhu-tog-au-di, not to be outdone in extravagance, registered an oath that whosoever captured Ta-kem-ena, the beautiful daughter of his enemy, should be rewarded with her patrimonial rights, and also be associated with him in ruling his own dominions.

As is universally the case with all American Indians, the females are equally warlike and sometimes quite as brave as the males. Ta-kem-ena was no exception to this rule, and she accordingly made instant preparations to capture or kill the heir to the throne of her enemy. For this purpose she selected a small, light bark canoe, and resolved all alone to make the attempt. Nor did she communicate her intention to any one else. Her father, even, was kept in profound ignorance of his daughter's design.

About the same time, a desire for fame, and a thirsting for supreme power, allured young Mo-ca-ru-po into the lists of those who became candidates for the recent reward offered by his father. He, too, determined to proceed alone.

It was just at midnight, of a beautiful moonlight evening, that the young scions of royalty set forth from opposite shores of the lake, and stealthily paddled for the dominions of their enemies. When about half across the boats came violently into collision. Each warrior seized arms for the conflict. The light of the full moon, riding at mid-heavens, fell softly upon the features of the Princess, and at the same time illuminated those of the young Prince.

The blows from the uplifted battle-axes failed to descend. The poisoned arrows were returned to their quivers. Surprise gave place quickly to admiration—that to something more human—pity followed close in the rear, and love, triumphant everywhere, paralyzed the muscles, benumbed the faculties, and captured the souls of his victims. Pouring a handful of the pure water of the lake upon each other's heads, as a pledge of love, and a ceremonial of marriage, in another moment the two were locked in each other's arms, made man and wife by the yearnings of the soul, and by a destiny which naught but Omnipotent Power could avert. What were the commands of kings, their threats, or their punishments, in the scale with youth, and hope, and love?

Never did those transparent waters leap more lightly beneath the moonbeams than upon this auspicious night. Hate, revenge, fame, power, all were forgotten in the supreme delights of love.

Who, indeed, would not be a lover? The future takes the hue of the rainbow, and spans the whole earth with its arch. The past fades into instant oblivion, and its dark scenes are remembered no more. Every beautiful thing looks lovelier—spring's breath smells sweeter—the heavens bend lower—the stars shine brighter. The eyes, the lips, the smiles of the loved one, bankrupt all nature. The diamond's gleam, the flower's blush, the fountain's purity, are all *her* own! The antelope's swiftness, the buffalo's strength, the lion's bravery, are but the reflex of *his* manly soul!

Fate thus had bound these two lovers in indissoluble bonds: let us now see what it had left in reserve.

The plashing of paddles aroused the lovers from their caressing. Quickly leaping into his own boat, side by side, they flew over the exultant waves, careless for the moment whither they went, and really aimless in their destination. Having safely eluded their pursuers, if such they were, the princes now consulted as to their future course. After long and anxious debate it was finally determined that they should part for the present, and would each night continue to meet at midnight at the majestic rock which towered up from the waves high into the heavens, not far from what is now known as Pray's Farm, that being the residence and headquarters of the O-kak-oni-ta tribe.

Accordingly, after many protestations of eternal fidelity, and warned by the ruddy gleam along the eastern sky, they parted.

Night after night, for many weeks and months, the faithful lovers met at the appointed place, and proved their affection by their constancy. They soon made the discovery that the immense rock was hollow, and contained a magnificent cave. Here, safe from all observation, the tardy months rolled by, both praying for peace, yet neither daring to mention a termination of hostilities to their sires. Finally, the usual concomitants of lawful wedlock began to grow manifest in the rounded form of the Princess—in her sadness, her drooping eyes, and her perpetual uneasiness whilst in the presence of her father. Not able any longer to conceal her griefs, they became the court scandal, and she was summoned to the royal presence and required to name her lover. This, of course, she persisted in refusing, but spies having been set upon her movements, herself and lover were surrounded and entrapped in the fatal cave.

In vain did she plead for the life of the young prince, regardless of her own. His doom was sealed. An embassador was sent to Rhu-tog-au-di, announcing the treachery of his son, and inviting that chief to be present at the immolation of both victims. He willingly consented to assist in the ceremonies. A grand council of the two nations was immediately called, in order to determine in what manner the death penalty should be inflicted. After many and grave debates, it was resolved that the lovers should be incarcerated in the dark and gloomy cave where they had spent so many happy hours, and there starve to death.

It was a grand gala-day with the Okak-oni-tas and the Gra-sop-o-itas. The mighty chiefs had been reconciled, and the wealth, power and beauty of the two realms turned out in all the splendor of fresh paint and brilliant feathers, to do honor to the occasion. The young princes were to be put to death. The lake in the vicinity of the rock was alive with canoes. The hills in the neighborhood were crowded with spectators. The two old kings sat in the same splendid barge, and followed close after the bark canoe in which the lovers were being conveyed to their living tomb. Silently they gazed into each other's faces and smiled. For each other had they lived; with one another were they now to die. Without food, without water, without light, they were hurried into their bridal chamber, and huge stones rolled against the only entrance.

Evening after evening the chiefs sat upon the grave

portals of their children. At first they were greeted with loud cries, extorted by the gnawing of hunger and the agony of thirst. Gradually the cries gave way to low moans, and finally, after ten days had elapsed, the tomb became as silent as the lips of the lovers. Then the huge stones were, by the command of the two kings, rolled away, and a select body of warriors ordered to enter and bring forth their lifeless forms. But the west wind had sprung up, and just as the stones were taken from the entrance, a low, deep, sorrowful sigh issued from the mouth of the cave. Startled and terrified beyond control, the warriors retreated hastily from the spot; and the weird utterances continuing, no warriors could be found brave enough to sound the depths of that dreadful sepulchre. Day after day canoes crowded about the mouth of the cave, and still the west wind blew, and still the sighs and moans continued to strike the souls of the trembling warriors.

Finally, no canoe dared approach the spot. In paddling past they would always veer their canoes seaward, and hurry past with all the speed they could command.

Centuries passed away; the level of the lake had sunk many feet; the last scions of the O-kak-oni-tas and the Gra-sop-o-itas had mouldered many years in the burying-grounds of their sires, and a new race had usurped their old hunting grounds. Still no one had ever entered the haunted cave.

One day, late in the autumn of 1849, a company of emigrants on their way to California, were passing, toward evening, the mouth of the cavern, and hearing a strange, low, mournful sigh, seeming to issue thence, they landed their canoe and resolved to solve the mystery. Lighting some pitch-pine torches, they proceeded cautiously to explore the cavern. For a long time they could discern nothing. At length, in the furthest corner of the gloomy recess, they found two human skeletons, with their bony arms entwined, and their fleshless skulls resting upon each other's bosoms. The lovers are dead, but the old cave still echoes with their dying sobs.

II.—DICK BARTER'S YARN; OR, THE LAST OF THE MERMAIDS.

WELL, Dick began, you see I am an old salt, having sailed the seas for more than forty-nine years, and being entirely unaccustomed to living upon the land. By some accident or other, I found myself, in the winter of 1849, cook for a party of miners who were sluicing high up the North Fork of the American. We had a hard time all winter, and when spring opened, it was agreed that I and a comrade named Liehard should cross the summit and spend a week fishing at the lake. We took along an old Washoe Indian, who spoke Spanish, as a guide. This old man had formerly lived on the north margin of the lake, near where Tahoe City is now situated, and was perfectly familiar with all the most noted fishing grounds and chief points of interest throughout its entire circuit.

We had hardly got started before he commenced telling us of a remarkable struggle, which he declared had been going on for many hundred years between a border tribe of Indians and the inhabitants of the lake, whom he designated as Water-men, or "*hombres de las aguas.*" On asking if he really meant to say that human beings lived and breathed like fish in Lake Bigler, he declared without any hesitation that such was the fact; that he had often seen them; and went on to describe a terrific combat he witnessed a great many years ago, between a Pol-i-wog chief and *a man of the water*. On my expressing some doubt as to the veracity of the statement, he proffered to show us the very spot where it occurred; and at the same time expressed a belief that by manufacturing a whistle from the bark of the mountain chinquapin, and blowing it as the Pol-i-wogs did, we might entice some of their old enemies from the depths of the lake. My curiosity now being raised tip-toe, I proceeded to interrogate Juan more closely, and in answer I succeeded in obtaining the following curious particulars:

The tribe of border Indians called the Pol-i-wogs were a sort of amphibious race, and a hybrid between the Pi-Utes and the mermaids of the lake. They were of a much lighter color than their progenitors, and were distinguished by a great many peculiar characteristics. Exceedingly few in number, and quarrelsome in the extreme, they resented every intrusion upon the waters of the lake as a personal affront, and made perpetual war upon neighboring tribes. Hence, as Juan remarked, they soon became extinct after the invasion of the Washoes. The last of them disappeared about twenty-five years ago. The most noted of their peculiarities were the following:

First. Their heads were broad and extremely flat; the eyes protuberant, and the ears scarcely perceptible —being a small opening closed by a movable valve shaped like the scale of a salmon. Their mouths were very large, extending entirely across the cheeks, and bounded by a hard rim of bone, instead of the common lip. In appearance, therefore, the head did not look unlike an immense catfish head, except there were no fins about the jaws, and no feelers, as we call them.

Second. Their necks were short, stout, and chubby,

and they possessed the power of inflating them at will, and thus distending them to two or three times their ordinary size.

Third. Their bodies were long, round, and flexible. When wet, they glistened in the sun like the back of an eel, and seemed to possess much greater buoyancy than those of common men. But the greatest wonder of all was a kind of loose membrane, that extended from beneath their shoulders all the way down their sides, and connected itself with the upper portion of their thighs. This loose skin resembled the wings of the common house bat, and when spread out, as it always did in the water, looked like the membrane lining of the legs and fore feet of the chipmunk.

Fourth. The hands and feet were distinguished for much greater length of toe and finger; and their extremities grew together like the toes of a duck, forming a complete web betwixt all the fingers and toes.

The Pol-i-wogs lived chiefly upon fish and oysters, of which there was once a great abundance in the lake. They were likewise cannibals, and ate their enemies without stint or compunction. A young Washoe girl was considered a feast, but a lake maiden was the *ne plus ultra* of luxuries. The Washoes reciprocated the compliment, and fattened upon the blubber of the Pol-i-wogs. It is true that they were extremely difficult to capture, for, when hotly pursued, they plunged into the lake, and by expert swimming and extraordinary diving, they generally managed to effect their escape.

Juan having exhausted his budget concerning the Pol-i-wogs, I requested him to give us as minute a description of the Lake Mermaids. This he declined for the present to do, alleging as an excuse that we would first attempt to capture, or at least to see one for ourselves, and if our hunt was unsuccessful, he would then gratify our curiosity.

It was some days before we came in sight of this magnificent sheet of water. Finally, however, after many perilous adventures in descending the Sierras, we reached the margin of the lake. Our first care was to procure trout enough to last until we got ready to return. That was an easy matter, for in those days the lake was far more plentifully supplied than at present. We caught many thousands at a place where a small brook came down from the mountains, and formed a pool not a great distance from its entrance into the lake, and this pool was alive with them. It occupied us but three days to catch, clean, and sun-dry as many as our single mule could carry, and having still nearly a week to spare we determined to start off in pursuit of the mermaids.

Our guide faithfully conducted us to the spot where he beheld the conflict between the last of the Pol-i-wogs and one of the water-men. As stated above, it is nearly on the spot where Tahoe City now stands. The battle was a fierce one, as the combatants were equally matched in strength and endurance, and was finally terminated only by the interposition of a small party of Washoes, our own guide being of the number. The struggle was chiefly in the water, the Pol-i-wog being better able to swim than the mermaid was to walk. Still, as occasion required, a round or two took place on the gravelly beach. Never did old Spain and England engage in fiercer conflict for the dominion of the seas, than now occurred between Pol-i-wog and Merman for the mastery of the lake. Each fought, as the Roman fought, for Empire. The Pol-i-wog, like the last of the Mohicans, had seen his tribe melt away, until he stood, like some solitary column at Persepolis, the sole monument of a once gorgeous temple. The water chieftain also felt that upon his arm, or rather tail, everything that made life desirable was staked. Above all, the trident of his native sea was involved.

The weapons of the Pol-i-wog were his teeth and his hind legs. Those of the Merman were all concentrated in the flop of his scaly tail. With the energy of a dying alligator, he would encircle, with one tremendous effort, the bruised body of the Pol-i-wog, and floor him beautifully on the beach. Recovering almost instantly, the Pol-i-wog would seize the Merman by the long black hair, kick him in the region of the stomach, and grapple his windpipe between his bony jaws, as the mastiff does the infuriated bull.

Finally, after a great many unsuccessful attempts to drag the Pol-i-wog into deep water, the mermaid was seized by her long locks and suddenly jerked out upon the beach in a very battered condition. At this moment, the Washoes with a yell rushed toward the combatants, but the Pol-i-wog seeing death before him upon water and land equally, preferred the embraces of the water nymphs to the stomachs of the landsmen, and rolling over rapidly was soon borne off into unfathomable depths by the triumphant Merman.

Such was the story of Juan. It resembled the condition of the ancient Britons, who, being crowded by the Romans from the sea, and attacked by the Picts from the interior, lamented their fate as the most unfortunate of men. "The Romans," they said, "drive us into the land; there we are met by the Picts, who in turn drive us into the sea. We must perish in either event. Those whom enemies spare, the waves devour."

Our first step was to prepare a chinquapin whistle. The flute was easily manufactured by Juan himself, thuswise: He cut a twig about eighteen inches in length, and not more than half an inch in diameter, and peeling the bark from the ends an inch or so, proceeded to rub the bark rapidly with a dry stick peeled perfectly smooth. In a short time the sap in the twig commenced to exude from both ends. Then placing the large end between his teeth he pulled suddenly, and the bark slipped off with a crack in it. Then cutting a small hole in the form of a parallelogram, near the upper end, he adjusted a stopper with flattened surface so as to fit exactly the opening. Cutting off the end of the stopple even with the bark and filling the lower opening nearly full of clay, he declared the work was done. As a proof of this, he blew into the hollow tube, and a low, musical sound was emitted, very flute-like and silvery. When blown harshly, it could be heard at a great distance, and filled the air with melodious echoes.

Thus equipped, we set out upon our search. The first two days were spent unsuccessfully. On the third we found ourselves near what is now called Agate Beach. At this place a small cove indents the land, which sweeps round in the form of a semi-circle. The shore is literally packed with agates and crystals. We dug some more than two feet deep in several places, but still could find no bottom to the glittering floor. They are of all colors, but the prevailing hues are red and yellow. Here Juan paused, and lifting his whistle to his lips, he performed a multitude of soft, gentle airs, which floated across the calm waves like a lover's serenade breathes o'er the breast of sleeping beauty. It all seemed in vain. We had now entirely circumnavigated the lake, and were on the eve of despairing utterly, when suddenly we beheld the surface of the lake, nearly a quarter of a mile from the shore, disturbed violently, as if some giant whale were floundering with a harpoon in its side. In a moment more the head and neck of one of those tremendous serpents that of late years have infested the lake, were uplifted some ten or fifteen feet above the surface. Almost at the same instant we beheld the head, face and hair, as of a human being, emerge quickly from the water, and look back toward the pursuing foe. The truth flashed upon us instantaneously. Here was a mermaid pursued by a serpent. On they came, seemingly regardless of our presence, and had approached to within twenty yards of the spot where we stood, when suddenly both came to a dead halt. Juan had never ceased for a moment to blow his tuneful flute, and it now became apparent that the notes had struck their hearing at the same time. To say that they were charmed would but half express their ecstatic condition. They were absolutely entranced.

The huge old serpent lolled along the waters for a hundred feet or so, and never so much as shook the spray from his hide. He looked like Milton's portrait of Satan, stretched out upon the burning marl of hell. In perfect contrast with the sea monster, the beautiful mermaiden lifted her pallid face above the water, dripping with the crystal tears of the lake, and gathering her long raven locks, that floated like the train of a meteor down her back, she carelessly flung them across her swelling bosom, as if to reproach us for gazing upon her beauteous form. But there my eyes were fastened! If she were entranced by the music, I was not less so with her beauty. Presently the roseate hues of a dying dolphin played athwart her brow and cheeks, and ere long a gentle sigh, as if stolen from the trembling chords of an Eolian harp, issued from her coral lips. Again and again it broke forth, until it beat in full symphony with the cadences of Juan's rustic flute.

My attention was at this moment aroused by the suspicious clicking of my comrade's rifle. Turning around suddenly, I beheld Liehard, with his piece leveled at the unconscious mermaid.

"Great God!" I exclaimed! "Liehard, would you commit murder?" But the warning came too late, for instantaneously the quick report of his rifle and the terrific shriek of the mermaid broke the noontide stillness; and, rearing her bleeding form almost entirely out of the water, she plunged headlong forwards, a corpse. Beholding his prey, powerless within his grasp, the serpent splashed toward her, and, ere I could cock my rifle, he had seized her unresisting body, and sank with it into the mysterious caverns of the lake. At this instant, I gave a loud outcry, as if in pain. On opening my eyes, my wife was bending over me, the midday sun was shining in my face, Dick Barter was spinning some confounded yarn about the Bay of Biscay and the rum trade of Jamaica, and the sloop *Edith Beaty* was still riding at anchor off the wild glen, and gazing tranquilly at her ugly image in the crystal mirror of Lake Bigler.

X.

ROSENTHAL'S ELAINE.

I STOOD and gazed far out into the waste;
No dip of oar broke on the listening ear;
But the quick rippling of the inward flood
Gave warning of approaching argosy.

Adown the west, the day's last fleeting gleam
Faded and died, and left the world in gloom.
Hope hung no star up in the murky east
To cheer the soul, or guide the pilgrim's way.
Black frown'd the heavens, and black the answering
earth
Reflected from her watery wastes the night.

Sudden, a plash! then silence. Once again
The dripping oar dipped in its silver blade,
Parting the waves, as smiles part beauty's lips.
Betwixt me and the curtain of the cloud,
Close down by the horizon's verge, there crept
From out the darkness, barge and crew and freight,
Sailless and voiceless, all!
Ah! Then I knew
I stood upon the brink of Time. I saw
Before me Death's swift river sweep along
And bear its burden to the grave.
"Elaine!"
One seamew screamed, in solitary woe;
"Elaine! Elaine!" stole back the echo, weird
And musical, from off the further shore.
Then burst a chorus wild, "Elaine! Elaine!"
And gazing upward through the twilight haze,

Mine eyes beheld King Arthur's phantom Court.
There stood the sturdy monarch: he who drove
The hordes of Hengist from old Albion's strand;
And, leaning on his stalwart arm, his queen,
The fair, the false, but trusted Guinevere!
And there, like the statue of a demi-god,
In marble wrought by some old Grecian hand,
With eyes downcast, towered Lancelot of the Lake.
Lavaine and Torre, the heirs of Astolat,
And he, the sorrowing Sire of the Dead,
Together with a throng of valiant knights
And ladies fair, were gathered as of yore,
At the Round Table of bold Arthur's Court.
There, too, was Tristram, leaning on his lance,
Whose eyes alone of all that weeping host
Swam not in tears; but indignation burned
Red in their sockets, like volcanic fires,
And from their blazing depths a Fury shot
Her hissing arrows at the guilty pair.
Then Lancelot, advancing to the front,
With glance transfixed upon the canvas true
That sheds immortal fame on ROSENTHAL,
Thus chanted forth his Requiem for the Dead:

Fresh as the water in the fountain,
Fair as the lily by its side,
Pure as the snow upon the mountain,
Is the angel
Elaine!
My spirit bride!

Day after day she grew fairer,
As she pined away in sorrow, at my side;
No pearl in the ocean could be rarer
Than the angel
Elaine!
My spirit bride!

The hours passed away all unheeded,
For love hath no landmarks in its tide.
No child of misfortune ever pleaded
In vain
To Elaine!
My spirit bride!

Here, where sad Tamesis is rolling
The wave of its sorrow-laden tide,
Forever on the air is heard tolling
The refrain
Of Elaine!
My spirit bride!

XI.

THE TELESCOPIC EYE.

A LEAF FROM A REPORTER'S NOTE-BOOK.

FOR the past five or six weeks, rumors of a strange abnormal development of the powers of vision of a youth named Johnny Palmer, whose parents reside at South San Francisco, have been whispered around in scientific circles in the city, and one or two short notices have appeared in the columns of some of our contemporaries relative to the prodigious *lusus naturæ*, as the scientists call it.

Owing to the action taken by the California College of Sciences, whose members comprise some of our most scientific citizens, the affair has assumed such importance as to call for a careful and exhaustive investigation.

Being detailed to investigate the flying stories, with regard to the powers of vision claimed for a lad named John or "Johnny" Palmer, as his parents call him, we first of all ventured to send in our card to Professor Gibbins, the President of the California College of Sciences. It is always best to call at the fountain-head for useful information, a habit which our two hundred thousand readers on this coast can never fail to see and appreciate. An estimable gentleman of the African persuasion, to whom we handed our "pasteboard," soon returned with the polite message, "Yes, sir; *in*. Please walk up." And so we followed our conductor through several passages almost as dark as the face of the *cicerone,* and in a few moments found ourselves in the presence of, perhaps, the busiest man in the city of San Francisco.

Without any flourish of trumpets, the Professor inquired our object in seeking him and the information we desired. "Ah," said he, "that is a long story. I have no time to go into particulars just now. I am computing the final sheet of Professor Davidson's report of the Transit of Venus, last year, at Yokohama and Loo-Choo. It must be ready before May, and it requires six months' work to do it correctly."

"But," I rejoined, "can't you tell me where the lad is to be found?"

"And if I did, they will not let you see him."

"Let me alone for that," said I, smiling; "a reporter, like love, finds his way where wolves would fear to tread."

"Really, my dear sir," quickly responded the Doctor, "I have no time to chat this morning. Our special committee submitted its report yesterday, which is on file in that book-case; and if you will promise not to publish it until after it has been read in open session of the College, you may take it to your sanctum, run it over, and clip from it enough to satisfy the public for the present."

Saying this, he rose from his seat, opened the case, took from a pigeon-hole a voluminous written document tied up with red tape, and handed it to me, adding, "Be careful!" Seating himself without another word, he turned his back on me, and I sallied forth into the street.

Reaching the office, I scrutinized the writing on the envelope, and found it as follows: "Report of Special Committee—Boy Palmer—Vision—Laws of Light—

Filed February 10, 1876—Stittmore, Sec." Opening the document, I saw at once that it was a full, accurate, and, up to the present time, complete account of the phenomenal case I was after, and regretted the promise made not to publish the entire report until read in open session of the College. Therefore, I shall be compelled to give the substance of the report in my own words, only giving *verbatim* now and then a few scientific phrases which are not fully intelligible to me, or susceptible of circumlocution in common language.

The report is signed by Doctors Bryant, Gadbury and Golson, three of our ablest medical men, and approved by Professor Smyth, the oculist. So far, therefore, as authenticity and scientific accuracy are concerned, our readers may rely implicitly upon the absolute correctness of every fact stated and conclusion reached.

The first paragraph of the report gives the name of the child, "John Palmer, age, nine years, and place of residence, South San Francisco, Culp Hill, near Catholic Orphan Asylum;" and then plunges at once into *in medias res.*

It appears that the period through which the investigation ran was only fifteen days; but it seems to have been so thorough, by the use of the ophthalmoscope and other modern appliances and tests, that no regrets ought to be indulged as to the brevity of the time employed in experiments. Besides, we have superadded a short and minute account of our own, verifying some of the most curious facts reported, with several tests proposed by ourselves and not included in the statement of the scientific committee.

To begin, then, with the beginning of the inquiries by the committee. They were conducted into a small back room, darkened by old blankets hung up at the window, for the purpose of the total exclusion of daylight; an absurd remedy for blindness, recommended by a noted quack whose name adorns the extra fly-leaf of the San Francisco *Truth Teller*. The lad was reclining upon an old settee, ill-clad and almost idiotic in expression. As the committee soon ascertained, his mother only was at home, the father being absent at his customary occupation—that of switch-tender on the San Jose Railroad. She notified her son of the presence of strangers and he rose and walked with a firm step toward where the gentlemen stood, at the entrance of the room. He shook them all by the hand and bade them good morning. In reply to questions rapidly put and answered by his mother, the following account of the infancy of the boy and the accidental discovery of his extraordinary powers of vision was given:

He was born in the house where the committee found him, nine years ago the 15th of last January. Nothing of an unusual character occurred until his second year, when it was announced by a neighbor that the boy was completely blind, his parents never having been suspicious of the fact before that time, although the mother declared that for some months anterior to the discovery she had noticed some acts of the child that seemed to indicate mental imbecility rather than blindness. From this time forward until a few months ago nothing happened to vary the boy's existence except a new remedy now and then prescribed by neighbors for the supposed malady. He was mostly confined to a darkened chamber, and was never trusted alone out of doors. He grew familiar, by touch and sound, with the forms of most objects about him, and could form very accurate guesses of the color and texture of them all. His conversational powers did not seem greatly impaired, and he readily acquired much useful knowledge from listening attentively to everything that was said in his presence. He was quite a musician, and touched the harmonicon, banjo and accordeon with skill and feeling. He was unusually sensitive to the presence of light, though incapable of seeing any object with any degree of distinctness; and hence the attempt to exclude light as the greatest enemy to the recovery of vision. It was very strange that up to the time of the examination of the committee, no scientific examination of the boy's eye had been made by a competent oculist, the parents contenting themselves with the chance opinions of visitors or the cheap nostrums of quacks. It is perhaps fortunate for science that this was the case, as a cure for the eye might have been an extinction of its abnormal power.

On the evening of the 12th of December last (1875), the position of the child's bed was temporarily changed to make room for a visitor. The bed was placed against the wall of the room, fronting directly east, with the window opening at the side of the bed next to the head. The boy was sent to bed about seven o'clock, and the parents and their visitor were seated in the front room, spending the evening in social intercourse. The moon rose full and cloudless about half-past seven o'clock, and shone full in the face of the sleeping boy.

Something aroused him from slumber, and when he opened his eyes the first object they encountered was the round disk of her orb. By some oversight the curtain had been removed from the window, and probably for the first time in his life he beheld the lustrous queen of night swimming in resplendent radiance, and bathing hill and bay in effulgent glory. Uttering a cry, equally of terror and delight, he sprang up in bed and sat there like a statue, with eyes aglare, mouth open, finger pointed, and astonishment depicted on every feature. His sudden, sharp scream brought his mother to his side, who tried for some moments in vain to distract his gaze from the object before him. Failing even to attract notice, she called in her husband and friend, and together they besought the boy to lie down and go to sleep, but to no avail. Believing him to be ill and in convulsions, they soon seized him, and were on the point of immersing him in a hot bath, when, with a sudden spring, he escaped from their grasp and ran out the front door. Again he fixed his unwinking eyes upon the moon, and remained speechless for several seconds. At length, having seemingly satisfied his present curiosity, he turned on his mother, who stood wringing her hands in the doorway and moaning piteously, and exclaimed, "I can see the moon yonder, and it is so beautiful that I am going there to-morrow morning, as soon as I get up."

"How big does it look?" said his mother.

"So big," he replied, "that I cannot see it all at one glance—as big as all out of doors."

"How far off from you does it seem to be?"

"About half a car's distance," he quickly rejoined.

It may be here remarked that the boy's idea of distance had been measured all his life by the distance from his home to the street-car station at the foot of the hill. This was about two hundred yards, so that the reply indicated that the moon appeared to be only one hundred yards from the spectator. The boy then proceeded of his own accord to give a very minute description of the appearance of objects which he beheld, corresponding, of course, to his poverty of words with which to clothe his ideas.

His account of things beheld by him was so curious, wonderful and apparently accurate, that the little group about him passed rapidly from a conviction of his insanity to a belief no less absurd—that he had become, in the cant lingo of the day, a seeing, or "clairvoyant" medium. Such was the final conclusion to which his parents had arrived at the time of the visit of the scientific committee. He had been classed with that credulous school known to this century as spiritualists, and had been visited solely by persons of that ilk heretofore.

The committee having fully examined the boy, and a number of independent witnesses, as to the facts, soon set about a scientific investigation of the true causes of of the phenomenon. The first step, of course, was to examine the lad's eye with the modern ophthalmoscope, an invention of Professor Helmholtz, of Heidelberg, a few years ago, by means of which the depths of this organ can be explored, and the smallest variations from a healthy or normal condition instantaneously detected.

The mode of using the instrument is as follows: The room is made perfectly dark; a brilliant light is then placed near the head of the patient, and the rays are reflected by a series of small mirrors into his eye, as if they came from the eye of the observer; then, by looking through the central aperture of the instrument, the oculist can examine the illuminated interior of the eyeball, and perceive every detail of structure, healthy or morbid, as accurately and clearly as we can see any part of the exterior of the body. No discomfort arises to the organ examined, and all its hidden mysteries can be studied and understood as clearly as those of any other organ of the body.

This course was taken with John Palmer, and the true secret of his mysterious power of vision detected in an instant.

On applying the ophthalmoscope, the committee ascertained in a moment that the boy's eye was abnormally shaped. A natural, perfect eye is perfectly round. But the eye examined was exceedingly flat, very thin, with large iris, flat lens, immense petira, and wonderfully dilated pupil. The effect of the shape was at once apparent. It was utterly impossible to see any object with distinctness at any distance short of many thousands of miles. Had the eye been elongated inward, or shaped like an egg—to as great an extent, the boy would have been effectually blind, for no combination of lens power could have placed the image of the object beyond the coat of the retina. In other words, there are two common imperfections of the human organ of sight; one called *myopia*, or "near-sightedness;" the *presbyopia*, or "far-sightedness."

"The axis being too long," says the report, "in myopic eyes, parallel rays, such as proceed from distant objects, are brought to a focus at a point so far in front of the retina, that only confused images are formed upon it. Such a malformation, constituting an excess of refractive power, can only be neutralized by concave glasses, which give such a direction to rays entering the eye as will allow of their being brought to a focus at a proper point for distant perception."

"Presbyopia is the reverse of all this. The antero-posterior axis of such eyes being too short, owing to the flat plate-like shape of the ball, their refractive power is not sufficient to bring even parallel rays to a focus upon the retina, but is adapted for convergent rays only. Convex glasses, in a great measure, compensate for this quality by rendering parallel rays convergent; and such glasses, in ordinary cases, bring the rays to a focus at a convenient distance from the glass, corresponding to its degree of curvature. But in the case under examination, no glass or combination of glasses could be invented sufficiently concave to remedy the malformation. By a mathematical problem of easy solution, it was computed that the nearest distance from the unaided eye of the patient at which a distinct image could be formed upon the retina, was two hundred and forty thousand miles, a fraction short of the mean distance of the moon from the earth; and hence it became perfectly clear that the boy could see with minute distinctness whatever was transpiring on the surface of the moon.

Such being the undeniable truth as demonstrated by science, the declaration of the lad assumed a far higher value than the mere dicta of spiritualists, or the mad ravings of a monomaniac; and the committee at once set to work to glean all the astronomical knowledge they could by frequent and prolonged night interviews with the boy.

It was on the night of January 9, 1876, that the first satisfactory experiment was tried, testing beyond all cavil or doubt the powers of the subject's eye. It was full moon, and that luminary rose clear and dazzlingly bright. The committee were on hand at an early hour, and the boy was in fine condition and exuberant spirits. The interview was secret, and none but the members of the committee and the parents of the child were present. Of course the first proposition to be settled was that of the inhabitability of that sphere. This the boy had frequently declared was the case, and he had on several previous occasions described minutely the form, size and means of locomotion of the Lunarians. On this occasion he repeated in almost the same language, what he had before related to his parents and friends, but was more minute, owing to the greater transparency of the atmosphere and the experience in expression already acquired.

The Lunarians are not formed at all like ourselves. They are less in height, and altogether of a different appearance. When fully grown, they resemble somewhat a chariot wheel, with four spokes, converging at the center or axle. They have four eyes in the head, which is the axle, so to speak, and all the limbs branch out directly from the center, like some sea-forms known as "Radiates." They move by turning rapidly like a wheel, and travel as fast as a bird through the air. The children are undeveloped in form, and are perfectly round, like a pumpkin or orange. As they grow older, they seem to drop or absorb the rotundity of the whole body, and finally assume the appearance of a chariot wheel.

They are of different colors, or nationalties—bright red, orange and blue being the predominant hues. The reds are in a large majority. They do no work, but sleep every four or five hours. They have no houses, and need none. They have no clothing, and do not require it. There being no night on the side of the moon fronting the sun, and no day on the opposite side, all the inhabitants, apparently at a given signal of some kind, form into vast armies, and flock in myriads to the sleeping grounds on the shadow-side of the planet. They do not appear to go very far over the dark rim, for they reappear in immense platoons in a few hours, and soon spread themselves over the illuminated surface. They sleep and wake about six times in one ordinary day of twenty-four hours. Their occupations cannot be discerned; they must be totally different from anything upon the earth.

The surface of the moon is all hill and hollow. There are but few level spots, nor is there any water visible. The atmosphere is almost as refined and light as hydrogen gas. There is no fire visible, nor are there any volcanoes. Most of the time of the inhabitants seems to be spent in playing games of locomotion, spreading themselves into squares, circles, triangles, and other mathematical figures. They move always in vast crowds. No one or two are ever seen separated from the main bodies. The children also flock in herds, and seem to be all of one family. Individualism is unknown. They seem to spawn like herring or shad, or to be propagated like bees, from the queen, in myriads. Motion is their normal condition. The moment after a mathematical figure is formed, it is dissolved, and fresh combinations take place, like the atoms in a kaleidoscope. No other species of animal, bird, or being exist upon the illuminated face of the moon.

The shrubbery and vegetation of the moon is all metallic. Vegetable life nowhere exists; but the forms of some of the shrubs and trees are exceedingly beautiful. The highest trees do not exceed twenty-five feet, and they appear to have all acquired their full growth. The ground is strewn with flowers, but they are all formed of metals—gold, silver, copper, and tin predominating. But there is a new kind of metal seen everywhere on tree, shrub and flower, nowhere known on the earth. It is of a bright vermilion color, and is semi-transparent. The mountains are all of bare and burnt granite, and appear to have been melted with fire. The committee called the attention of the boy to the bright "sea of glass" lately observed near the northern rim of the moon, and inquired of what it is composed. He examined it carefully, and gave such a minute description of it that it became apparent at once to the committee that it was pure mercury or quicksilver. The reason why it has but very recently shown itself to astronomers is thus accounted for: it appears close up to the line of demarcation separating the light and shadow upon the moon's disk; and on closer inspection a distinct cataract of the fluid—in short, a metallic Niagara, was clearly seen falling from the night side to the day side of the luminary. It has already filled up a vast plain—one of the four that exist on the moon's surface—and appears to be still emptying itself with very great rapidity and volume. It covers an area of five by seven hundred miles in extent, and may possibly deluge one half the entire surface of the moon. It does not seem to occasion much apprehension to the inhabitants, as they were seen skating, so to speak, in platoons and battalions, over and across it. In fact, it presents the appearance of an immense park, to which the Lunarians flock, and disport themselves with great gusto upon its polished face. One of the most beautiful sights yet seen by the lad was the formation of a new figure, which he drew upon the sand with his finger.

The central heart was of crimson-colored natives; the one to the right of pale orange, and the left of bright blue. It was ten seconds in forming, and five seconds in dispersing. The number engaged in the evolution could not be less than half a million.

Thus has been solved one of the great astronomical questions of the century.

The next evening the committee assembled earlier, so as to get a view of the planet Venus before the moon rose. It was the first time that the lad's attention had been drawn to any of the planets, and he evinced the liveliest joy when he first beheld the cloudless disk of that resplendent world. It may here be stated that his power of vision, in looking at the fixed stars, was no greater or less than that of an ordinary eye. They appeared only as points of light, too far removed into the infinite beyond to afford any information concerning their pròperties. But the committee were doomed to a greater disappointment when they inquired of the boy what he beheld on the surface of Venus. He replied, "Nothing clearly; all is confused and watery; I see nothing with distinctness." The solution of the difficulty was easily apprehended, and at once surmised. The focus of the eye was fixed by nature at 240,000 miles, and the least distance of Venus from the earth being 24,293,000 miles, it was, of course, impossible to observe that planet's surface with distinctness. Still she appeared greatly enlarged, covering about one hundredth part of the heavens, and blazing with unimaginable splendor.

Experiments upon Jupiter and Mars were equally futile, and the committee half sorrowfully turned again to the inspection of the moon.

The report then proceeds at great length to give full descriptions of the most noted geographical peculiarities of the lunar surface, and corrects many errors fallen into by Herschel, Leverrier and Proctor. Professor Secchi informs us that the surface of the moon is much better known to astronomers than the surface of the earth is to geographers; for there are two zones on the globe within the Arctic and Antarctic circles, that we can never examine. But every nook and cranny of the illuminated face of the moon has been fully delineated, examined and named, so that no object greater than sixty feet square exists but has been seen and photographed by means of Lord Rosse's telescope and De la

Ruis' camera and apparatus. As the entire report will be ordered published at the next weekly meeting of the College, we refrain from further extracts, but now proceed to narrate the results of our own interviews with the boy.

It was on the evening of the 17th of February, 1876, that we ventured with rather a misgiving heart to approach Culp Hill, and the humble residence of a child destined, before the year is out, to become the most celebrated of living beings. We armed ourselves with a pound of sugar candy for the boy, some *muslin-delaine* as a present to the mother, and a box of cigars for the father. We also took with us a very large-sized opera-glass, furnished for the purpose by M. Muller. At first we encountered a positive refusal; then, on exhibiting the cigars, a qualified negative; and finally, when the muslin and candy were drawn on the enemy, we were somewhat coldly invited in and proffered a seat. The boy was pale and restless, and his eyes without bandage or glasses. We soon ingratiated ourself into the good opinion of the whole party, and henceforth encountered no difficulty in pursuing our investigations. The moon being nearly full, we first of all verified the tests by the committee. These were all perfectly satisfactory and reliable. Requesting, then, to stay until after midnight, for the purpose of inspecting Mars with the opera-glass, we spent the interval in obtaining the history of the child, which we have given above.

The planet Mars being at this time almost in dead opposition to the sun, and with the earth in conjunction, is of course as near to the earth as he ever approaches, the distance being thirty-five millions of miles. He rises toward midnight, and is in the constellation Virgo, where he may be seen to the greatest possible advantage, being in perigee. Mars is most like the earth of all the planetary bodies. He revolves on his axis in a little over twenty-four hours, and his surface is pleasantly variegated with land and water, pretty much like our own world—the land, however, being in slight excess. He is, therefore, the most interesting of all the heavenly bodies to the inhabitants of the earth.

Having all things in readiness, we directed the glass to the planet. Alas, for all our calculations, the power was insufficient to clear away the obscurity resulting from imperfect vision and short focus.

Swallowing the bitter disappointment, we hastily made arrangements for another interview, with a telescope, and bade the family good night.

There is but one large telescope properly mounted in the city, and that is the property and pride of its accomplished owner, J. P. Manrow, Esq. We at once procured an interview with that gentleman, and it was agreed that on Saturday evening the boy should be conveyed to his residence, picturesquely situated on Russian Hill, commanding a magnificent view of the Golden Gate and the ocean beyond.

At the appointed hour the boy, his parents and myself presented ourselves at the door of that hospitable mansion. We were cordially welcomed, and conducted without further parley into the lofty observatory on the top of the house. In due time the magnificent tube was presented at the planet, but it was discovered that the power it was set for was too low. It was then gauged for 240,000 diameters, being the full strength of the telescope, and the eye of the boy observer placed at the eye-glass. One cry of joy, and unalloyed delight told the story! Mars, and its mountains and seas, its rivers, vales, and estuaries, its polar snow-caps and grassy plains—its inhabitants, palaces, ships, villages and cities, were all revealed, as distinctly, clearly and certainly, as the eye of Kit Carson, from the summits of the Sierra Nevada range, beheld the stupendous panorama of the Sacramento Valley, and the snow-clad summits of Mount Hood and Shasta Butte.

XII.

THE EMERALD ISLE.

CHAOS was ended. From its ruins rolled
The central Sun, poised on his throne of gold;
The changeful Moon, that floods the hollow dome
Of raven midnight with her silvery foam;
Vast constellations swarming all around,
In seas of azure, without line or bound,
And this green globe, rock-ribbed and mountain-crown'd.

The eye of God, before His hand had made
Man in His image, this wide realm surveyed;
O'er hill and valley, over stream and wood,
He glanced triumphant, and pronounced it "good."
But ere He formed old Adam and his bride,
He called a shining seraph to His side,
And pointing to our world, that gleamed afar,
And twinkled on creation's verge, a star,
Bade him float 'round this new and narrow span
And bring report if all were ripe for Man.
The angel spread his fluttering pinions fair,
And circled thrice the circumambient air;
Quick, then, as thought, he stood before the gate
Where cherubs burn, and minist'ring spirits wait.
Nor long he stood, for God beheld his plume,
Already tarnished by terrestrial gloom,
And beck'ning kindly to the flurried aid,
Said, "Speak your wish; if good, be it obeyed."
The seraph raised his gem-encircled hand,
Obeisance made, at heaven's august command,
And thus replied, in tones so bold and clear,
That angels turned and lent a listening ear:

"Lord of all systems, be they near or far,
Thrice have I circled 'round yon beauteous Star,
I've seen its mountains rise, its rivers roll,
Its oceans sweep majestic to each pole;
Its floors in mighty continents expand,
Or dwindle into specs of fairy-land;
Its prairies spread, its forests stretch in pride,
And all its valleys dazzle like a bride;
Hymns have I heard in all its winds and streams,
And beauty seen in all its rainbow gleams.
But whilst the LAND can boast of every gem
That sparkles in each seraph's diadem;
Whilst diamonds blaze 'neath dusk Golconda's skies,
And rubies bleed where Alps and Andes rise;
Whilst in Brazilian brooks the topaz shines,
And opals burn in California mines;
Whilst in the vales of Araby the Blest
The sapphire flames beside the amethyst:
The pauper Ocean sobs forever more,
Ungemm'd, unjeweled, on its wailing shore!"

"What wouldst thou do?" responded heaven's great King.
"Add music to the song the breakers sing!",
The strong-soul'd seraph cried, "I'd make yon sea
Rival in tone heaven's sweetest minstrelsy;
I'd plant within the ocean's bubbling tide
An island gem, of every sea the pride!
So bright in robes of ever-living green,
In breath so sweet, in features so serene,
Such crystal streams to course its valleys fair,
Such healthful gales to purify its air,
Such fertile soil, such ever-verdant trees,
Angels should name it 'EMERALD OF THE SEAS!'"

The seraph paused, and downward cast his eyes,
Whilst heav'nly hosts stood throbbing with surprise.

Again the Lord of all the realms above,
Supreme in might, but infinite in love,
With no harsh accent in His tones replied:
"Go, drop this Emerald in the envious tide!"

Quick as the lightning cleaves the concave blue,
The seraph seized the proffer'd gem, and flew
Until he reached the confines of the earth,
Still struggling in the throes of turbid birth;
And there, upon his self-sustaining wing,
Sat poised, and heard our globe her matins sing;
Beheld the sun traverse the arching sky,
The sister Moon walk forth in majesty;
Saw every constellation rise and roll
Athwart the heaven, or circle round the pole.
Nor did he move, until our spotted globe
Had donned for him her morn and evening robe;
Till on each land his critic eye was cast,
And every ocean rose, and heav'd, and pass'd;
Then, like some eagle pouncing on its prey,
He downward sail'd, through bellowing clouds and spray,
To where he saw the billows bounding free,
And dropped the gem within the stormy sea!

And would'st thou know, Chief of St. Patrick's band,
Where fell this jewel from the seraph's hand?
What ocean caught the world-enriching prize?
O! Child of Moina, homeward cast your eyes!
Lo! in the midst of wat'ry deserts wide,
Behold the EMERALD bursting through the tide,
And bearing on its ever vernal-sod
The monogram of seraph, and of God!

Its name, the sweetest human lips e'er sung,
First trembled on an angel's fervid tongue;
Then chimed Æolian on the evening air,
Lisped by an infant, in its mother prayer;

Next roared in war, with battle's flag unfurl'd;
Now, gemm'd with glory, gather'd through the world!
What name! Perfidious Albion, blush with shame:
It is thy sister's! Erin is the name!

Once more the seraph stood before the throne
Of dread Omnipotence, pensive and alone.
"What hast thou done?" Heaven's Monarch sadly sigh'd.
"I dropped the jewel in the flashing tide,"
The seraph said; but saw with vision keen
A mightier angel stalk upon the scene,
Whose voice like grating thunder smote his ear
And taught his soul the mystery of fear.

"Because thy heart with impious pride did swell,
And dared make better what thy God made well;
Because thy hand did fling profanely down
On Earth a jewel wrenched from Heaven's bright crown,
The Isle which thine own fingers did create
Shall reap a blessing and a curse from fate!"

THE CURSE.

Far in the future, as the years roll on,
And all the pagan ages shall have flown;
When Christian virtues, flaming into light,
Shall save the world from superstition's night;
Erin, oppress'd, shall bite the tyrant's heel,
And for a thousand years enslaved shall kneel;
Her sons shall perish in the field and flood,
Her daughters starve in city, wold, and wood;
Her patriots, with their blood, the block shall stain,
Her matrons fly behind the Western main;
Harpies from Albion shall her strength consume,
And thorns and thistles in her gardens bloom.
But, curse of curses thine, O! fated land:
Traitors shall thrive where statesmen ought to stand!

THE BLESSING.

But past her heritage of woe and pain,
A far more blest millennium shall reign;
Seedlings of heroes shall her exiles be,
Where'er they find a home beyond the sea;
Bright paragons of beauty and of truth,
Her maidens all shall dazzle in their youth;
And when age comes, to dim the flashing eye,
Still gems of virtue shall they live, and die!
No braver race shall breathe beneath the sun
Than thine, O! Erin, ere the goal be won.

Wherever man shall battle for the right,
There shall thy sons fall thickest in the fight;
Wherever man shall perish to be free,
There shall thy martyrs foremost be!
And O! when thy redemption is at hand,
Soldiers shall swell thy ranks from every land!
Heroes shall flock in thousands to thy shore,
And swear thy soil is FREE FOREVERMORE!
Then shall thy harp be from the willow torn,
And in yon glitt'ring galaxy be borne!
Then shall the Emerald change its verdant crest,
And blaze a Star co-equal with the rest!

The sentence pass'd, the doomsman felt surprise,
For tears were streaming from the seraph's eyes.

"Weep not for Erin," once again he spoke,
"But for thyself, that did'st her doom provoke;
I bear a message, seraph, unto thee,
As unrelenting in its stern decree.
For endless years it is thy fate to stand,
The chosen guardian of the SHAMROCK land.
Three times, as ages wind their coils away.
Incarnate on yon Island shalt thou stray.

"First as a Saint, in majesty divine,
The world shall know thee by this potent sign:
From yonder soil, where pois'nous reptiles dwell,
Thy voice shall snake and slimy toad expel.
Next as a Martyr, pleading in her cause,
Thy blood shall flow to build up Albion's laws.
Last as a Prophet and a Bard combined,
Rebellion's fires shall mould thy patriot mind.
In that great day, when Briton's strength shall fail,
And all her glories shiver on the gale;
When winged chariots, rushing through the sky,
Shall drop their faggots, blazing as they fly,
Thy form shall tower, a hero 'midst the flames,
And add one more to Erin's deathless names!"

Exiles of Erin! gathered here in state,
Such is the story of your country's fate.
Six thousand years in strife have rolled away,
Since Erin sprang from billowy surf and spray;
In that drear lapse, her sons have never known
One ray of peace to gild her crimson zone.
Cast back your glance athwart the tide of years,
Behold each billow steeped with Erin's tears,
Inspect each drop that swells the mighty flood,
Its purple globules smoke with human blood!

Come with me now, and trace the seraph's path,
That has been trodden since his day of wrath.
Lo! in the year when Attila the Hun
Had half the world in terror overrun,
On Erin's shore there stood a noble youth,
The breath of honor and the torch of truth.
His was the tongue that taught the Celtic soul
Christ was its Saviour, Heaven was its goal!
His was the hand that drove subdued away,
The venom horde that lured but to betray;

His were the feet that sanctified the sod,
Erin redeemed, and gave her back to God!
The gray old Earth can boast no purer fame
Than that whose halos gild St. Patrick's name!

Twelve times the centuries builded up their store
Of plots, rebellions, gibbets, tears and gore;
Twelve times centennial annivers'ries came,
To bless the seraph in St. Patrick's name.
In that long night of treach'ry and gloom,
How many myriads found a martyr's tomb!
Beside the waters of the dashing Rhone
In exile starved the bold and blind Tyrone.
Beneath the glamour of the tyrant's steel
Went out in gloom the soul of great O'Neill.
What countless thousands, children of her loin,
Sank unanneal'd beneath the bitter Boyne!
What fathers fell, what mothers sued in vain,
In Tredah's walls, on Wexford's gory plain,
When Cromwell's shaven panders slaked their lust,
And Ireton's fiends despoiled the breathless dust!

Still came no seraph, incarnate in man,
To rescue Erin from the bandit clan.
Still sad and lone, she languished in her chains,
That clank'd in chorus o'er her martyrs' manes.

At length, when Freedom's struggle was begun
Across the seas, by conq'ring Washington,
When Curran thunder'd, and when Grattan spoke,
The guardian seraph from his slumber woke.
Then guilty Norbury from his vengeance fled,
Fitzgerald fought, and glorious Wolfe Tone bled.
Then Emmet rose, to start the battle-cry,
To strike, to plead, to threaten, and to die!
Immortal Emmet! happier in thy doom,
Though uninscrib'd remains thy seraph tomb,

Than the long line of Erin's scepter'd foes,
Whose bones in proud mausoleums repose;
More noble blood through Emmet's pulses rings
Than courses through ten thousand hearts of kings!

Thus has the seraph twice redeem'd his fate,
And roamed a mortal through this low estate;
Again obedient to divine command,
His final incarnation is at hand.

THE PROPHECY.

Scarce shall yon sun *five times* renew the year,
Ere Erin's guardian Angel shall appear,
Not as a priest, in holy garb arrayed;
Not as a patriot, by his cause betray'd,
Shall he again assume a mortal guise,
And tread the earth, an exile from the skies.
But like the lightning from the welkin hurl'd,
His eye shall light, his step shall shake the world!

Ye sons of Erin! from your slumbers start!
Feel ye no vengeance burning in your heart?
Are ye but scions of degenerate slaves?
Shall tyrants spit upon your fathers' graves?
Is all the life-blood stagnant in your veins?
Love ye no music but the clank of chains?
Hear ye no voices ringing in the air,
That chant in chorus wild, *Prepare*, PREPARE!
Hark! on the winds there comes a prophet sound,—
The blood of Abel crying from the ground,—
Pealing in tones of thunder through the world,
"ARM! ARM! The Flag of Erin is unfurl'd!"

On some bold headland do I seem to stand,
And watch the billows breaking 'gainst the land;
Not in lone rollers do their waters pour,
But the vast ocean rushes to the shore.

So flock in millions sons of honest toil,
From ev'ry country, to their native soil;
Exiles of Erin, driven from her sod,
By foes of justice, mercy, man, and God!
Ærial chariots spread their snowy wings,
And drop torpedoes in the halls of kings.
On every breeze a thousand banners fly,
And Erin's seraph swells the battle-cry:—
"Strike! till the Unicorn shall lose the crown!
Strike! till the Eagle tears the Lion down!
Strike! till proud Albion bows her haughty head!
Strike! for the living and the martyr'd dead!
Strike! for the bones that fill your mothers' graves!
Strike! till your kindred are no longer slaves!
Strike! till fair Freedom on the world shall smile!
For God! for Truth! and FOR THE EMERALD ISLE!"

XIII.

THE EARTH'S HOT CENTER.

THE following extracts from the report of the Hon. John Flannagan, United States Consul at Bruges, in Belgium, to the Secretary of State, published in the Washington City *Telegraph* of a late date, will fully explain what is meant by the "Great Scare in Belgium."

Our extracts are not taken continuously, as the entire document would be too voluminous for our pages. But where breaks appear we have indicated the hiatus in the usual manner by asterisks, or by brief explanations.

GEN. FLANNAGAN'S REPORT.

BRUGES, December 12, 1872.

TO THE HON. HAMILTON FISH,
Secretary of State.

SIR: In pursuance of special instructions recently received from Washington (containing inclosures from Prof. Henry of the Smithsonian Institute, and Prof. Lovering of Harvard), I proceeded on Wednesday last to the scene of operations at the "International Exploring Works," and beg leave to submit the following circumstantial report:

Before proceeding to detail the actual state of affairs at Dudzeele, near the line of canal connecting Bruges with the North Sea, it may not be out of place to furnish a succinct history of the origin of the explorations out of which the present alarming events have arisen. It will be remembered by the State Department that during the short interregnum of the provisional government of France, under Lamartine and Cavaignac, in 1848, a proposition was submitted by France to the governments of the United States, Great Britain and Russia, and which was subsequently extended to King Leopold of Belgium, to create an "International Board for Subterranean Exploration" in furtherance of science, and in order, primarily, to test the truth of the theory of igneous central fusion, first propounded by Leibnitz, and afterward embraced by most of contemporary geologists; but also with the further objects of ascertaining the magnetic condition of the earth's crust, the variations of the needle at great depths, and finally to set at rest the doubts of some of the English mineralogists concerning the permanency of the coal measures, about which considerable alarm had been felt in all the manufacturing centers of Europe.

The protocol of a quintuple treaty was finally drawn by Prof. Henry, of the Smithsonian Institute, and approved by Sir Roderick Murchison, at that time President of the Royal Society of Great Britain. To this project Arago lent the weight of his great name, and Nesselrode affixed the approval of Russia, it being one of the last official acts performed by that veteran statesman.

The programme called for annual appropriations by each of the above-named powers of 100,000 francs (about $20,000 each), the appointment of commissioners and a general superintendent, the selection of a site for prosecuting the undertaking, and a board of scientific visitors, consisting of one member from each country.

It is unnecessary to detail the proceedings for the first few months after the organization of the commission. Prof. Watson, of Chicago, the author of a scientific treatise called "Prairie Geology," was selected by President Fillmore, as the first representative of the United States; Russia sent Olgokoff; France, Ango Jeuno; England, Sir Edward Sabine, the present President of the Royal Society; and Belgium, Dr. Secchi, since so famous for his spectroscopic observations on the fixed stars. These gentlemen, after organizing at Paris, spent almost an entire year in traveling before a site for the scene of operations was selected. Finally, on the 10th of April, 1849, the first ground was broken for actual work at Dudzeele, in the neighborhood of Bruges, in the Kingdom of Belgium.

The considerations which led to the choice of this locality were the following: First, it was the most central, regarding the capitals of the parties to the protocol; secondly, it was easy of access and connected by rail with Brussels, Paris and St. Petersburg, and by line of steamers with London, being situated within a short distance of the mouth of the Hond or west Scheldt; thirdly, and perhaps as the most important consideration of all, it was the seat of the deepest shaft in the world, namely, the old salt mine at Dudzeele, which had been worked from the time of the Romans down to the commencement of the present century, at which time it was abandoned, principally on account of the intense heat at the bottom of the excavation, and which could not be entirely overcome except by the most costly scientific appliances.

There was still another reason, which, in the estimation of at least one member of the commission, Prof. Watson, overrode them all—the exceptional increase of heat with depth, which was its main characteristic.

The scientific facts upon which this great work was projected, may be stated as follows: It is the opinion of the principal modern geologists, based primarily upon the hypothesis of Kant (that the solar universe was originally an immense mass of incandescent vapor gradually cooled and hardened after being thrown off from the grand central body—afterward elaborated by La Place into the present nebular hypothesis)—that "the globe was once in a state of igneous fusion, and that as its heated mass began to cool, an exterior crust was formed, first very thin, and afterward gradually increasing until it attained its present thickness, which has been variously estimated at from ten to two hundred miles. During the process of gradual refrigeration, some portions of the crust cooled more rapidly than others, and the pressure on the interior igneous mass being unequal, the heated matter or lava burst through the thinner parts, and caused high-peaked mountains; the same cause also producing all volcanic action." The arguments in favor of this doctrine are almost innumerable; these are among the most prominent:

First. The form of the earth is just that which an igneous liquid mass would assume if thrown into an orbit with an axial revolution similar to that of our earth. Not many years ago Professor Faraday, assisted by Wheatstone, devised a most ingenious apparatus by which, in the laboratory of the Royal Society, he actually was enabled, by injecting a flame into a vacuum, to exhibit visibly all the phenomena of the formation of the solar universe, as contended for by La Place and by Humboldt in his "Cosmos."

Secondly. It is perfectly well ascertained that heat increases with depth, in all subterranean excavations. This is the invariable rule in mining shafts, and preventive measures must always be devised and used, by means generally of air apparatus, to temper the heat as the depth is augmented, else deep mining would have to be abandoned. The rate of increase has been variously estimated by different scientists in widely distant portions of the globe. A few of them may be mentioned at this place, since it was upon a total miscalculation on this head that led to the present most deplorable results.

The editor of the *Journal of Science*, in April, 1832, calculated from results obtained in six of the deepest coal mines in Durham and Northumberland, the mean rate of increase at one degree of Fahrenheit for a descent of forty-four English feet.

In this instance it is noticeable that the bulb of the thermometer was introduced into cavities purposely cut into the solid rock, at depths varying from two hundred to nine hundred feet. The Dolcoath mine in Cornwall, as examined by Mr. Fox, at the depth of thirteen hundred and eighty feet, gave an average result of four degrees for every seventy-five feet.

Kupffer compared results obtained from the silver mines in Mexico, Peru and Freiburg, from the salt wells of Saxony, and from the copper mines in the Caucasus, together with an examination of the tin mines of Cornwall and the coal mines in the north of England, and found the average to be at least one degree of Fahrenheit for every thirty-seven English feet. Cordier, on the contrary, considers this amount somewhat overstated and reduces the general average to one degree Centigrade for every twenty-five metres, or about one degree of Fahrenheit for every forty-five feet English measure.

Thirdly. That the lavas taken from all parts of the world, when subjected to chemical analysis, indicate that they all proceed from a common source; and

Fourthly. On no other hypothesis can we account for the change of climate indicated by fossils.

The rate of increase of heat in the Dudzeele shaft was no less than one degree Fahrenheit for every thirty feet English measure.

At the time of recommencing sinking in the shaft on the 10th of April, 1849, the perpendicular depth was twenty-three hundred and seventy feet, the thermometer marking forty-eight degrees Fahrenheit at the surface; this would give the enormous heat of one hundred and twenty-seven degrees Fahrenheit at the bottom of the mine. Of course, without ventilation no human being could long survive in such an atmosphere, and the first operations of the commission were directed to remedy this inconvenience.

The report then proceeds to give the details of a very successful contrivance for forcing air into the shaft at the greatest depths, only a portion of which do we deem it important to quote, as follows:

The width of the Moer-Vater, or Lieve, at this point, was ten hundred and eighty yards, and spanned by an old bridge, the stone piers of which were very near together, having been built by the emperor Hadrian in the early part of the second century. The rise of the tide in the North Sea, close at hand, was from fifteen to eighteen feet, thus producing a current almost as rapid as that of the Mersey at Liverpool. The commissioners determined to utilize this force, in preference to the erection of expensive steam works at the mouth of the mine. A plan was submitted by Cyrus W. Field, and at once adopted. Turbine wheels were built, covering the space betwixt each arch, movable, and adapted to the rise and fall of the tide. Gates were also constructed between each arch, and a head of water, ranging from ten to fifteen feet fall, provided for each turn of the tide—both in the ebb and the flow, so that there should be a continuous motion to the machinery. Near the mouth of the shaft two large boiler-iron reservoirs were constructed, capable of holding from one hundred and fifty thousand to two hundred thousand cubic feet of compressed air, the average rate of condensation being about two hundred atmospheres. These reservoirs were properly connected with the pumping apparatus of the bridge by large cast-iron mains, so that the supply was continuous, and at an almost nominal cost. It was by the same power of compressed air that the tunneling through Mount St. Gothard was effected for the Lyons and Turin Railway, just completed.

The first operations were to enlarge the shaft so as to form an opening forty by one hundred feet, English measure. This consumed the greater part of the year 1849, so that the real work of sinking was not fairly under way until early in 1850. But from that period down to the memorable 5th of November, 1872, the excavation steadily progressed. I neglected to state at the outset that M. Jean Dusoloy, the State engineer of Belgium, was appointed General Superintendent, and continued to fill that important office until he lost his life, on the morning of the 6th of November, the melancholly details of which are hereinafter fully narrated.

As the deepening progressed the heat of the bottom continued to increase, but it was soon observed in a different ratio from the calculations of the experts. After attaining the depth of fifteen thousand six hundred and fifty feet, —about the height of Mt. Blanc—which was reached early in 1864, it was noticed, for the first time, that the laws of temperature and gravitation were synchronous; that is, that the heat augmented in a ratio proportioned to the square of the distance from the surface downward. Hence the increase at great depths bore no relation at all to the apparently gradual augmentation near the surface. As early as June, 1868, it became apparent that the sinking, if carried on at all, would have to be protected by some atheromatous or adiathermic covering. Professor Tyndall was applied to, and, at the request of Lord Palmerston, made a vast number of experiments on non-conducting bodies. As the result of his labors, he prepared a compound solution about the density of common white lead, composed of selenite alum and sulphate of copper, which was laid on three or four thicknesses, first upon the bodies of the naked miners —for in all deep mines the operatives work *in puris naturalibus*—and then upon an oval-shaped cage made of papier mache, with a false bottom, enclosed within which the miners were enabled to endure the intense heat for a shift of two hours each day. The drilling was all done by means of the diamond-pointed instrument, and the blasting by nitro-glycerine from the outset; so that the principal labor consisted in shoveling up the debris and keeping the drill-point *in situ*.

Before proceeding further it may not be improper to enumerate a few of the more important scientific facts which, up to the 1st of November of the past year, had been satisfactorily established. First in importance is the one alluded to above—the rate of increase of temperature as we descend into the bowels of the earth. This law, shown above to correspond exactly with the law of attraction or gravitation, had been entirely overlooked by all the scientists, living or dead. No one had for a moment suspected that heat followed the universal law of physics as a material body ought to do, simply because, from the time of De Saussure, heat had been regarded only as a force or *vis viva* and not as a ponderable quality.

But not only was heat found to be subject to the law of inverse ratio of the square of the distance from the surface, but the amosphere itself followed the same invariable rule. Thus, while we know that water boils at the level of the sea at two hundred and twelve degrees Fahrenheit, it readily vaporizes at one hundred and eighty-five degrees on the peak of Teneriffe, only fifteen thousand feet above that level. This, we know, is owing to the weight of the superincumbent atmosphere, there being a heavier burden at the surface than at any height above it. The rate of decrease above the surface is perfectly regular, being one degree for every five hundred and ninety feet of ascent. But the amazing fact was shown that the weight of the atmosphere increased in a ratio proportioned to the square of the distance downward. . . . . The magnetic needle also evinced some curious disturbance, the dip being invariably upward. Its action also was exceedingly feeble, and the day before the operations ceased it lost all polarity whatever, and the finest magnet would not meander from the point of the compass it happened to be left at for the time being. As Sir Edward Sabine finely said, "The hands of the magnetic clock stopped." But the activity of the needle gradually increased as the surface was approached.

All electrical action also ceased, which fully confirms the theory, of Professor Faraday, that "electricity is a force generated by the rapid axial revolution of the earth, and that magnetic attraction in all cases points or operates at right angles to its current." Hence electricity, from the nature of its cause, must be superficial.

Every appearance of water disappeared at the depth of only 9000 feet. From this depth downward the rock was of a basaltic character, having not the slightest appearance of granite formation—confirming, in a most remarkable manner, the discovery made only last year, that all *granites* are of *aqueous*, instead of *igneous* deposition. As a corollary from the law of atmospheric pressure, it was found utterly impossible to vaporize water at a greater depth than

24,000 feet, which point was reached in 1869. No amount of heat affected it in the least perceptible manner, and on weighing the liquid at the greatest depth attained, by means of a nicely adjusted scale, it was found to be of a density expressed thus: 198,073, being two degrees or integers of atomic weight heavier than gold, at the surface.

The report then proceeds to discuss the question of the true figure of the earth, whether an oblate spheroid, as generally supposed, or only truncated at the poles; the length of a degree of longitude at the latitude of Dudzeele, 51 deg. 20 min. N., and one or two other problems. The concluding portion of the report is reproduced in full.

For the past twelve months it was found impossible to endure the heat, even sheltered as the miners were by the atmospheric cover and cage, for more than fifteen minutes at a time, so that the expense of sinking had increased geometrically for the past two years. However, important results had been obtained, and a perpendicular depth reached many thousands of feet below the deepest sea soundings of Lieutenant Brooks. In fact, the enormous excavation, on the 1st of November, 1872, measured perpendicularly, no less than 37,810 feet and 6 inches from the floor of the shaft building! The highest peak of the Himalayas is only little over 28,000 feet, so that it can at once be seen that no time had been thrown away by the Commissioners since the inception of the undertaking, in April, 1849.

The first symptoms of alarm were felt on the evening of November 1. The men complained of a vast increase of heat, and the cages had to be dropped every five minutes for the greater part of the night; and of those who attempted to work, at least one half were extricated in a condition of fainting, but one degree from cyncope. Toward morning, hoarse, profound and frequent subterranean explosions were heard, which had increased at noon to one dull, threatening and continuous roar. But the miners went down bravely to their tasks, and resolved to work as long as human endurance could bear it. But this was not to be much longer; for late at night, on the 4th, after hearing a terrible explosion, which shook the whole neighborhood, a hot sirocco issued from the bottom, which drove them all out in a state of asphyxia. The heat at the surface became absolutely unendurable, and on sending down a cage with only a dog in it, the materials of which it was composed took fire, and the animal perished in the flames. At 3 o'clock A. M. the iron fastenings to another cage were found fused, and the wire ropes were melted for more than 1000 feet at the other end. The detonations became more frequent, the trembling of the earth at the surface more violent, and the heat more oppressive around the mouth of the orifice. A few minutes before 4 o'clock a subterranean crash was heard, louder than Alpine thunder, and immediately afterward a furious cloud of ashes, smoke and gaseous exhalation shot high up into the still darkened atmosphere of night. At this time at least one thousand of the terrified and half-naked inhabitants of the neighboring village of Dudzeele had collected on the spot, and with wringing hands and fearful outcries bewailed their fate, and threatened instant death to the officers of the commission, and even to the now terrified miners. Finally, just before dawn, on the 5th of November, or, to be more precise, at exactly twenty minutes past 6 A. M., molten lava made its appearance at the surface!

The fright now became general, and as the burning buildings shed their ominous glare around, and the languid stream of liquid fire slowly bubbled up and rolled toward the canal, the scene assumed an aspect of awful sublimity and grandeur. The plains around were lit up for many leagues, and the foggy skies intensified and reduplicated the effects of the illumination. Toward sunrise the flow of lava was suspended for nearly an hour, but shortly after ten o'clock it suddenly increased its volume, and, as it cooled, formed a sort of saucer-shaped funnel, over the edges of which it boiled up, broke, and ran off in every direction. It was at this period that the accomplished Dusoloy, so long the Superintendent, lost his life. As the lava slowly meandered along, he attempted to cross the stream by stepping from one mass of surface cinders to another. Making a false step, the floating rock upon which he sprang suddenly turned over, and before relief could be afforded his body was consumed to a crisp. I regret to add that his fate kindled no sympathy among the assembled multitude; but they rudely seized his mutilated remains, and amid jeers, execrations, and shouts of triumph, attached a large stone to the half-consumed corpse and precipitated it into the canal. Thus are the heroes of science frequently sacrificed to the fury of a plebeian mob.

It would afford me a pleasure to inform the department that the unforeseen evils of our scientific convention terminated here. But I regret to add that such is very far from being the case. Indeed, from the appearance of affairs this morning at the volcanic crater—for such it has now become—the possible evils are almost incalculable. The Belgian Government was duly notified by telegraph of the death of the Superintendent and the mutinous disposition of the common people about Bruges, and early on the morning of the 6th of November a squad of flying horse was dispatched to the spot to maintain order. But this interference only made matters worse. The discontent, augmented by the wildest panic, became universal, and the mob reigned supreme. Nor could the poor wretches be greatly condemned; for toward evening the lava current reached the confines of the old village of Dudzeele, and about midnight set the town on fire. The lurid glare of the conflagration awakened the old burghers of Bruges from their slumbers and spread consternation in the city, though distant several miles from the spot. A meeting was called at the Guildhall at dawn, and the wildest excitement prevailed. But after hearing explanations from the members of the commission, the populace quietly but doggedly dispersed. The government from this time forward did all that power and prudence combined could effect to quell the reign of terror around Bruges. In this country the telegraph, being a government monopoly, has been rigorously watched and a cordon of military posts established around the threatened district, so that it has been almost impossible to convey intelligence of this disaster beyond the limits of the danger. In the mean time, a congress of the most experienced scientists was invited to the scene for the purpose of suggesting some remedy against the prospective spread of the devastation. The first meeting took place at the old Guildhall in Bruges and was strictly private, none being admitted except the diplomatic representatives of foreign governments, and the members elect of the college. As in duty bound, I felt called on to attend, and shall in this place attempt a short synopsis of the proceedings.

Professor Palmieri, of Naples, presided, and Dr. Kirchoff officiated as secretary.

Gassiot, of Paris, was the first speaker, and contended that the theory of nucleatic fusion, now being fully established, it only remained to prescribe the laws governing its superficial action. "There is but one law applicable, that I am aware of," said he, "and that is the law which drives from the center of a revolving body all fluid matter toward the circumference, and forcibly ejects it into space, if possible, in the same manner that a common grindstone in rapid motion will drive off from its rim drops of water or other foreign unattached matter. Thus, whenever we find a vent or open orifice, as in the craters of active volcanoes, the incandescent lava boils up and frequently overflows the top of the highest peak of the Andes."

Palmieri then asked the speaker "if he wished to be understood as expressing the unqualified opinion that an orifice once being opened would continue to flow forever, and that there was no law governing the quantity or regulating the level to which it could rise?"

Gassiot replied in the affirmative.

The Neapolitan philosopher then added: "I dissent *in toto* from the opinion of M. Gassiot. For more than a quarter of a century I have studied the lava-flows of Vesuvius, Ætna and Stromboli, and I can assure the Congress that the Creator has left no such flaw in His mechanism of the globe. The truth is, that molten lava can only rise about 21,000 feet above the level of the sea, owing to the balance-wheel of terrestrial gravitation, which counteracts at that height all centrifugal energy. Were this not so, the entire contents of the globe would gush from the incandescent center and fly off into surrounding space."

M. Gassiot replied, "that true volcanoes were supplied by nature with *circumvalvular lips*, and hence, after filling their craters, they ceased to flow. But in the instance before us no such provision existed, and the only protection which he could conceive of consisted in the smallness of the orifice; and he would therefore recommend his Majesty King Leopold to direct all his efforts to confine the aperture to its present size."

Palmieri again responded, "that he had no doubt but that the crater at Dudzeele would continue to flow until it had built up around itself basaltic walls to the height of many hundreds, perhaps thousands, of feet, and that the idea of setting bounds to the size of the mouth of the excavation was simply ridiculous."

Gassiot interrupted, and was about to answer in a very excited tone, when Prof. Palmieri "disclaimed any intention of personal insult, but spoke from a scientific standpoint." He then proceeded: "The lava bed of Mount Ætna maintains a normal level of 7000 feet, while Vesuvius calmly reposes at a little more than one half that altitude. On the other hand, according to Prof. Whitney, of the Pacific Survey, Mount Kilauea, in the Sandwich Islands, bubbles up to the enormous height of 17,000 feet. It cannot be contended that the crater of Vesuvius is not a true nucleatic orifice, because I have demonstrated that the molten bed regularly rises and falls like the tides of the ocean when controlled by the moon." It was seen at once that the scientists present were totally unprepared to discuss the question in its novel and most important aspects; and on taking a vote, at the close of the session, the members were equally divided between the opinions of Gassiot and Palmieri. A further session will take place on the arrival of Prof. Tyndall, who has been telegraphed for from New York, and of the great Russian geologist and astronomer, Tugenieff.

In conclusion, the damage already done may be summed up as follows: The destruction of the Bruges and Hond Canal by the formation of a basaltic dyke across it more than two hundred feet wide, the burning of Dudzeele, and the devastation of about thirty thousand acres of valuable land. At the same time it is utterly impossible to predict where the damage may stop, inasmuch as early this morning the mouth of the crater had fallen in, and the flowing stream had more than doubled in size.

In consideration of the part hitherto taken by the Government of the United States in originating the work that led to the catastrophe, and by request of M. Musenheim, the Belgian Foreign Secretary, I have taken the liberty of drawing upon the State Department for eighty-seven thousand dollars, being the sum agreed to be paid for the cost of emigration to the United States of two hundred families (our own pro rata) rendered homeless by the conflagration of Dudzeele.

I am this moment in receipt of your telegram dated yesterday, and rejoice to learn that Prof. Agassiz has returned from the South Seas, and will be sent forward without delay.

With great respect, I have the honor to be your obedient servant,

JOHN FLANNAGAN,
United States Consul at Bruges.

P.S.—Since concluding the above dispatch, Professor Palmieri did me the honor of a special call, and, after some desultory conversation, approached the all-absorbing topic of the day, and cautiously expressed his opinion as follows: Explaining his theory, as announced at the Congress, he said that "Holland, Belgium, and Denmark, being all low countries, some portions of each lying below the sea-level, he would not be surprised if the present outflow of lava devastated them all, and covered the bottom of the North Sea for many square leagues with a bed of basalt." The reason given was this: "That lava must continue to flow until, by its own action, it builds up around the volcanic crater a rim or cone high enough to afford a counterpoise to the centrifugal tendency of axial energy; and that, as the earth's crust was demonstrated to be exceptionally thin in the north of Europe, the height required in this instance would be so great that an enormous lapse of time must ensue before the self-created cone could obtain the necessary altitude. Before Ætna attained its present secure height, it devastated an area as large as France; and Prof. Whitney has demonstrated that some center of volcanic action, now extinct, in the State of California, threw out a stream that covered a much greater surface, as the basaltic table mountains, vulgarly so called, extend north and south for a distance as great as from Moscow to Rome." In concluding his remarks, he ventured the prediction that "the North Sea would be completely filled up, and the British Islands again connected with the Continent."

J. F., U.S.C.

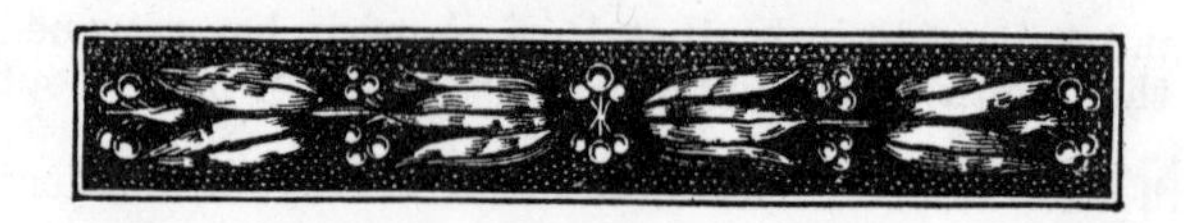

XIV.

WILDEY'S DREAM.

A BLACKSMITH stood, at his anvil good,
Just fifty years ago,
And struck in his might, to the left and right,
The iron all aglow.
And fast and far, as each miniature star
Illumined the dusky air,
The sparks of his mind left a halo behind,
Like the aureola of prayer.

And the blacksmith thought, as he hammered and wrought,
Just fifty years ago,
Of the sins that start in the human heart
When *its* metal is all aglow;
And he breathed a prayer, on the evening air,
As he watched the fire-sparks roll,
That with hammer and tongs, *he* might right the wrongs
That environ the human soul!

When he leaned on his sledge, not like minion or drudge,
With center in self alone,
But with vision so grand, it embraced every land,
In the sweep of its mighty zone;
O'er mountain and main, o'er forest and plain,
He gazed from his swarthy home,
Till rafter and wall, grew up in a hall,
That covered the world with its dome!

'Neath that bending arch, with a tottering march
All peoples went wailing by,
To the music of groan, of sob, and of moan,
To the grave that was yawning nigh,
When the blacksmith rose and redoubled his blows
On the iron that was aglow,
Till his senses did seem to dissolve in a dream,
Just fifty years ago.

He thought that he stood upon a mountain chain,
And gazed across an almost boundless plain;
Men of all nations, and of every clime,
Of ancient epochs, and of modern time,
Rose in thick ranks before his wandering eye,
And passed, like waves, in quick succession by.

First came Osiris, with his Memphian band
Of swarth Egyptians, darkening all the land;
With heads downcast they dragged their limbs along,
Laden with chains, and torn by lash and thong.
From morn till eve they toiled and bled and died,
And stained with blood the Nile's encroaching tide.
Slowly upon the Theban plain there rose
Old Cheop's pride, a pyramid of woes;
And millions sank unpitied in their graves,
With tombs inscribed—"Here lies a realm of slaves."

Next came great Nimrod prancing on his steed,
His serried ranks, Assyrian and Mede,
By bold Sennacherib moulded into one,
By bestial Sardanapalus undone.
He saw the walls of Babylon arise,
Spring from the earth, invade the azure skies,
And bear upon their airy ramparts old
Gardens and vines, and fruit, and flowers of gold.
Beneath their cold and insalubrious shade
All woes and vices had their coverts made;

Lascivious incest o'er the land was sown,
From peasant cabin to imperial throne,
And that proud realm, so full of might and fame,
Went down at last in blood, and sin, and shame.

Then came the Persian, with his vast array
Of armed millions, fretting for the fray,
Led on by Xerxes and his harlot horde,
Where billows swallowed, and where battle roared.
On every side there rose a bloody screen,
Till mighty Alexander closed the scene.
Behold that warrior! in his pomp and pride,
Dash through the world, and over myriads ride;
Plant his proud pennon on the Gangean stream,
Pierce where the tigers hide, mount where the eagles scream,
And happy only amid war's alarms,
The clank of fetters, and the clash of arms;
And moulding man by battle-fields and blows,
To one foul mass of furies, fiends and foes.
Such, too, the Roman, vanquishing mankind,
Their fields to ravage, and their limbs to bind;
Whose proudest trophy, and whose highest good,
To write his fame with pencil dipped in blood;
To stride the world, like Ocean's turbid waves,
And sink all nations into servient slaves.

As passed the old, so modern realms swept by,
Woe in all hearts, and tears in every eye;
Crimes stained the noble, famine crushed the poor;
Poison for kings, oppression for the boor;
Force by the mighty, fraud by the feebler shown;
Mercy a myth, and charity unknown.

The Dreamer sighed, for sorrow filled his breast;
Turned from the scene and sank to deeper rest.
"Come!" cried a low voice full of music sweet,
"Come!" and an angel touched his trembling feet.

Down the steep hills they wend their toilsome way,
Cross the vast plain that on their journey lay;
Gain the dark city, through its suburbs roam,
And pause at length within the dreamer's home.

Again he stood at his anvil good
  With an angel by his side,
And rested his sledge on its iron edge
  And blew up his bellows wide;
He kindled the flame till the white heat came,
  Then murmured in accent low:
"All ready am I your bidding to try
  So far as a mortal may go."

'Midst the heat and the smoke the angel spoke,
  And breathed in his softest tone,
"Heaven caught up your prayer on the evening air
  As it mounted toward the throne.
God weaveth no task for mortals to ask
  Beyond a mortal's control,
And with hammer and tongs you shall right the wrongs
  That encompass the human soul.

"But go you first forth 'mong the sons of the earth,
  And bring me a human heart
That throbs for its kind, spite of weather and wind,
  And acts still a brother's part.
The night groweth late, but here will I wait
  Till dawn streak the eastern skies;
And lest you should fail, spread *my* wings on the gale,
  And search with *my* angel eyes."

The dreamer once more passed the open door,
  But plumed for an angel's flight;
He sped through the world like a thunderbolt hurled
  When the clouds are alive with light;

He followed the sun till his race was won,
  And probed every heart and mind;
But in every zone man labored alone
  For himself and not for his kind.

All mournful and flushed, his dearest hopes crushed,
  The dreamer returned to his home,
And stood in the flare of the forge's red glare,
  Besprinkled with dew and foam.
"The heart you have sought must be tempered and taught
  In the flame that is all aglow."
"No heart could I find that was true to its kind,
  So I left all the world in its woe."

Then the stern angel cried: "In your own throbbing side
  Beats a heart that is sound to the core;
Will you give your own life to the edge of the knife
  For the widowed, the orphaned, and poor?"
"Most unworthy am I for my brothers to die,
  And sinful my sorrowing heart;
But strike, if you will, to redeem or to kill,
  With life I am willing to part."

Then he threw ope his vest and bared his broad breast
  To the angel's glittering blade;
Soon the swift purple tide gushed a stream red and wide
  From the wound that the weapon had made.
With a jerk and a start he then plucked out his heart,
  And buried it deep in the flame
That flickered and fell like the flashes of hell
  O'er the dreamer's quivering frame.

"Now with hammer and tongs you may right all the wrongs
  That environ the human soul;
But first, you must smite with a Vulcan's might
  The heart in yon blistering bowl."

Quick the blacksmith arose, and redoubling his blows,
  Beat the heart that was all aglow,
Till its fiery scars like a shower of stars
  Illumined the night with their flow.

Every sling of his sledge reopened the edge
  Of wounds that were healed long ago;
And from each livid chasm leaped forth a phantasm
  Of passion, of sin, or of woe.
But he heeded no pain as he hammered amain,
  For the angel was holding the heart,
And cried at each blow, "Strike high!" or "Strike low!"
  "Strike hither!" or "Yonder apart!"

So he hammered and wrought, and he toiled and fought
  Till Aurora peeped over the plain;
When the angel flew by and ascended the sky,
  But left on the anvil a chain!
Its links were as bright as heaven's own light,
  As pure as the fountain of youth;
And bore on each fold in letters of gold,
  This token—LOVE, FRIENDSHIP AND TRUTH.

The dreamer awoke, and peered through the smoke
  At the anvil that slept by his side;
And then in a wreath of flower-bound sheath,
  The triple-linked chain he espied.
Odd Fellowship's gem is that bright diadem,
  Our emblem in age and in youth;
For our hearts we must prove in the fire of LOVE,
  And mould with the hammer of TRUTH.

XV.

WHITHERWARD.

BY pursuing the analogies of nature, the human mind reduces to order the vagaries of the imagination, and bodies them forth in forms of loveliness and in similitudes of heaven.

By an irrevocable decree of Nature's God, all his works are progressive in the direction of himself. This law is traceable from the molehill up to the mountain, from the mite up to the man. Geology, speaking to us from the depths of a past eternity, from annals inscribed upon the imperishable rock, utters not one syllable to contradict this tremendous truth. Millions of ages ago, she commenced her impartial record, and as we unroll it to-day, from the coal-bed and the marble quarry, we read in creation's dawn as plainly as we behold in operation around us, the mighty decree—ONWARD AND UPWARD, FOREVER!

In the shadowy past this majestic globe floated through the blue ether, a boiling flood of lava. The elements were then unborn. Time was not; for as yet the golden laws of Kepler had not emerged from chaos. The sun had not hemmed his bright-eyed daughters in, nor marked out on the azure concave the paths they were to tread. The planets were not worlds, but shot around the lurid center liquid masses of flame and desolation. Comets sported at random through the sky, and trailed after them their horrid skirts of fire. The Spirit of God had not "moved upon the face of the waters," and rosy Chaos still held the scepter in his hand. But changes were at work. As the coral worm toils on in the unfathomable depths of ocean, laying in secret the foundations of mighty continents, destined as the ages roll by to emerge into light and grandeur, so the laws of the universe carried on their everlasting work.

An eternity elapsed, and the age of fire passed away. A new era dawned upon the earth. The gases were generated, and the elements of air and water overspread the globe. Islands began to appear, at first presenting pinnacles of bare and blasted granite; but gradually, by decay and decomposition, changing into dank marshes and fertile plains.

One after another the sensational universe now springs into being. This but prepared the way for the animated, and that in turn formed the groundwork and basis for the human. Man then came forth, the result of all her previous efforts—nature's pet, her paragon and her pride.

Reason sits enthroned upon his brow, and the soul wraps its sweet affections about his heart; angels spread their wings above him, and God calls him His child. He treads the earth its acknowledged monarch, and commences its subjection. One by one the elements have yielded to his sway, nature has revealed her hoariest secrets to his ken, and heaven thrown wide its portals to his spirit. He stands now upon the very acme of the visible creation, and with straining eye, and listening ear, and anxious heart, whispers to himself that terrific and tremendous word—WHITHERWARD!

Late one afternoon in April, I was sitting on the grassy slope of Telegraph Hill, watching the waves of sunset as they rolled in from the west, and broke in crimson spray upon the peaks of the Contra Costa hills. I was alone; and, as my custom is, was ruminating upon the grand problem of futurity. The broad and beautiful bay spread out like a sea of silver at my feet, and the distant mountains, reflecting the rays of the setting sun, seemed to hem it in with barriers of gold. The city lay like a tired infant at evening in its mother's arms, and only at intervals disturbed my reflections by its expiring sobs. The hours of business I well knew had passed, and the heavy iron door had long since grated on its hinges, and the fire-proof shutter been bolted for the night. But I felt that my labors had just commenced. The duties of my profession had swallowed up thought throughout the long hours devoted to the cares of life, and it was not until I was released from their thraldom that I found myself in truth a slave. The one master-thought came back into my brain, until it burned its hideous image there in letters of fire—WHITHERWARD! WHITHERWARD!

The past came up before me with its long memories of Egyptian grandeur, with its triumphs of Grecian art, with its burden of Roman glory. Italy came with her republics, her "starry" Galileo, and her immortal Buonarotti. France flashed by, with her garments dyed in blood, and her Napoleons in chains. England rose up with her arts and her arms, her commerce and her civilization, her splendor and her shame. I beheld Newton gazing at the stars, heard Milton singing of Paradise, and saw Russell expiring on the scaffold. But ever and anon a pale, thorn-crowned monarch, arrayed in mock-purple, and bending beneath a cross, would start forth at my side, and with uplifted eye, but speechless lip, point with one hand to the pages of a volume I had open on my knee, and with the other to the blue heaven above. Judea would then pass with solemn tread before me. Her patriarchs, her prophets and her apostles, her judges, her kings, and her people, one by one came and went like the phantasmagoria of a dream. The present then rose up in glittering robes, its feet resting upon the mounds of Nimrod, its brow encircled with a coronet of stars, pillaging, with one hand, the cloud above of its lightnings, and sending them forth with the other, bridled and subdued, to the uttermost ends of the earth.

But this was not all. Earth's physical history also swept by in full review. All nature lent her stores, and with an effort of mind, by no means uncommon for those who have long thought upon a single subject, I seemed to possess the power to generalize all that I had ever heard, read or seen, into one gorgeous picture, and hang it up in the wide heavens before me.

The actual scenery around me entirely disappeared, and I beheld an immense pyramid of alabaster, reared to the very stars, upon whose sides I saw inscribed a faithful history of the past. Its foundations were in deep shadow, but the light gradually increased toward the top, until its summit was bathed in the most refulgent lustre.

Inscribed in golden letters I read on one of its sides these words, in alternate layers, rising gradually to the apex: "*Granite, Liquid, Gas, Electricity;*" on another, "*Inorganic, Vegetable, Animal, Human;*" on the third side, "*Consciousness, Memory, Reason, Imagination;*" and on the fourth, "*Chaos, Order, Harmony, Love.*"

At this moment I beheld the figure of a human being

standing at the base of the pyramid, and gazing intently upward. He then placed his foot upon the foundation, and commenced climbing toward the summit. I caught a distinct view of his features, and perceived that they were black and swarthy like those of the most depraved Hottentot. He toiled slowly upward, and as he passed the first layer, he again looked toward me, and I observed that his features had undergone a complete transformation. They now resembled those of an American Indian. He passed the second layer; and as he entered the third, once more presented his face to me for observation. Another change had overspread it, and I readily recognized in him the tawny native of Malacca or Hindoostan. As he reached the last layer, and entered its region of refulgent light, I caught a full glimpse of his form and features, and beheld the high forehead, the glossy ringlets, the hazel eye, and the alabaster skin of the true Caucasian.

I now observed for the first time that the pyramid was left unfinished, and that its summit, instead of presenting a well-defined peak, was in reality a level plain. In a few moments more, the figure I had traced from the base to the fourth layer, reached the apex, and stood with folded arms and upraised brow upon the very summit. His lips parted as if about to speak, and as I leaned forward to hear, I caught, in distinct tone and thrilling accent, that word which had so often risen to my own lips for utterance, and seared my very brain, because unanswered—WHITHERWARD!

"Whitherward, indeed!" exclaimed I, aloud, shuddering at the sepulchral sound of my voice. "Home," responded a tiny voice at my side, and turning suddenly around, my eyes met those of a sweet little school-girl, with a basket of flowers upon her arm, who had approached me unobserved, and who evidently imagined I had addressed her when I spoke. "Yes, little daughter," replied I, "'tis time to proceed homeward, for the sun has ceased to gild the summit of Diavolo, and the evening star is visible in the west. I will attend you home," and taking her proffered hand, I descended the hill, with the dreadful word still ringing in my ears, and the fadeless vision still glowing in my heart.

Midnight had come and gone, and still the book lay open on my knee. The candle had burned down close to the socket, and threw a flickering glimmer around my chamber; but no indications of fatigue or slumber visited my eyelids. My temples throbbed heavily, and I felt the hot and excited blood playing like the piston-rod of an engine between my heart and brain.

I had launched forth on the broad ocean of speculation, and now perceived, when too late, the perils of my situation. Above me were dense and lowering clouds, which no eye could penetrate; around me howling tempests, which no voice could quell; beneath me heaving billows, which no oil could calm. I thought of Plato struggling with his doubts; of Epicurus sinking beneath them; of Socrates swallowing his poison; of Cicero surrendering himself to despair. I remembered how all the great souls of the earth had staggered beneath the burden of the same thought, which weighed like a thousand Cordilleras upon my own; and as I pressed my hand upon my burning brow, I cried again and again—WHITHERWARD! WHITHERWARD!

I could find no relief in philosophy; for I knew her maxims by heart from Zeno and the Stagirite down to Berkeley and Cousin. I had followed her into all her hiding-places, and courted her in all her moods. No coquette was ever half so false, so fickle, and so fair. Her robes are woven of the sunbeams, and a star adorns her brow; but she sits impassive upon her icy throne, and wields no scepter but despair. The light she throws around is not the clear gleam of the sunshine, nor the bright twinkle of the star; but glances in fitful glimmerings on the soul, like the aurora on the icebergs of the pole, and lightens up the scene only to show its utter desolation.

The Bible lay open before me, but I could find no comfort there. Its lessons were intended only for the meek and humble, and my heart was cased in pride. It reached only to the believing; I was tossed on an ocean of doubt. It required, as a condition to faith, the innocence of an angel and the humility of a child; I had long ago seared my conscience by mingling in the busy scenes of life, and was proud of my mental acquirements. The Bible spoke comfort to the Publican; I was of the straight sect of the Pharisees. Its promises were directed to the poor in spirit, whilst mine panted for renown.

At this moment, whilst heedlessly turning over its leaves and scarcely glancing at their contents, my attention was arrested by this remarkable passage in one of Paul's epistles: "That was not *first* which is spiritual, but that which was natural, and *afterward* that which is spiritual. Behold, I show you a mystery: *we shall not all sleep*, but we shall all be changed, in a moment, in the twinkling of an eye, at the last trump."

Again and again I read this text, for it promised more by reflection than at first appeared in the words. Slowly a light broke in on the horizon's verge, and I felt, for the first time in my whole life, that the past was not all inexplicable, nor the future a chaos, but that the human soul, lit up by the torch of science, and guided by the prophecies of Holy Writ, might predict the path it is destined to tread, and read in advance the history of its final enfranchisement. St. Paul evidently intended to teach the doctrine of *progress*, even in its applicability to man. He did not belong to that narrow-minded sect in philosophy, which declares that the earth and the heavens are finished; that man is the crowning glory of his Maker, and the utmost stretch of His creative power; that henceforth the globe which he inhabits is barren, and can produce no being superior to himself. On the contrary, he clearly intended to teach the same great truth which modern science is demonstrating to all the world, that progression is nature's first law, and that even in the human kingdom the irrevocable decree has gone forth—ONWARD AND UPWARD, FOREVER!

Such were my reflections when the last glimmer of the candle flashed up like a meteor, and then as suddenly expired in night. I was glad that the shadows were gone. Better, thought I, is utter darkness than that poor flame which renders it visible. But I had suddenly grown rich in thought. A clue had been furnished to the labyrinth in which I had wandered from a child; a hint had been planted in the mind which it would be impossible ever to circumscribe or extinguish. One letter had been identified by which, like Champollion le Jeune, I could eventually decipher the inscription on the pyramid. What are these spectral apparitions which rear themselves in the human mind, and are called by mortals *hints?* Whence do they come? Who lodges them in the chambers of the mind, where they sprout and germinate, and bud and blossom, and bear?

The Florentine caught one as it fell from the stars, and invented the telescope to observe them. Columbus caught another, as it was whispered by the winds, and they wafted him to the shores of a New World. Franklin beheld one flash forth from the cloud, and he traced the lightnings to their bourn. Another dropped from the skies into the brain of Leverrier, and he scaled the very heavens, till he unburied a star.

Rapidly was my mind working out the solution of the problem which had so long tortured it, based upon the intimation it had derived from St. Paul's epistle, when most unexpectedly, and at the same time most unwelcomely, I fell into one of those strange moods which can neither be called sleep nor consciousness, but which leave their impress far more powerfully than the visions of the night or the events of the day.

I beheld a small egg, most beautifully dotted over, and stained. Whilst my eye rested on it, it cracked; an opening was made *from within*, and almost immediately afterward a bird of glittering plumage and mocking song flew out, and perched on the bough of a rose-tree, beneath whose shadow I found myself reclining. Before my surprise had vanished, I beheld a painted worm at my feet, crawling toward the root of the tree which was blooming above me. It soon reached the trunk, climbed into the branches, and commenced spinning its cocoon. Hardly had it finished its silken home, ere it came forth in the form of a gorgeous butterfly, and, spreading its wings, mounted toward the heavens. Quickly succeeding this, the same pyramid of alabaster, which I had seen from the summit of Telegraph Hill late in the afternoon, rose gradually upon the view. It was in nowise changed; the inscriptions on the sides were the same, and the identical figure stood with folded arms and uplifted brow upon the top. I now heard a rushing sound, such as stuns the ear at Niagara, or greets it during a hurricane at sea, when the shrouds of the ship are whistling to the blast, and the flashing billows are dashing against her sides.

Suddenly the pyramid commenced changing its form, and before many moments elapsed it had assumed the rotundity of a globe, and I beheld it covered with seas, and hills, and lakes, and mountains, and plains, and fertile fields. But the human figure still stood upon its crest. Then came forth the single blast of a bugle, such as the soldier hears on the morn of a world-changing battle. Cæsar heard it at Pharsalia, Titus at Jerusalem, Washington at Yorktown, and Wellington at Waterloo.

No lightning flash ever rended forest king from crest to root quicker than the transformation which now overspread the earth. In a second of time it became as transparent as crystal, and as brilliant as the sun. But in every other respect it preserved its identity. On casting my eyes toward the human being, I perceived that he still preserved his position, but his feet did not seem to touch the earth. He appeared to be floating upon its arch, as the halcyon floats in the atmosphere. His features were lit up with a heavenly radiance, and assumed an expression of superhuman beauty.

The thought crossed my mind, Can this be a spirit? As sudden as the question came forth the response, "I am." But, inquired my mind, for my lips did not move, you have never passed the portals of the grave? Again I read in his features the answer, "For ages this earth existed as a natural body, and all its inhabitants partook of its characteristics; gradually it approached the spiritual state, and by a law like that which transforms the egg into the songster, or the worm into the butterfly, it has just accomplished one of its mighty cycles, and now gleams forth with the refulgence of the stars. I did not die, but passed as naturally into the spiritual world as the huge earth itself. Prophets and apostles predicted this change many hundred years ago; but the blind infatuation of our race did not permit them to realize its truth. Your own mind, in common with the sages of all time, long brooded over the idea, and oftentimes have you exclaimed, in agony and dismay—WHITHERWARD! WHITHERWARD!

"The question is now solved. The revolution may not come in the year allotted you, but so surely as St. Paul spoke inspiration, so surely as science elicits truth, so surely as the past prognosticates the future, the natural world must pass into the spiritual, and everything be changed in the twinkling of an eye. Watch well! your own ears may hear the clarion note, your own eyes witness the transfiguration."

Slowly the vision faded away, and left me straining my gaze into the dark midnight which now shrouded the world, and endeavoring to calm my heart, which throbbed as audibly as the hollow echoes of a drum. When the morning sun peeped over the Contra Costa range, I still sat silent and abstracted in my chair, revolving over the incidents of the night, but thankful that, though the reason is powerless to brush away the clouds which obscure the future, yet the imagination may spread its wings, and, soaring into the heavens beyond them, answer the soul when in terror she inquires—WHITHERWARD!

XVI.

OUR WEDDING-DAY.

I.

A DOZEN springs, and more, dear Sue,
  Have bloomed, and passed away,
Since hand in hand, and heart to heart,
  We spent our wedding-day.
Youth blossomed on our cheeks, dear Sue,
  Joy chased each tear of woe,
When first we promised to be true,
  That morning long ago.

II.

Though many cares have come, dear Sue,
  To checker life's career,
As down its pathway we have trod,
  In trembling and in fear.
Still in the darkest storm, dear Sue,
  That lowered o'er the way,
We clung the closer, while it blew,
  And laughed the clouds away.

III.

'Tis true, our home is humble, Sue,
  And riches we have not,
But children gambol round our door,
  And consecrate the spot.
Our sons are strong and brave, dear Sue,
  Our daughters fair and gay,
But none so beautiful as you,
  Upon our wedding-day.

IV.

No grief has crossed our threshold, Sue,
  No crape festooned the door,
But health has waved its halcyon wings,
  And plenty filled our store.
Then let's be joyful, darling Sue,
  And chase-dull cares away,
And kindle rosy hope anew,
  As on our wedding-day.

XVII.

THE OLD YEAR AND THE NEW.

ONE more flutter of time's restless wing,
One more furrow in the forehead of spring;
One more step in the journey of fate,
One more ember gone out in life's grate;
One more gray hair in the head of the sage,
One more round in the ladder of age;
One leaf more in the volume of doom,
And one span less in the march to the tomb,
Since brothers, we gathered around bowl and tree,
And Santa Claus welcomed with frolic and glee.

How has thy life been speeding
Since Aurora, at the dawn,
Peeped within thy portals, leading
The babe year, newly born?

Has thy soul been scorched by sorrow,
Has some spectre nestled there?
And with every new to-morrow,
Sowed the seeds of fresh despair?
Rise from thy grief, my brothers!
Burst its chain with strength sublime,
For behold! I bring another,
And a fairer child of time.

Has the year brought health and riches?
Have thy barns been brimming o'er?
Will thy stature fit the niches
Hewn for Hercules of yore?

Are thy muscles firm as granite?
  Are thy thousands safe and sound?
Behold! the rolling planet
  Starts on a nobler round.

But perhaps across thy vision
  Death had cast its shadow there,
And thy home, once all elysian,
  Now crapes an empty chair;
Or happier, thy dominions,
  Spreading broad and deep and strong,
Re-echo 'neath love's pinions
  To a pretty cradle song!

Whate'er thy fortunes, brother!
  God's blessing on your head;
Joy for the living mother,
  Peace with the loving dead.

XVIII.

A PAIR OF MYTHS:

BEING A CHAPTER FROM AN UNPUBLISHED WORK.

EIGHT days passed away unreckoned, and still I remained unconscious of everything occurring around me. The morning of the ninth dawned, dragged heavily along, and noon approached, whilst I lay in the same comatose state. No alteration had taken place, except that a deeper and sounder sleep seemed to have seized upon me; a symptom hailed by my physician with joy, but regarded by my mother with increased alarm.

Suddenly, the incautious closing of my chamber door, as my sister, Miss Lucy Stanly, then in her fifteenth year, entered the apartment, aroused me from slumber and oblivion.

Abed at noonday! What did it betoken? I endeavored to recall something of the past, but memory for a long time refused its aid, and I appeared as fatally and irremediably unconscious as ever. Gradually, however, my shattered mind recovered its faculties, and in less than an hour after my awakening, I felt perfectly restored. No pain tormented me, and no torpor benumbed my faculties. I rapidly reviewed, mentally, the occurrences of the day before, when, as I imagined, the disaster had happened, and resolved at once to rise from my bed and prosecute my intended journey.

At this moment my father entered the apartment,

and observing that I was awake, ventured to speak to me kindly and in a very low tone. I smiled at his uneasiness, and immediately relieved him from all apprehension, by conversing freely and intelligibly of the late catastrophe. His delight knew no bounds. He seized my hand a thousand times, and pressed it again and again to his lips. At length, remembering that my mother was ignorant of my complete restoration, he rushed from the room, in order to be the first to convey the welcome intelligence.

My bed was soon surrounded by the whole family, chattering away, wild with joy, and imprinting scores of kisses on my lips, cheeks and forehead. The excitement proved too severe for me in my weak condition, and had not the timely arrival of the physician intervened to clear my chamber of every intruder, except Mamma Betty, as we all called the nurse, these pages in all probability would never have arrested the reader's eye. As it was, I suddenly grew very sick and faint; everything around me assumed a deep green tinge, and I fell into a deathlike swoon.

Another morning's sun was shining cheerily in at my window, when consciousness again returned. The doctor was soon at my side, and instead of prescribing physic as a remedy, requested my sister to sit at my bedside, and read in a low tone any interesting little story she might select. He cautioned her not to mention, even in the most casual manner, *Mormonism*, *St. Louis*, or the *Moselle*, which order she most implicitly obeyed; nor could all my ingenuity extract a solitary remark in relation to either.

My sister was not very long in making a selection; for, supposing what delighted herself would not fail to amuse me, she brought in a manuscript, carefully folded, and proceeded at once to narrate its history. It was written by my father, as a sort of model or sampler for my brothers and sisters, which they were to imitate when composition-day came round, instead of "hammering away," as he called it, on moral essays and metaphysical commonplaces. It was styled

THE KING OF THE NINE-PINS: A MYTH.

Heinrich Schwarz, or Black Hal, as he was wont to be called, was an old toper, but he was possessed of infinite good humor, and related a great many very queer stories, the truth of which no one, that I ever heard of, had the hardihood to doubt; for Black Hal had an uncommon share of "Teutonic pluck" about him, and was at times very unceremonious in the display of it. But Hal had a weakness—it was not liquor, for that was his strength—which he never denied; *Hal was too fond of nine-pins.* He had told me, in confidence, that "many a time and oft" he had rolled incessantly for weeks together. I think I heard him say that he once rolled for a month, day and night, without stopping a single moment to eat or to drink, or even to catch his breath.

I did not question his veracity at the time; but since, on reflection, the fact seems almost incredible; and were it not that this sketch might accidentally fall in his way, I might be tempted to show philosophically that such a thing could not possibly be. And yet I have read of very long fasts in my day—that, for instance, of Captain Riley in the Great Sahara, and others, which will readily occur to the reader. But I must not episodize, or I shall not reach my story.

Black Hal was sitting late one afternoon in a Nine-Pin Alley, in the little town of Kaatskill, in the State of

New York—it is true, for he said so—when a tremendous thunder-storm invested his retreat. His companions, one by one, had left him, until, rising from his seat and gazing around, he discovered that he was alone. The alley-keeper, too, could nowhere be found, and the boys who were employed to set up the pins had disappeared with the rest. It was growing very late, and Hal had a long walk, and he thought it most prudent to get ready to start home. The lightning glared in at the door and windows most vividly, and the heavy thunder crashed and rumbled and roared louder than he had ever heard it before. The rain, too, now commenced to batter down tremendously, and just as night set in, Hal had just got ready to set out. Hal first felt uneasy, next unhappy, and finally miserable. If he had but a boy to talk to! I'm afraid Hal began to grow scared. A verse that he learned in his boyhood, across the wide sea, came unasked into his mind. It always came there precisely at the time he did not desire its company. It ran thus:

> "Oh ! for the might of dread Odin
> The powers upon him shed,
> For a sail in the good ship Skidbladnir,*
> And a talk with Mimir's head !" †

This verse was repeated over and over again inaudibly. Gradually, however, his voice became a little louder, and a little louder still, until finally poor Hal hallooed it vociferously forth so sonorously that it drowned the very thunder. He had repeated it just seventy-seven

* The ship Skidbladnir was the property of Odin. He could sail in it on the most dangerous seas, and yet could fold it up and carry it in his pocket.

† Mimir's head was always the companion of Odin. When he desired to know what was transpiring in distant countries, he inquired of Mimir, and always received a correct reply.

times, when suddenly a monstrous head was thrust in at the door, and demanded, in a voice that sounded like the maelstrom, "What do *you* want with Odin?" "Oh, nothing—nothing in the world, I thank you, sir," politely responded poor Hal, shaking from head to foot. Here the head was followed by the shoulders, arms, body and legs of a giant at least forty feet high. Of course he came in on all fours, and approached in close proximity to Black Hal. Hal involuntarily retreated, as far as he could, reciting to himself the only prayer he remembered, "Now I lay me down to sleep," etc.

The giant did not appear desirous of pursuing Hal, being afraid—so Hal said—that he would draw his knife on him. But be the cause what it might, he seated himself at the head of the nine-pin alley, and shouted, "Stand up!" As he did so, the nine-pins at the other end arose and took their places.

"Now, sir," said he, turning again to Hal, "I'll bet you an ounce of your blood I can beat you rolling."

Hal trembled again, but meekly replied, "Please, sir, we don't bet *blood* nowadays—we bet *money*."

"Blood's my money," roared forth the giant. "Fee, fo, fum!" Hal tried in vain to hoist the window.

"Will you bet?"

"Yes, sir," said Hal; and he thought as it was only *an ounce*, he could spare that without much danger, and it might appease the monster's appetite.

"Roll first!" said the giant.

"Yes, sir," replied Hal, as he seized what he supposed to be the largest and his favorite ball.

"What are you doing with Mimir's head?" roared forth the monster.

"I beg your pardon, most humbly," began Hal, as he let the bloody head fall; "I did not mean any harm."

"Rumble, bang-whang!" bellowed the thunder.

Hal fell on his knees and recited most devoutly, "Now I lay me down," etc.

"Roll on! roll on! I say," and the giant seized poor Hal by the collar and set him on his feet.

He now selected a large ball, and poising it carefully in his hand, ran a few steps, and sent it whirling right in among the nine-pins; but what was his astonishment to behold them jump lightly aside, and permit the ball to pass in an avenue directly through the middle of the alley. Hal shuddered. The second and third ball met with no better success. Odin—for Hal said it was certainly he, as he had Mimir's head along—now grasped a ball and rolled it with all his might; but long before it reached the nine-pins, they had, every one of them, tumbled down, and lay sprawling on the alley.

"Two spares!" said the giant, as he grinned most gleefully at poor Hal. "Get up!" and up the pins all stood instantly. Taking another ball, he hurled it down the alley, and the same result followed. "Two more spares!" and Odin shook his gigantic sides with laughter.

"I give up the game," whined out Hal.

"Then you lose double," rejoined Odin.

Hal readily consented to pay two ounces, for he imagined, by yielding at once, he would so much the sooner get rid of his grim companion. As he said so, Odin pulled a pair of scales out of his coat pocket, made proportionably to his own size. He poised them upon a beam in the alley, and drew forth what he denominated two ounces, and put them in one scale. Each ounce was about the size of a twenty-eight pound weight, and was quite as heavy.

"Ha! ha! ha!! Ha! ha! ha!!! Ha! ha! ha!!!!"

shouted the giant, as he grasped the gasping and terrified gambler. He soon rolled up his sleeves, and bound his arm with a pocket handkerchief. Next he drew forth a lancet as long as a sword, and drove the point into the biggest vein he could discover. Hal screamed and fainted. When he returned to consciousness, the sun was shining brightly in at the window, and the sweet rumbling of the balls assured him that he still lay where the giant left him. On rising to his feet he perceived that a large coagulum of blood had collected where his head rested all night, and that he could scarcely walk from the effects of his exhaustion. He returned immediately home and told his wife all that had occurred; and though, like some of the neighbors, she distrusted the tale, yet she never intimated her doubts to Black Hal himself. The alley-keeper assured me in a whisper, one day, that upon the very night fixed on by Hal for the adventure, he was beastly drunk, and had been engaged in a fight with one of his boon companions, who gave him a black eye and a bloody nose. But the alley-keeper was always jealous of Black Hal's superiority in story telling; besides, he often drank too much himself, and I suspect he originated the report he related to me in a fit of wounded pride, or drunken braggadocio. One thing is certain, he never ventured to repeat the story in the presence of Black Hal himself.

In spite of the attention I endeavored to bestow on the marvelous history of Black Hal and his grim companion, my mind occasionally wandered far away, and could only find repose in communing with her who I now discovered for the first time held in her own hands the thread of my destiny. Lucy was not blind to these fits of abstraction, and whenever they gained entire control of my attention, she would pause, lay down the manuscript, and threaten most seriously to discontinue the perusal, unless I proved a better listener. I ask no man's pardon for declaring that my sister was an excellent reader. Most brothers, perhaps, think the same of most sisters; but there *was* a charm in Lucy's accent and a distinctness in her enunciation I have never heard excelled. Owing to these qualities, as much, perhaps, as to the strangeness of the story, I became interested in the fate of the drunken gambler, and when Lucy concluded, I was ready to exclaim, "And pray where is Black Hal now?"

My thoughts took another direction, however, and I impatiently demanded whether or not the sample story had been imitated. A guilty blush assured me quite as satisfactorily as words could have done, that Miss Lucy had herself made an attempt, and I therefore insisted that as she had whetted and excited the appetite, it would be highly unfraternal—(particularly in my present very precarious condition)—that parenthesis settled the matter—to deny me the means of satisfying it.

"But you'll laugh at me," timidly whispered my sister.

"Of course I shall," said I, "if your catastrophe is half as melancholy as Black Hal's. But make haste, or I shall be off to St. Louis. But pray inform me, what is the subject of your composition?"

"The Origin of Marriage."

"I believe, on my soul," responded I, laughing outright, "you girls never think about anything else."

I provoked no reply, and the manuscript being unfolded, my sister thus attempted to elucidate

THE ORIGIN OF MARRIAGE.

Professor Williams having ceased his manipulations, my eyes involuntarily closed, and I became unconscious to everything occurring around me. There's truth in mesmerism, after all, thought I, and being in the clairvoyant state, I beheld a most beautiful comet at this moment emerging from the constellation Taurus, and describing a curve about the star Zeta, one of the Pleiades. Now for a trip through infinite space! and as this thought entered my brain, I grasped a hair in the tail of the comet as it whizzed by me.

I climbed up the glittering hair until I found myself seated very comfortably on the comet's back, and was beginning to enjoy my starlit ramble exceedingly, when I was suddenly aroused from my meditations by the song of a heavenly minstrel, who, wandering from star to star and system to system, sang the fate of other worlds and other beings to those who would listen to his strains and grant him the rites of hospitality. As I approached, his tones were suddenly changed, his voice lowered into a deeper key, and gazing intently at me, or at what evidenced my presence to his sight, thus began:

The flaming sword of the cherub, which had waved so frightfully above the gate of the garden of Eden, had disappeared; the angel himself was gone; and Adam, as he approached the spot where so lately he had enjoyed the delights of heaven, beheld with astonishment and regret that Paradise and all its splendors had departed from the earth forever. Where the garden lately bloomed, he could discover only the dark and smouldering embers of a conflagration; a hard lava had incrusted itself along the golden walks; the birds were flown, the flowers withered, the fountains dried up, and desolation brooded over the scene.

"Ah!" sighed the patriarch of men, "where are now the pleasures which I once enjoyed along these peaceful avenues? Where are all those beautiful spirits, given by Heaven to watch over and protect me? Each guardian angel has deserted me, and the rainbow glories of Paradise have flown. No more the sun shines out in undimmed splendor, for clouds array him in gloom; the earth, forgetful of her verdure and her flowers, produces thorns to wound and frosts to chill me. The very air, once all balm and zephyrs, now howls around me with the voice of the storm and the fury of the hurricane. No more the notes of peace and happiness greet my ears, but the harsh tones of strife and battle resound on every side. Nature has kindled the flames of discord in her own bosom, and universal war has begun his reign!"

And then the father of mankind hid his face in the bosom of his companion, and wept the bitter tears of contrition and repentance.

"Oh, do not weep so bitterly, my Adam," exclaimed his companion. "True, we are miserable, but all is not yet lost; we have forfeited the smiles of Heaven, but we may yet regain our lost place in its affections. Let us learn from our misfortunes the anguish of guilt, but let us learn also the mercy of redemption. We may yet be happy."

"Oh, talk not of happiness now," interrupted Adam; "that nymph who once waited at our side, attentive to the beck, has disappeared, and fled from the companionship of such guilty, fallen beings as ourselves, forever."

"Not forever, Adam," kindly rejoined Eve; "she may yet be lurking among these groves, or lie hid behind yon hills."

"Then let us find her," quickly responded Adam; "you follow the sun, sweet Eve, to his resting-place, whilst I will trace these sparkling waters to their bourn. Let us ramble this whole creation o'er; and when we have found her, let us meet again on this very spot, and cling to her side, until the doom of death shall overtake us."

And the eye of Adam beamed with hope, then kindled for the first time on earth in the bosom of man; and he bade Eve his first farewell, and started eastward in his search.

Eve turned her face to the west, and set out on her allotted journey.

The sun had shone a hundred times in midsummer splendor, and a hundred times had hid himself in the clouds of winter, and yet no human foot had trod the spot where the garden of Eden once bloomed. Adam had in vain traced the Euphrates to the sea, and climbed the Himalaya Mountains. In vain had he endured the tropical heats on the Ganges, and the winter's cold in Siberia. He stood at last upon the borders of that narrow sea which separates Asia from America, and casting a wistful glance to the far-off continent, exclaimed: "In yon land, so deeply blue in the distance, that it looks like heaven, Happiness may have taken refuge. Alas! I cannot pursue her there. I will return to Eden, and learn if Eve, too, has been unsuccessful."

And then he took one more look at the distant land, sighed his adieu, and set out on his return.

Poor Eve! First child of misery, first daughter of despair! Poor Eve, with the blue of heaven in her eye, and the crimson of shame upon her lip! Poor Eve, arrayed in beauty, but hastening to decay—she, too, was unsuccessful.

Wandering in her westward way, the azure waters of the Mediterranean soon gleamed upon her sight. She stood at length upon the pebbly shore, and the glad waves, silent as death before, when they kissed her naked feet, commenced that song still heard in their eternal roar. A mermaid seemed to rise from the waters at her feet, and to imitate her every motion. Her long dark tresses, her deep blue eyes, her rosy cheek, her sorrowful look, all were reflected in the mermaid before her.

"Sweet spirit," said Eve, "canst thou inform me where the nymph Happiness lies concealed? She always stood beside us in the garden of Eden; but when we were driven from Paradise we beheld her no more."

The lips of the mermaid moved, but Eve could hear no reply.

Ah! mother of mankind, the crystal waters of every sea, reflecting thy lovely image, still faithful to their trust, conceal a mermaid in their bosom for every daughter of beauty who looks upon them!

Neither the orange groves of the Arno, nor the vineyards of France; neither the forests of Germania, nor the caves of Norway, concealed the sought-for nymph. Eve explored them all. Her track was imprinted in the sands of Sahara, by the banks of the Niger, on the rocks of Bengola, in the vales of Abyssinia—but all in vain.

"O Happiness! art thou indeed departed from our earth? How can we live without thee? Come, Death," cried Eve; "come now, and take me where thou wilt. This world is a desert, for Happiness has left it desolate."

A gentle slumber soon overcame the wearied child of sorrow, and in her sleep a vision came to comfort her. She dreamed that she stood before an aged man, whose hoary locks attested that the snows of many winters had whitened them, and in whose glance she recognized the spirit of Wisdom.

"Aged Father," said Eve, "where is Happiness?" and then she burst into a flood of tears.

"Comfort thyself, Daughter," mildly answered the old man; "Happiness yet dwells on earth, but she is no longer visible. A temple is built for her in every mortal's bosom, but she never ascends her throne until welcomed there by the child of Honor and Love."

The morning sun aroused Eve from her slumber, but did not dispel the memory of her dream. "I will return to Eden, and there await until the child of Honor and Love shall enthrone in my bosom the lost nymph Happiness;" and saying this, she turned her face to the eastward, and thinking of Adam and her vision, journeyed joyfully along.

The sun of Spring had opened the flowers and clothed the woods in verdure; had freed the streams from their icy fetters, and inspired the warbling world with harmony, when two forlorn and weary travelers approached the banks of the river Pison; that river which had flowed through the garden of Eden when the first sunshine broke upon the world. A hundred years had rolled away, and the echo of no human voice had resounded through the deserted groves. At length the dusky figures emerged from the overshadowing shrubbery, and raised their eyes into each other's faces. One bound—one cry—and they weep for joy in each other's arms.

Adam related his sad and melancholy story, and then Eve soon finished hers. But no sooner had she told her dream, than Adam, straining her to his bosom, exclaimed:

"There is no mystery here, my Eve. If Happiness

on earth be indeed the child of Honor and Love, it must be in Matrimony alone. What else now left us on earth can lay claim to the precious boon? Approved by heaven, and cherished by man, in the holy bonds of Matrimony it must consist; and if this be all, we need seek no further; it is ours!"

They then knelt in prayer, and returned thanks to Heaven, that though the garden of Eden was a wild, and the nymph Happiness no longer an angel at their side, yet that her spirit was still present in every bosom where the heart is linked to Honor and Love by the sacred ties of Matrimony.

XIX.

THE LAST OF HIS RACE.

NO further can fate tempt or try me,
With guerdon of pleasure or pain;
Ere the noon of my life has sped by me,
The last of my race I remain.
To that home so long left I might journey;
But they for whose greeting I yearn,
Are launched on that shadowy ocean
Whence voyagers never return.

My life is a blank in creation,
My fortunes no kindred may share;
No brother to cheer desolation,
No sister to soften by prayer;
No father to gladden my triumphs,
No mother my sins to atone;
No children to lean on in dying—
I must finish my journey alone!

In that hall, where their feet tripp'd before me,
How lone would now echo my tread!
While each fading portrait threw o'er me
The chill, stony smile of the dead.
One sad thought bewilders my slumbers,
From eve till the coming of dawn:
I cry out in visions, "*Where are they?*"
And echo responds, "*They are gone!*"

But fain, ere the life-fount grows colder,
  I'd wend to that lone, distant place,
That row of green hillocks, where moulder
  The rest of my early doom'd race.
There slumber the true and the manly,
  There slumber the spotless and fair;
And when my last journey is ended,
  My place of repose be it there!

XX.

THE TWO GEORGES.

BETWEEN the years of our Lord 1730 and 1740, two men were born on opposite sides of the Atlantic Ocean, whose lives were destined to exert a commanding influence on the age in which they lived, as well as to control the fortunes of many succeeding generations.

One was by birth a plain peasant, the son of a Virginia farmer; the other an hereditary Prince, and the heir of an immense empire. It will be the main object of this sketch to trace the histories of these two individuals, so dissimilar in their origin, from birth to death, and show how it happened that one has left a name synonymous with tyranny, whilst the other will descend to the latest posterity, radiant with immortal glory, and renowned the world over as the friend of virtue, the guardian of liberty, and the benefactor of his race.

Go with me for one moment to the crowded and splendid metropolis of England. It is the evening of the 4th of June, 1734. Some joyful event must have occurred, for the bells are ringing merrily, and the inhabitants are dressed in holiday attire. Nor is the circumstance of a private nature, for banners are everywhere displayed, the vast city is illuminated, and a thousand cannon are proclaiming it from their iron throats. The population seem frantic with joy, and rush tumultuously into each other's arms, in token of a national jubilee. Tens of thousands are hurrying along toward a splendid marble pile, situated on a commanding eminence, near the river Thames, whilst from the loftiest towers of St. James's Palace the national ensigns of St. George and the Red Cross are seen floating on the breeze. Within one of the most gorgeously furnished apartments of that royal abode, the wife of Frederic, Prince of Wales, and heir apparent to the British Empire, has just been delivered of a son. The scions of royalty crowd into the bed-chamber, and solemnly attest the event as one on which the destiny of a great empire is suspended. The corridors are thronged with dukes, and nobles, and soldiers, and courtiers, all anxious to bend the supple knee, and bow the willing neck, to power just cradled into the world. A Royal Proclamation soon follows, commemorating the event, and commanding British subjects everywhere, who acknowledge the honor of Brunswick, to rejoice, and give thanks to God for safely ushering into existence George William Frederic, heir presumptive of the united crowns of Great Britain and Ireland. Just twenty-two years afterward that child ascended the throne of his ancestors as King George the Third.

Let us now turn our eyes to the Western Continent, and contemplate a scene of similar import, but under circumstances of a totally different character. It is the 22d February, 1732. The locality is a distant colony, the spot the verge of an immense, untrodden and unexplored wilderness, the habitation a log cabin, with its chinks filled in with clay, and its sloping roof patched over with clapboards. Snow covers the ground, and a chill wintery wind is drifting the flakes, and moaning through the forest. Two immense chimneys stand at either end of the house, and give promise of cheerful comfort and primitive hospitality within, totally in contrast with external nature. There are but four small rooms in the dwelling, in one of which Mary Ball, the wife of Augustine Washington, has just given birth to a son. No dukes or marquises or earls are there to attest the humble event. There are no princes of the blood to wrap the infant in the insignia of royalty, and fold about his limbs the tapestried escutcheon of a kingdom. His first breath is not drawn in the center of a mighty capitol, the air laden with perfume, and trembling to the tones of soft music and the "murmurs of low fountains." But the child is received from its mother's womb by hands imbrowned with honest labor, and laid upon a lowly couch, indicative only of a backwoodsman's home and an American's inheritance. He, too, is christened George, and forty-three years afterward took command of the American forces assembled on the plains of old Cambridge.

But if their births were dissimilar, their rearing and education were still more unlike. From his earliest recollection the Prince heard only the language of flattery, moved about from palace to palace, just as caprice dictated, slept upon the cygnet's down, and grew up in indolence, self-will and vanity, a dictator from his cradle. The peasant boy, on the other hand, was taught from his infancy that labor was honorable, and hardships indispensable to vigorous health. He early learned to sleep alone amid the dangers of a boundless wilderness, a stone for his pillow, and the naked sod his bed; whilst the voices of untamed nature around him sang his morning and his evening hymns. Truth, courage and constancy were early implanted in his mind by a mother's counsels, and the important lesson of life was taught by a father's example, that when existence ceases to be useful it ceases to be happy.

Early manhood ushered them both into active life; the one as king over extensive dominions, the other as a modest, careful, and honest district surveyor.

Having traced the two Georges to the threshold of their career, let us now proceed one step further, and take note of the first great public event in the lives of either.

For a long time preceding the year 1753 the French had laid claim to all the North American continent west of the Alleghany Mountains, stretching in an unbroken line from Canada to Louisiana. The English strenuously denied this right, and when the French commandant on the Ohio, in 1753, commenced erecting a fort near where the present city of Pittsburg stands, and proceeded to capture certain English traders, and expel them from the country, Dinwiddie, Governor of Virginia, deemed it necessary to dispatch an agent on a diplomatic visit to the French commandant, and demand by what authority he acted, by what title he claimed the country, and order him immediately to evacuate the territory.

George Washington, then only in his twenty-second year, was selected by the Governor for this important mission.

It is unnecessary to follow him, in all his perils, during his wintery march through the wilderness. The historian of his life has painted in imperishable colors his courage, his sagacity, his wonderful coolness in the midst of danger, and the success which crowned his undertaking. The memory loves to follow him through the trackless wilds of the forest, accompanied by only a single companion, and making his way through wintery snows, in the midst of hostile savages and wild beasts, for more than five hundred miles, to the residence of the French commander. How often do we not shudder, as we behold the treacherous Indian guide, on his return, deliberately raising his rifle, and leveling it at that majestic form; thus endeavoring, by an act of treachery and cowardice, to deprive Virginia of her young hero! And oh! with what fervent prayers do we not implore a kind Providence to watch over his desperate encounter with the floating ice, at midnight, in the swollen torrent of the Alleghany, and rescue him from the wave and the storm. Standing bareheaded on the frail raft, whilst in the act of dashing aside some floating ice that threatened to ingulf him, the treacherous oar was broken in his hand, and he is precipitated many feet into the boiling current. Save! oh, save him heaven! for the destinies of millions yet unborn hang upon that noble arm!

Let us now recross the ocean. In the early part of the year 1764 a ministerial crisis occurs in England, and Lord Bute, the favorite of the British monarch, is driven from the administration of the government. The troubles with the American colonists have also just commenced to excite attention, and the young King grows angry, perplexed, and greatly irritated. A few days after this, a rumor starts into circulation that the monarch is sick. His attendants look gloomy, his friends terrified, and even his physicians exhibit symptoms of doubt and danger. Yet he has no fever, and is daily observed walking with uncertain and agitated step along the corridors of the palace. His conduct becomes gradually more and more strange, until doubt gives place to certainty, and the royal medical staff report to a select committee of the House of Commons that the King is threatened with *insanity*. For six weeks the cloud obscures his mental faculties, depriving him of all interference with the administration of the government, and betokening a sad disaster in the future. His reason is finally restored, but frequent fits of passion, pride and obstinacy indicate but too surely that the disease is seated, and a radical cure impossible.

Possessed now of the chief characteristics of George Washington and George Guelph, we are prepared to review briefly their conduct during the struggle that ensued between the two countries they respectively represented.

Let us now refer to the first act of disloyalty of Washington, the first indignant spurn his high-toned spirit evinced under the oppressions of a king.

Not long after his return from the west, Washington was offered the chief command of the forces about to be raised in Virginia, to expel the French; but, with his usual modesty, he declined the appointment, on account of his extreme youth, but consented to take the post of lieutenant-colonel. Shortly afterward, on the death of Colonel Fry, he was promoted to the chief command, but through no solicitations of his own. Subsequently, when the war between France and England broke out in Europe, the principal seat of hostilities was transferred to America, and his Gracious Majesty George III sent over a large body of troops, *under the command of favorite officers*. But this was not enough. An edict soon followed, denominated an "Order to settle the rank of the officers of His Majesty's forces serving in America." By one of the articles of this order, it was provided "that all officers commissioned by the King, should take precedence of those of the same grade commissioned by the governors of the respective colonies, although their commissions might be of junior date;" and it was further provided, that "when the trôops served together, the provincial officers should enjoy no rank at all." This order was scarcely promulgated—indeed, before the ink was dry —ere the Governor of Virginia received a communication informing him that *George Washington was no longer a soldier*. Entreaties, exhortations, and threats were all lavished upon him in vain; and to those who, in their expostulations, spoke of the defenseless frontiers of his native State, he patriotically but nobly replied: "I will serve my country when I can do so without dishonor."

In contrast with this attitude of Washington, look at the conduct of George the Third respecting the colonies, after the passage of the Stamp Act. This act was no sooner proclaimed in America, than the most violent opposition was manifested, and combinations for the purpose of effectual resistance were rapidly organized from Massachusetts to Georgia. The leading English patriots, among whom were Burke and Barré, protested against the folly of forcing the colonies into rebellion, and the city of London presented a petition to the King, praying him to dismiss the Granville ministry, and repeal the obnoxious act. "It is with the utmost astonishment," replied the King, "that I find any of my subjects capable of encouraging the rebellious disposition that unhappily exists in some of my North American colonies. Having entire confidence in the wisdom of my parliament, the great council of the realm, I will steadily pursue those measures which they have recommended for the support of the constitutional rights of Great Britain." He heeded not the memorable words of Burke, that afterward became prophetic. "There are moments," exclaimed this great statesman, "critical moments in the fortunes of all states, when they who are too weak to contribute to your prosperity may yet be strong enough to complete your ruin." The Boston port bill passed, and the first blood was spilt at Lexington.

It is enough to say of the long and bloody war that followed, that George the Third, by his obstinacy, contributed more than any other man in his dominion to prolong the struggle, and affix to it the stigma of cruelty, inhumanity and vengeance; whilst Washington was equally the soul of the conflict on the other side, and by his imperturbable justice, moderation and firmness, did more than by his arms to convince England that her revolted colonists were invincible.

It is unnecessary to review in detail the old Revolution. Let us pass to the social position of the two Georges in after-life.

On the 2d August, 1786, as the King was alighting from his carriage at the gate of St. James, an attempt was made on his life by a woman named Margaret Nicholson, who, under pretense of presenting a petition, endeavored to stab him with a knife which was concealed in the paper. The weapon was an old one, and so rusty that, on striking the vest of the King, it bent double, and thus preserved his life. On the 29th October, 1795, whilst his majesty was proceeding to the House of Lords, a ball passed through both windows of the carriage. On his return to St. James the mob threw stones into the carriage, several of which struck the King, and one lodged in the cuff of his coat. The state carriage was completely demolished by the mob. But it was on the 15th May, 1800, that George the

Third made his narrowest escapes. In the morning of that day, whilst attending the field exercise of a battalion of guards, one of the soldiers loaded his piece with a bullet and discharged it at the King. The ball fortunately missed its aim, and lodged in the thigh of a gentleman who was standing in the rear. In the evening of the same day a more alarming circumstance occurred at the Drury Lane Theatre. At the moment when the King entered the royal box, a man in the pit, on the right-hand side of the orchestra, suddenly stood up and discharged a large horse-pistol at him. The hand of the would-be assassin was thrown up by a bystander, and the ball entered the box just above the head of the King.

Such were the public manifestations of affection for this royal tyrant. He was finally attacked by an enemy that could not be thwarted, and on the 20th December, 1810, he became a confirmed lunatic. In this dreadful condition he lingered until January, 1820, when he died, having been the most unpopular, unwise and obstinate sovereign that ever disgraced the English throne. He was forgotten as soon as life left his body, and was hurriedly buried with that empty pomp which but too often attends a despot to the grave.

His whole career is well summed up by Allan Cunningham, his biographer, in few words: "Throughout his life he manifested a strong disposition to be his own minister, and occasionally placed the kingly prerogatives in perilous opposition to the resolutions of the nation's representatives. His interference with the deliberations of the upper house, as in the case of Fox's Indian bill, was equally ill-judged and dangerous. *The separation of America from the mother country, at the time it took place, was the result of the King's personal feel-*

ings and interference with the ministry. The war with France was, in part at least, attributable to the views and wishes of the sovereign of England. His obstinate refusal to grant any concessions to his Catholic subjects, kept his cabinet perpetually hanging on the brink of dissolution, and threatened the dismemberment of the kingdom. He has been often praised for firmness, but it was in too many instances the firmness of obstinacy; a dogged adherence to an opinion once pronounced, or a resolution once formed."

The mind, in passing from the unhonored grave of the prince to the last resting-place of the peasant boy, leaps from a kingdom of darkness to one of light.

Let us now return to the career of Washington. Throughout the Revolutionary War he carried, like Atropos, in his hand the destinies of millions; he bore, like Atlas, on his shoulders the weight of a world. It is unnecessary to follow him throughout his subsequent career. Honored again and again by the people of the land he had redeemed from thraldom, he has taken his place in death by the side of the wisest and best of the world's benefactors. Assassins did not unglory him in life, nor has oblivion drawn her mantle over him in death. The names of his great battle-fields have become nursery words, and his principles have imbedded themselves forever in the national character. Every pulsation of our hearts beats true to his memory. His mementoes are everywhere around and about us. Distant as we are from the green fields of his native Westmoreland, the circle of his renown has spread far beyond our borders. In climes where the torch of science was never kindled; on shores still buried in primeval bloom; amongst barbarians where the face of liberty was never seen, the Christian missionary of

America, roused perhaps from his holy duties by the distant echo of the national salute, this day thundering amidst the billows of every sea, or dazzled by the gleam of his country's banner, this day floating in every wind of heaven, pauses over his task as a Christian, and whilst memory kindles in his bosom the fires of patriotism, pronounces in the ear of the enslaved pagan the venerated name of WASHINGTON!

Nor are the sons of the companions of Washington alone in doing justice to his memory. Our sisters, wives and mothers compete with us in discharging this debt of national gratitude. With a delicacy that none but woman could exhibit, and with a devotion that none but a daughter could feel, they are now busy in executing the noble scheme of purchasing his tomb, in order for endless generations to stand sentinel over his remains. Take them! take them to your hearts, oh! ye daughters of America; enfold them closer to your bosom than your first-born offspring; build around them a mausoleum that neither time nor change can overthrow; for within them germinates the seeds of liberty for the benefit of millions yet unborn. Wherever tyranny shall lift its Medusan head, wherever treason shall plot its hellish schemes, wherever disunion shall unfurl its tattered ensign, there, oh there, sow them in the hearts of patriots and republicans! For from these pale ashes there shall spring, as from the dragon's teeth sown by Cadmus of old on the plains of Heber, vast armies of invincible heroes, sworn upon the altar and tomb at Mount Vernon, to live as freemen, or as such to die!

XXI.

MASONRY.

OH, sacred spirit of Masonic love,
Offspring of Heaven, the angels' bond above,
Guardian of peace and every social tie,
How deep the sources of thy fountains lie!
How wide the realms that 'neath thy wings expand,
Embracing every clime, encircling every land!

Beneath the aurora of the Polar skies,
Where Greenland's everlasting glaciers rise,
The Lodge mysterious lifts its snow-built dome,
And points the brother to a sunnier home;
Where Nilus slays the sacrificial kid,
Beneath the shadow of her pyramid,
Where magian suns unclasp the gaping ground,
And far Australia's golden sands abound;
Where breakers thunder on the coral strand,
To guard the gates of Kamehameha's land;
Wherever man, in lambskin garb arrayed,
Strikes in defense of innocence betrayed;
Lifts the broad shield of charity to all,
And bends in anguish o'er a brother's fall;
Where the bright symbol of Masonic truth,
Alike for high and low, for age or youth,
Flames like yon sun at tropic midday's call,
And opes the universal eye on all!
What though in secret all your alms be done,
Your foes all vanquished and your trophies won?
What though a veil be o'er your Lodges thrown,
And brother only be to brother known?

In secret, God built up the rolling world;
In secret, morning's banners are unfurled;
In secret, spreads the leaf, unfolds the flower,
Revolve the spheres, and speeds the passing hour.
The day is noise, confusion, strife, turmoil,
Struggles for bread, and sweat beneath the toil.
The night is silence—progress without jars,
The rest of mortals and the march of stars!
The day for work to toiling man was given;
But night, to lead his erring steps to Heaven.
All hail! ye brethren of the mystic tie!
Who feed the hungry, heed the orphan's cry;
Who clothe the naked, dry the widow's tear,
Befriend the exile, bear the stranger's bier;
Stand round the bedside when the fluttering soul
Bursts her clay bonds and parteth for her goal;
God speed you in the noble path you tread,
Friends of the living, mourners o'er the dead.

May all your actions, measured on the square,
Be just and righteous, merciful and fair;
Your thoughts flow pure, in modesty of mind,
Along the equal level of mankind;
Your words be troweled to truth's perfect tone,
Your fame be chiseled in unblemished stone,
Your hearts be modeled on the plummet's line,
Your faith be guided by the Book divine;
And when at last the gavel's beat above
Calls you from labor to the feast of love,
May mighty Boaz, pillar'd at that gate
Which seraphs tyle and where archangels wait,
Unloose the bandage from your dazzled eyes,
Spell out the *Password* to Arch-Royal skies;
Upon your bosom set the signet steel,
Help's sign disclose, and Friendship's grip reveal;
Place in your grasp the soul's unerring rod,
And light you to the Temple of your God!

XXII.

POLLOCK'S EUTHANASIA.

HE is gone! the young, and gifted!
By his own strong pinions lifted
To the stars;

Where he strikes, with minstrels olden,
Choral harps, whose strings are golden,
Deathless bars.

There, with Homer's ghost all hoary,
Not with years, but fadeless glory,
Lo! he stands;

And through that open portal,
We behold the bards immortal
Clasping hands!

Hark! how Rome's great epic master
Sings, that death is no disaster
To the wise;

Fame on earth is but a menial,
But it reigns a king perennial
In the skies!

Albion's blind old bard heroic,
Statesman, sage, and Christian stoic,
Greets his son;

Whilst in pæans wild and glorious,
Like his "Paradise victorious,"
Sings, Well done!

Lo! a bard with forehead pendent,
But with glory's beams resplendent
As a star;

Slow descends from regions higher,
With a crown and golden lyre
In his car.

All around him, crowd as minions,
Thrones and sceptres, and dominions,
Kings and Queens;

Ages past and ages present,
Lord and dame, and prince and peasant,
His demesnes!

Approach! young bard hesperian,
Welcome to the heights empyrean,
Thou did'st sing,

Ere yet thy trembling fingers
Struck where fame immortal lingers,
In the string.

Kneel! I am the bard of Avon,
And the Realm of song in Heaven
Is my own;

Long thy verse shall live in story,
And thy Lyre I crown with glory,
And a throne!

XXIII.

SCIENCE, LITERATURE AND ART DURING THE FIRST HALF OF THE NINETEENTH CENTURY.

LOOKING back into the past, and exploring by the light of authentic history, sacred as well as profane, the characteristics of former ages, the merest tyro in learning cannot fail to perceive that certain epochs stand prominently out on the "sands of time," and indicate vast activity and uncommon power in the human mind.

These epochs are so well marked that history has given them a designation, and to call them by their name, conjures up, as by the wand of an enchanter, the heroic representatives of our race.

If, for instance, we should speak of the era of Solomon, in sacred history, the memory would instantly picture forth the pinnacles of the Holy Temple, lifting themselves into the clouds; the ear would listen intently to catch the sweet intonations of the harp of David, vocal at once with the prophetic sorrows of his race, and swelling into sublime ecstasy at the final redemption of his people; the eye would glisten at the pomp and pageantry of the foreign potentates who thronged his court, and gloat with rapture over the beauty of the young Queen of Sheba, who journeyed from a distant land to seek wisdom at the feet of the wisest monarch that ever sat upon a throne. We should behold his ships traversing every sea, and pouring into the lap of

Israel the gold of Ophir, the ivory of Senegambia, and the silks, myrrh, and spices of the East.

So, too, has profane history its golden ages, when men all seemed to be giants, and their minds inspired.

What is meant when we speak of the age of Pericles? We mean all that is glorious in the annals of Greece. We mean Apelles with his pencil, Phidias with his chisel, Alcibiades with his sword. We seem to be strolling arm-in-arm with Plato, into the academy, to listen to the divine teachings of Socrates, or hurrying along with the crowd toward the theatre, where Herodotus is reading his history, or Euripides is presenting his tragedies. Aspasia rises up like a beautiful apparition before us, and we follow willing slaves at the wheels of her victorious chariot. The whole of the Peloponnesus glows with intellect like a forge in blast, and scatters the trophies of Grecian civilization profusely around us. The Parthenon lifts its everlasting columns, and the Venus and Apollo are moulded into marble immortality.

Rome had her Augustan age, an era of poets, philosophers, soldiers, statesmen, and orators. Crowded into contemporary life, we recognize the greatest general of the heathen world, the greatest poet, the greatest orator, and the greatest statesman of Rome. Cæsar and Cicero, Virgil and Octavius, all trod the pavement of the capitol together, and lent their blended glory to immortalize the Augustan age.

Italy and Spain and France and England have had their golden age. The eras of Lorenzo the Magnificent, of Ferdinand and Isabella, of Louis Quatorze and of Elizabeth, can never be forgotten. They loom up from the surrounding gloom like the full moon bursting upon the sleeping seas; irradiating the night, clothing the meanest wave in sparkling silver, and dimming the lustre of the brightest stars. History has also left in its track mementoes of a different character. In sacred history we have the age of Herod; in profane, the age of Nero. We recognize at a glance the talismanic touch of the age of chivalry, and the era of the Crusades, and mope our way in darkness and gloom along that opaque track, stretching from the reign of Justinian, in the sixth century, to the reign of Edward the Third, in the fourteenth, and known throughout Christendom as the "Dark Ages." Let us now take a survey of the field we occupy, and ascertain, if possible, the category in which our age shall be ranked by our posterity.

But before proceeding to discuss the characteristics of our epoch, let us define more especially what that epoch embraces.

It does not embrace the American nor the French Revolution, nor does it include the acts or heroes of either. The impetus given to the human mind by the last half of the eighteenth century, must be carefully distinguished from the impulses of the first half of the nineteenth. The first was an era of almost universal war, the last of almost uninterrupted peace. The dying ground-swell of the waves after a storm belong to the tempest, not to the calm which succeeds. Hence the wars of Napoleon, the literature and art of his epoch, must be excluded from observation, in properly discussing the true characteristics of our era.

De Staël and Goethe and Schiller and Byron; Pitt and Nesselrode, Metternich and Hamilton; Fichte and Stewart and Brown and Cousin; Canova, Thorwaldsen and La Place, though all dying since the beginning of this century, belong essentially to a former era. They were the ripened fruits of that grand uprising of the human mind which first took form on the 4th day of July, 1776. Our era properly commences with the downfall of the first Napoleon, and none of the events connected therewith, either before or afterward, can be philosophically classed in the epoch we represent, but must be referred to a former period. Ages hence, then, the philosophic critic will thus describe the first half of the nineteenth century:

"The normal state of Christendom was peace. The age of steel that immediately went before it had passed. It was the Iron age.

"Speculative philosophy fell asleep; literature declined; Skepticism bore sway in religion, politics, and morals; Utility became the universal standard of right and wrong, and the truths of every science and the axioms of every art were ruthlessly subjected to the *experimentum crucis*. Everything was liable to revision. The verdicts pronounced in the olden time against Mohammed and Mesmer and Robespierre were set aside, and a new trial granted. The ghosts of Roger Bacon and Emanuel Swedenborg were summoned from the Stygian shore to plead their causes anew before the bar of public opinion. The head of Oliver Cromwell was ordered down from the gibbet, the hump was smoothed down on the back of Richard III, and the sentence pronounced by Urban VIII against the 'starry Galileo' reversed forever. Aristotle was decently interred beneath a modern monument inscribed thus: '*In pace requiescat;*' whilst Francis Bacon was rescued from the sacrilegious hands of kings and peers and parliament, and canonized by the unanimous consent of Christendom. It was the age of tests. Experiment governed the world. Germany led the van, and Humboldt became the impersonation of his times."

Such unquestionably will be the verdict of the future, when the present time, with all its treasures and trash, its hopes and realizations, shall have been safely shelved and labeled amongst the musty records of bygone generations.

Let us now examine into the grounds of this verdict more minutely, and test its accuracy by exemplifications.

I. And first, who believes now in *innate ideas?* Locke has been completely superseded by the materialists of Germany and France, and all speculative moral philosophy exploded. The audiences of Edinburgh and Brown University interrupt Sir William Hamilton and Dr. Wayland in their discourses, and, stripping off the plumage from their theses, inquisitively demand, "*Cui bono?*" What is the use of all this? How can we apply it to the every-day concerns of life? We ask you for bread and you have given us a stone; and though that stone be a diamond, it is valueless, except for its glitter. No philosopher can speculate successfully or even satisfactorily to himself, when he is met at every turn by some vulgar intruder into the domains of Aristotle and Kant, who clips his wings just as he was prepared to soar into the heavens, by an offer of copartnership to "speculate," it may be, in the price of pork. Hence, no moral philosopher of our day has been enabled to erect any theory which will stand the assaults of logic for a moment. Each school rises for an instant to the surface, and sports out its little day in toss and tribulation, until the next wave rolls along, with foam on its crest and fury in its roar, and overwhelms it forever. As with its predecessor, so with itself.

> "The eternal surge
> Of Time and Tide rolls on and bears afar
> Their bubbles: as the old burst, new emerge,
> Lashed from the foam of ages."

II. But I have stated that this is an age of *literary decline.* It is true that more books are written and published, more newspapers and periodicals printed and circulated, more extensive libraries collected and incorporated, and more ink indiscriminately spilt, than at any former period of the world's history. In looking about us we are forcibly reminded of the sarcastic couplet of Pope, who complains—

> "That those who cannot write, and those who can,
> All scratch, all scrawl, and scribble to a man."

Had a modern gentleman all the eyes of Argus, all the hands of Briareus, all the wealth of Crœsus, and lived to the age of Methuselah, his eyes would all fail, his fingers all tire, his money all give out, and his years come to an end, long before he perused one tenth of the annual product of the press of Christendom at the present day. It is no figure of rhetoric to say that the press groans beneath the burden of its labors. Could the types of Leipsic and London, Paris and New York, speak out, the Litany would have to be amended, and a new article added, to which they would solemnly respond: "Spare us, good Lord!"

A recent publication furnishes the following statistical facts relating to the book trade in our own country: "Books have multiplied to such an extent in the United States that it now takes 750 paper-mills, with 2000 engines in constant operation, to supply the printers, who work day and night, endeavoring to keep their engagements with publishers. These tireless mills produce 270,000,000 pounds of paper every year. It requires a pound and a quarter of old rags for one pound of paper, thus 340,000,000 pounds of rags were consumed in this way last year. There are about 300 publishers in the United States, and near 10,000 booksellers who are engaged in the task of dispensing literary pabulum to the public."

It may appear somewhat paradoxical to assert that literature is declining whilst books and authors are multiplying to such a fearful extent. Byron wrote:

> " 'Tis pleasant, sure, to see one's name in print;
> A book 's a book, although there 's nothing in 't."

True enough; but books are not always literature. A man may become an author without ceasing to be an ignoramus. His name may adorn a title-page without being recorded *in œre perenne.* He may attempt to write himself up a very "lion" in literature, whilst good master Slender may be busily engaged "in writing him down an ass."

Not one book in a thousand is a success; not one success in ten thousand wreathes the fortunate author with the laurel crown, and lifts him up into the region of the immortals. Tell me, ye who prate about the *literary glory* of the nineteenth century, wherein it consists? Whose are

> "The great, the immortal names
> That were not born to die?"

I cast my eyes up the long vista toward the Temple of Fame, and I behold hundreds of thousands pressing on to reach the shining portals. They jostle each other by the way, they trip, they fall, they are overthrown and ruthlessly trampled into oblivion, by the giddy throng, as they rush onward and upward. One, it may be two, of the million who started out, stand trembling at the threshold, and with exultant voices cry aloud for admittance. One perishes before the summons can be answered; and the other, awed into immortality by the august presence into which he enters, is transformed into imperishable stone.

Let us carefully scan the rolls of the literature of our era, and select, if we can, poet, orator, or philosopher, whose fame will deepen as it runs, and brighten as it burns, until future generations shall drink at the fountain and be refreshed, and kindle their souls at the vestal flame and be purified, illuminated and ennobled.

In poetry, aye, in the crowded realms of song, who bears the sceptre?—who wears the crown? America, England, France and Germany can boast of bards *by the gross*, and rhyme *by the acre*, but not a single poet. The *poeta nascitur* is not here. He may be on his way—and I have heard that he was—but this generation must pass before he arrives. Is he in America? If so, which is he? Is it Poe, croaking sorrowfully with his "Raven," or Willis, cooing sweetly with his "Dove"? Is it Bryant, with his "Thanatopsis," or Prentice, with his "Dirge to the Dead Year"? Perhaps it is Holmes, with his "Lyrics," or Longfellow, with his "Idyls." Alas! is it not self-evident that we have no poet, when it is utterly impossible to discover any two critics in the land who can find him?

True, we have lightning-bugs enough, but no star; foot-hills, it may be, in abundance, but no Mount Shasta, with its base built upon the everlasting granite, and its brow bathed in the eternal sunlight.

In England, Tennyson, the Laureate, is the spokesman of a clique, the pet poet of a princely circle, whose rhymes flow with the docility and harmony of a limpid brook, but never stun like Niagara, nor rise into sublimity like the storm-swept sea.

Béranger, the greatest poet of France of our era, was a mere song-writer; and Heine, the pride of young Germany, a mere satirist and lyrist. Freiligrath can never rank with Goethe or Schiller; and Victor Hugo never attain the heights trodden by Racine, Corneille, or Boileau.

In oratory, where shall we find the compeer of Chatham or Mirabeau, Burke or Patrick Henry? I have not forgotten Peel and Gladstone, nor Lamartine and Count Cavour, nor Sargent S. Prentiss and Daniel Webster. But Webster himself, by far the greatest intellect of all these, was a mere debater, and the spokesman of a party. He was an eloquent speaker, but can never rank as an orator with the rhetoricians of the last century.

And in philosophy and general learning, where shall we find the equal of that burly old bully, Dr. Sam Johnson? and yet Johnson, with all his learning, was a third-rate philosopher.

In truth, the greatest author of our era was a mere essayist. Beyond all controversy, Thomas Babington Macaulay was the most polished writer of our times. With an intellect acute, logical and analytic; with an imagination glowing and rich, but subdued and under perfect control; with a style so clear and limpid and concise, that it has become a standard for all who aim to follow in the path he trod, and with a learning so full and exact, and exhaustive, that he was nicknamed, when an undergraduate, the "Omniscient Macaulay;" he still lacks the giant grasp of thought, the bold originality, and the intense, earnest enthusiasm which characterize the master-spirits of the race, and identify them with the eras they adorn.

III. As in literature, so in what have been denominated by scholars the *Fine Arts*. The past fifty years has not produced a painter, sculptor, or composer, who ranks above mediocrity in their respective vocations. Canova and Thorwaldsen were the last of their race;

Sir Joshua Reynolds left no successor, and the immortal Beethoven has been superseded by negro minstrelsy and senseless pantomime. The greatest architect of the age is a railroad contractor, and the first dramatist a cobbler of French farces.

IV. But whilst the highest faculty of the mind—the imagination—has been left uncultivated, and has produced no worthy fruit, the next highest, the casual, or the one that deals with causes and effects, has been stimulated into the most astonishing fertility.

Our age ignores fancy, and deals exclusively with fact. Within its chosen range it stands far, very far pre-eminent over all that have preceded it. It reaps the fruit of Bacon's labors. It utilizes all that it touches. It stands thoughtfully on the field of Waterloo, and estimates scientifically the manuring properties of bones and blood. It disentombs the mummy of Thotmes II, sells the linen bandages for the manufacture of paper, burns the asphaltum-soaked body for firewood, and plants the pint of red wheat found in his sarcophagus, to try an agricultural experiment. It deals in no sentimentalities; it has no appreciation of the sublime. It stands upon the ocean shore, but with its eyes fixed on the yellow sand searching for gold. It confronts Niagara, and, gazing with rapture at its misty shroud, exclaims, in an ecstasy of admiration, "Lord, what a place to sponge a coat!" Having no soul to save, it has no religion to save it. It has discovered that Mohammed was a great benefactor of his race, and that Jesus Christ was, after all, a mere man; distinguished, it is true, for his benevolence, his fortitude and his morality, but for nothing else. It does not believe in the Pope, nor in the Church, nor in the Bible. It ridicules the infallibility of the first, the despotism of the second, and the chronology of the third. It is possessed of the very spirit of Thomas; it must "touch and handle" before it will believe. It questions the existence of spirit, because it cannot be analyzed by chemical solvents; it questions the existence of hell, because it has never been scorched; it questions the existence of God, because it has never beheld Him.

It does, however, believe in the explosive force of gunpowder, in the evaporation of boiling water, in the head of the magnet, and in the heels of the lightnings. It conjugates the Latin verb *invenio* (to find out) through all its voices, moods and tenses. It invents everything; from a lucifer match in the morning to kindle a kitchen fire, up through all the intermediate ranks and tiers and grades of life, to a telescope that spans the heavens in the evening, it recognizes no chasm or hiatus in its inventions. It sinks an artesian well in the desert of Sahara for a pitcher of water, and bores through the Alleghanies for a hogshead of oil. From a fish-hook to the Great Eastern, from a pocket deringer to a columbiad, from a sewing machine to a Victoria suspension bridge, it oscillates like a pendulum.

Deficient in literature and art, our age surpasses all others in science. Knowledge has become the great end and aim of human life. "I want to know," is inscribed as legibly on the hammer of the geologist, the crucible of the chemist, and the equatorial of the astronomer, as it is upon the phiz of a regular "Down-Easter." Our age has inherited the chief failing of our first mother, and passing by the "Tree of Life in the midst of the Garden," we are all busily engaged in mercilessly plundering the Tree of Knowledge of all its fruit. The time is rapidly approaching when no man will be considered a gentleman who has not filed his *caveat* in the Patent Office.

The inevitable result of this spirit of the age begins already to be seen. The philosophy of a cold, blank, calculating materialism has taken possession of all the avenues of learning. Epicurus is worshiped instead of Christ. Mammon is considered as the only true savior. *Dum Vivimus Vivamus*, is the maxim we live by, and the creed we die by. We are all iconoclasts. St. Paul has been superseded by St. Fulton; St. John by St. Colt; St. James by St. Morse; St. Mark by St. Maury; and St. Peter has surrendered his keys to that great incarnate representative of this age, St. Alexandre Von Humboldt.

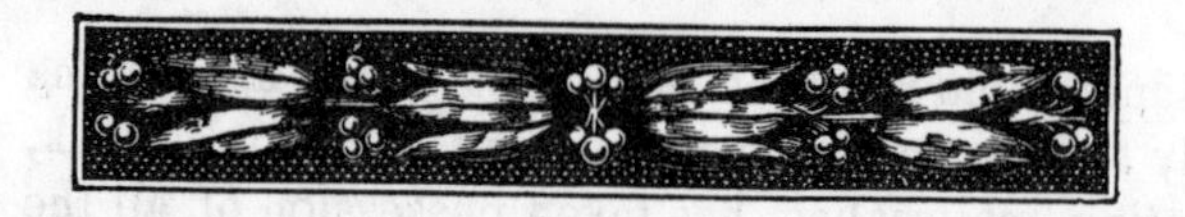

XXIV.

THE ENROBING OF LIBERTY.

THE war-drum was silent, the cannon was mute,
  The sword in its scabbard lay still,
And battle had gathered the last autumn fruit
  That crimson-dyed river and rill,
When a Goddess came down from her mansion on high,
  To gladden the world with her smile,
Leaving only her robes in the realm of the sky,
  That their sheen might no mortal beguile.

As she lit on the earth she was welcomed by Peace,
  Twin sisters in Eden of yore—
But parted forever when fetter-bound Greece
  Drove her exiled and chained from her shore;
Never since had the angel of liberty trod
  In virginal beauty below;
But, chased from the earth, she had mounted to God,
  Despoiled of her raiment of snow.

Our sires gathered round her, entranced by her smile,
  Remembering the footprints of old
She had graven on grottoes, in Scio's sweet Isle,
  Ere the doom of fair Athens was told.
"I am naked," she cried; "I am homeless on earth;
  Kings, Princes, and Lords are my foes,
But I stand undismayed, though an orphan by birth,
  And condemned to the region of snows."

"Hail, Liberty! hail"—our fathers exclaim—
"To the glorious land of the West!
With a diadem bright we will honor thy name,
And enthrone thee America's guest;
We will found a great nation and call it thine own,
And erect here an altar to thee,
Where millions shall kneel at the foot of thy throne
And swear to forever be free!"

Then each brought a vestment her form to enrobe,
And screen her fair face from the sun,
And thus she stood forth as the Queen of the globe
When the work of our Fathers was done.

A circlet of stars round her temples they wove,
That gleamed like Orion's bright band,
And an emblem of power, the eagle of Jove,
They perched like a bolt in her hand;
On her forehead, a scroll that contained but a line
Was written in letters of light,
That our great "Constitution" forever might shine,
A sun to illumine the night.

Her feet were incased in broad sandals of gold,
That riches might spring in her train;
While a warrior's casque, with its visor uproll'd,
Protected her tresses and brain;
Round her waist a bright girdle of satin was bound,
Formed of colors so blended and true,
That when as a banner the scarf was unwound,
It floated the "Red, White and Blue."

Then Liberty calm, leant on Washington's arm,
And spoke in prophetical strain:
"Columbia's proud hills I will shelter from ills,
Whilst her valleys and mountains remain;

But palsied the hand that would pillage the band
Of sisterhood stars in my crown,
And death to the knave whose sword would enslave,
By striking your great charter down.

"Your eagle shall soar this western world o'er,
And carry the sound of my name,
Till monarchs shall quake and its confines forsake,
If true to your ancestral fame!
Your banner shall gleam like the polar star's beam,
To guide through rebellion's Red sea,
And in battle 'twill wave, both to conquer and save,
If borne by the hands of the free!"

XXV.

A CAKE OF SOAP.

I STOOD at my washstand, one bright sunny morn,
And gazed through the blinds at the upspringing corn,
And mourn'd that my summers were passing away,
Like the dew on the meadow that morning in May.

I seized, for an instant, the Iris-hued soap,
That glowed in the dish, like an emblem of hope,
And said to myself, as I melted its snows,
"The longer I use it, the lesser it grows."

For life, in its morn, is full freighted and gay,
And fair as the rainbow when clouds float away;
Sweet-scented and useful, it sheds its perfume,
Till wasted or blasted, it melts in the tomb.

Thus day after day, whilst we lather and scrub,
Time wasteth and blasteth with many a rub,
Till thinner and thinner, the soap wears away,
And age hands us over to dust and decay.

Oh Bessie! dear Bess! as I dream of thee now,
With the spice in thy breath, and the bloom on thy brow,
To a cake of pure Lubin thy life I compare,
So fragrant, so fragile, and so debonair!

But fortune was fickle, and labor was vain,
And want overtook us, with grief in its train,
Till, worn out by troubles, death came in the blast;
But *thy* kisses, like Lubin's, were sweet to the last!

XXVI.

THE SUMMERFIELD CASE.

THE following additional particulars, as sequel to the Summerfield homicide, have been furnished by an Auburn correspondent:

MR. EDITOR: The remarkable confession of the late Leonidas Parker, which appeared in your issue of the 13th ultimo, has given rise to a series of disturbances in this neighborhood, which, for romantic interest and downright depravity, have seldom been surpassed, even in California. Before proceeding to relate in detail the late transactions, allow me to remark that the wonderful narrative of Parker excited throughout this county sentiments of the most profound and contradictory character. I, for one, halted between two opinions—horror and incredulity; and nothing but subsequent events could have fully satisfied me of the unquestionable veracity of your San Francisco correspondent, and the scientific authenticity of the facts related.

The doubt with which the story was at first received in this community—and which found utterance in a burlesque article in an obscure country journal, the Stars and Stripes, of Auburn—has finally been dispelled, and we find ourselves forced to admit that we stand even now in the presence of the most alarming fate. Too much credit cannot be awarded to our worthy coroner for the promptitude of his action, and we trust that the Governor of the State will not be less efficient in the discharge of his duty.

[Since the above letter was written the following proclamation has been issued.—P. J.]

PROCLAMATION OF THE GOVERNOR.

$10,000 REWARD!

DEPARTMENT OF STATE.

By virtue of the authority in me vested, I do hereby offer the above reward of ten thousand dollars, in gold coin of the United States, for the arrest of Bartholomew Graham, familiarly known as Black Bart. Said Graham is accused of the murder of C. P. Gillson, late of Auburn, county of Placer, on the 14th ultimo. He is five feet ten inches and a half in height, thick set, has a mustache sprinkled with gray, grizzled hair, clear blue eyes, walks stooping, and served in the late civil war, under Price and Quantrell, in the Confederate army. He may be lurking in some of the mining-camps near the foot-hills, as he was a Washoe teamster during the Comstock excitement. The above reward will be paid for him, *dead or alive*, as he possessed himself of an important secret by robbing the body of the late Gregory Summerfield.

By the Governor: H. G. NICHOLSON,
Secretary of State.

Given at Sacramento, this the fifth day of June, 1871.

Our correspondent continues:

I am sorry to say that Sheriff Higgins has not been so active in the discharge of his duty as the urgency of the case required, but he is perhaps excusable on account of the criminal interference of the editor above alluded to. But I am detaining you from more important matters. Your Saturday's paper reached here at 4 o'clock, Saturday, 13th May, and, as it now appears from the evidence taken before the coroner, several persons left Auburn on the same errand, but without any previous conference. Two of these were named respectively Charles P. Gillson and Bartholomew Graham, or, as he was usually called, "Black Bart." Gillson kept a saloon at the corner of Prickly Ash Street and the Old Spring Road; and Black Bart was in the employ of Conrad & Co., keepers of the Norfolk livery stable. Gillson was a son-in-law of ex-Governor Roberts, of Iowa, and leaves a wife and two children to mourn his untimely end. As for Graham, nothing certain is known of his antecedents. It is said that he was engaged in the late robbery of Wells & Fargo's express at Grizzly Bend, and that he was an habitual gambler. Only one thing about him is certainly well known: he was a lieutenant in the Confederate army, and served under General Price and the outlaw Quantrell. He was a man originally of fine education, plausible manners and good family; but strong drink seems early in life to have overmastered him, and left him but a wreck of himself. But he was not incapable of generous, or rather, romantic, acts; for, during the burning of the Putnam House, in this town, last summer, he rescued two ladies from the flames. In so doing he scorched his left hand so seriously as to contract the tendons of two fingers, and this very scar may lead to his apprehension. There is no doubt about his utter desperation of character, and, if taken at all, it will probably be not alive.

So much for the persons concerned in the tragedy at the Flat.

Herewith I inclose copies of the testimony of the witnesses examined before the coroner's jury, together with the statement of Gillson, taken *in articulo mortis:*

DEPOSITION OF DOLLIE ADAMS.

STATE OF CALIFORNIA, }
County of Placer. } ss.

Said witness, being duly sworn, deposed as follows, to wit: My name is Dollie Adams; my age forty-seven years; I am the wife of Frank G. Adams, of this township, and reside on the North Fork of the American River, below Cape Horn, on Thompson's Flat; about one o'clock P.M., May 14, 1871, I left the cabin to gather wood to cook dinner for my husband and the hands at work for him on the claim; the trees are mostly cut away from the bottom, and I had to climb some distance up the mountain side before I could get enough to kindle the fire; I had gone about five hundred yards from the cabin, and was searching for small sticks of fallen timber, when I thought I heard some one groan, as if in pain; I paused and listened; the groaning became more distinct, and I started at once for the place whence the sounds proceeded; about ten steps off I discovered the man whose remains lie there (pointing to the deceased), sitting up, with his back against a big rock; he looked so pale that I thought him already dead, but he continued to moan until I reached his side; hearing me approach, he opened his eyes, and begged me, "For God's sake, give me a drop of water!" I asked him, "What is the matter?" He replied, "I am shot in the back." "Dangerously?" I demanded. "Fatally!" he faltered. Without waiting to question him further, I returned to the cabin, told Zenie—my daughter—what I had seen, and sent her off on a run for the men. Taking with me a gourd of water, some milk and bread—for I thought the poor gentleman might be hungry and weak, as well as wounded—I hurried back to his side, where I remained until "father" —as we all call my husband—came with the men. We removed him as gently as we could to the cabin; then sent for Dr. Liebner, and nursed him until he died, yesterday, just at sunset.

Question by the Coroner: Did you hear his statement, taken down by the Assistant District Attorney?—A. I did.

Q. Did you see him sign it?—A. Yes, sir.

Q. Is this your signature thereto as witness?—A. It is, sir.

(Signed) DOLLIE ADAMS.

DEPOSITION OF MISS X. V. ADAMS.

Being first duly sworn, witness testified as follows: My name is Xixenia Volumnia Adams; I am the daughter of Frank G. Adams and the last witness; I reside with them on the Flat, and my age is eighteen years; a little past 1 o'clock on Sunday last my mother came running into the house and informed me that a man was dying from a wound, on the side-hill, and that I must go for father and the boys immediately. I ran as fast as my legs would carry me to where they were "cleaning up," for they never cleaned up week-days on the Flat, and told the news; we all came back together and proceeded to the spot where the wounded man lay weltering in his blood; he was cautiously removed to the cabin, where he lingered until yesterday sundown, when he died.

Question. Did he speak after he reached the cabin? A. He did frequently; at first with great pain, but afterward more audibly and intelligibly.

Q. What did he say? A. First, to send for Squire Jacobs, the Assistant District Attorney, as he had a statement to make; and some time afterward, to send for his wife; but we first of all sent for the doctor.

Q. Who was present when he died? A. Only myself; he had appeared a great deal easier, and his wife had lain down to take a short nap, and my mother had gone to the spring and left me alone to watch; suddenly he lifted himself spasmodically in bed, glared around wildly and muttered something inaudible; seeing me, he cried out, "Run! run! run! He has it! Black Bart has got the vial! Quick! or he'll set the world afire! See, he opens it! Oh, my God! Look! look! look! Hold his hands! tie him! chain him down! Too late! too late! oh the flames! Fire! fire! fire!" His tone of voice gradually strengthened until the end of his raving; when he cried "fire!" his eyeballs glared, his mouth quivered, his body convulsed, and before Mrs. Gillson could reach his bedside he fell back stone dead.

(Signed) X. V. ADAMS.

The testimony of Adams corroborated in every particular that of his wife and daughter, but set forth more fully the particulars of his demoniac ravings. He would taste nothing from a glass or bottle, but shuddered whenever any article of that sort met his eyes. In fact, they had to remove from the room the cups, tumblers, and even the castors. At times he spoke rationally, but after the second day only in momentary flashes of sanity.

The deposition of the attending physician, after giving the general facts with regard to the sickness of the patient and his subsequent demise, proceeded thus:

I found the patient weak, and suffering from loss of blood and rest, and want of nourishment; occasionally sane, but for the most part flighty and in a comatose condition. The wound was an ordinary gunshot wound, produced most probably by the ball of a navy revolver, fired at the distance of ten paces. It entered the back near the left clavicle, beneath the scapula, close to the vertebræ between the intercostal spaces of the fifth and sixth ribs; grazing the pericardium it traversed the mediastinum, barely touching the œsophagus, and vena azygos, but completely severing the thoracic duct, and lodging in the xiphoid portion of the sternum. Necessarily fatal, there was no reason, however, why the patient could not linger for a week or more; but it is no less certain that from the effect of the wound he ultimately died. I witnessed the execution of the paper shown to me—as the statement of deceased—at his request; and at the time of signing the same he was in his perfect senses. It was taken down in my presence by Jacobs, the Assistant District Attorney of Placer County, and read over to the deceased before he affixed his signature. I was not present when he breathed his last, having been called away by my patients in the town of Auburn, but I reached his bedside shortly afterward. In my judgment, no amount of care or medical attention could have prolonged his life more than a few days.

(Signed) KARL LIEBNER, M.D.

The statement of the deceased was then introduced to the jury as follows:

PEOPLE OF THE STATE OF CALIFORNIA
vs.
BARTHOLOMEW GRAHAM.

Statement and Dying Confession of Charles P. Gillson, taken in articulo mortis by George Simpson, Notary Public.

On the morning of Sunday, the 14th day of May, 1871, I left Auburn alone in search of the body of the late Gregory Summerfield, who was reported to have been pushed from the cars at Cape Horn, in this county, by one Leonidas Parker, since deceased. It was not fully light when I reached the track of the Central Pacific Railroad. Having mined at an early day on Thompson's Flat, at the foot of the rocky promontory now called Cape Horn, I was familiar with the zigzag paths leading down that steep precipice. One was generally used as a descent, the other as an ascent from the cañon below. I chose the latter, as being the freest from the chance of observation. It required the greatest caution to thread the narrow gorge; but I finally reached the rocky bench, about one thousand feet below the grade of the railroad. It was now broad daylight, and I commenced cautiously the search for Summerfield's body. There is quite a dense undergrowth of shrubs thereabouts, lining the interstices of the granite rocks so as to obscure the vision even at a short distance. Brushing aside a thick manzanita bush, I beheld the dead man at the same instant of time that another person arrived like an apparition upon the spot. It was Bartholomew Graham, known as "Black Bart." We suddenly confronted each other, the skeleton of Summerfield lying exactly between us. Our recognition was mutual. Graham advanced and I did the same; he stretched out his hand and we greeted one another across the prostrate corpse.

Before releasing my hand, Black Bart exclaimed in a hoarse whisper, "Swear, Gillson, in the presence of the dead, that you will forever be faithful, never betray me, and do exactly as I bid you, as long as you live!"

I looked him full in the eye. Fate sat there, cold and remorseless as stone. I hesitated; with his left hand he slightly raised the lappels of his coat, and grasped the handle of a navy revolver.

"Swear!" again he cried.

As I gazed, his eyeballs assumed a greenish tint, and his

brow darkened into a scowl. "As your confederate," I answered, "never as your slave."

"Be it so!" was his only reply.

The body was lying upon its back, with the face upwards. The vultures had despoiled the countenance of every vestige of flesh, and left the sockets of the eyes empty. Snow and ice and rain had done their work effectually upon the exposed surfaces of his clothing, and the eagles had feasted upon the entrails. But underneath, the thick beaver cloth had served to protect the flesh, and there were some decaying shreds left of what had once been the terrible but accomplished Gregory Summerfield. A glance told us all these things. But they did not interest me so much as another spectacle, that almost froze my blood. In the skeleton gripe of the right hand, interlaced within the clenched bones, gleamed the wide-mouthed vial which was the object of our mutual visit. Graham fell upon his knees, and attempted to withdraw the prize from the grasp of its dead possessor. But the bones were firm, and when he finally succeeded in securing the bottle, by a sudden wrench, I heard the skeleton fingers snap like pipe-stems.

"Hold this a moment, whilst I search the pockets," he commanded.

I did as directed.

He then turned over the corpse, and thrusting his hand into the inner breast-pocket, dragged out a roll of MSS., matted closely together and stained by the winter's rains. A further search eventuated in finding a roll of small gold coin, a set of deringer pistols, a rusted double-edged dirk, and a pair of silver-mounted spectacles. Hastily covering over the body with leaves and branches cut from the embowering shrubs, we shudderingly left the spot.

We slowly descended the gorge toward the banks of the American River, until we arrived in a small but sequestered thicket, where we threw ourselves upon the ground. Neither had spoken a word since we left the scene above described. Graham was the first to break the silence which to me had become oppressive.

"Let us examine the vial and see if the contents are safe."

I drew it forth from my pocket and handed it to him.

"Sealed hermetically, and perfectly secure," he added. Saying this he deliberately wrapped it up in a handkerchief and placed it in his bosom.

"What shall we do with our prize?" I inquired.

"*Our* prize?" As he said this he laughed derisively, and cast a most scornful and threatening glance toward me.

"Yes," I rejoined firmly; "*our* prize!"

"Gillson," retorted Graham, "you must regard me as a consummate simpleton, or yourself a Goliah. This bottle is mine, and *mine* only. It is a great fortune for *one*, but of less value than a toadstool for *two*. I am willing to divide fairly. This secret would be of no service to a coward. He would not dare to use it. Your share of the robbery of the body shall be these MSS.; you can sell them to some poor devil of a printer, and pay yourself for your day's work."

Saying this he threw the bundle of MSS. at my feet; but I disdained to touch them. Observing this, he gathered them up safely and replaced them in his pocket. "As you are unarmed," he said, "it would not be safe for you to be seen in this neighborhood during daylight. We will both spend the night here, and just before morning return to Auburn. I will accompany you part of the distance."

With the *sangfroid* of a perfect desperado, he then stretched himself out in the shadow of a small tree, drank deeply from a whisky flagon which he produced, and pulling his hat over his eyes, was soon asleep and snoring. It was a long time before I could believe the evidence of my own senses. Finally, I approached the ruffian, and placed my hand on his shoulder. He did not stir a muscle. I listened; I heard only the deep, slow breathing of profound slumber. Resolved not to be balked and defrauded by such a scoundrel, I stealthily withdrew the vial from his pocket, and sprang to my feet, just in time to hear the click of a revolver behind me. I was betrayed! I remember only a flash and an explosion—a deathly sensation, a whirl of the rocks and trees about me, a hideous imprecation from the lips of my murderer, and I fell senseless to the earth. When I awoke to consciousness it was past midnight. I looked up at the stars, and recognized Lyra shining full in my face. That constellation I knew passed the meridian at this season of the year after twelve o'clock, and its slow march told me that many weary hours would intervene before daylight. My right arm was paralyzed, but I put forth my left, and it rested in a pool of my own blood. "Oh, for one drop of water!" I exclaimed, faintly; but only the low sighing of the night blast responded. Again I fainted. Shortly after daylight I revived, and crawled to the spot where I was discovered on the next day by the kind mistress of this cabin. You know the rest. I accuse Bartholomew Graham of my assassination. I do this in the perfect possession of my senses, and with a full sense of my responsibility to Almighty God.

(Signed) C. P. GILLSON.

GEORGE SIMPSON, Notary Public.
CHRIS. JACOBS, Assistant District Attorney.

DOLLIE ADAMS,
KARL LIEBNER, } Witnesses.

The following is a copy of the verdict of the coroner's jury:

COUNTY OF PLACER,
Cape Horn Township. }

In re C. P. Gillson, late of said county, deceased.

We, the undersigned, coroner's jury, summoned in the foregoing case to examine into the causes of the death of said Gillson, do find that he came to his death at the hands of Bartholomew Graham, usually called "Black Bart," on Wednesday, the 17th May, 1871. And we further find said Graham guilty of murder in the first degree, and recommend his immediate apprehension.

(Signed) JOHN QUILLAN,
PETER MCINTYRE,
ABEL GEORGE,
ALEX. SCRIBER,
WM. A. THOMPSON.

(Correct:)
THOS. J. ALWYN,
Coroner.

The above documents constitute the papers introduced before the coroner. Should anything of further interest occur, I will keep you fully advised.

POWHATTAN JONES.

Since the above was in type we have received from

our esteemed San Francisco correspondent the following letter:

SAN FRANCISCO, June 8, 1871.

MR. EDITOR: On entering my office this morning I found a bundle of MSS. which had been thrown in at the transom over the door, labeled, "The Summerfield MSS." Attached to them was an unsealed note from one Bartholomew Graham, in these words:

DEAR SIR: These are yours; you have earned them. I commend to your especial notice the one styled "*De Mundo Comburendo.*" At a future time you may hear again from

BARTHOLOMEW GRAHAM.

A casual glance at the papers convinces me that they are of great literary value. Summerfield's fame never burned so brightly as it does over his grave. Will you publish the MSS.?

XXVII.

THE AVITOR.

HURRAH for the wings that never tire—
 For the nerves that never quail;
For the heart that beats in a bosom of fire—
For the lungs whose cast-iron lobes respire
 Where the eagle's breath would fail!

As the genii bore Aladdin away,
 In search of his palace fair,
On his magical wings to the land of Cathay,
So here I will spread out my pinions to-day
 On the cloud-borne billows of air.

Up! up! to its home on the mountain crag,
 Where the condor builds its nest,
I mount far fleeter than hunted stag,
I float far higher than Switzer flag—
 Hurrah for the lightning's guest!

Away, over steeple and cross and tower—
 Away, over river and sea;
I spurn at my feet the tempests that lower,
Like minions base of a vanquished power,
 And mutter their thunders at me!

Diablo frowns, as above him I pass,
 Still loftier heights to attain;
Calaveras' groves are but blades of grass—
Yosemite's sentinel peaks a mass
 Of ant-hills dotting a plain!

Sierra Nevada's shroud of snow,
  And Utah's desert of sand,
Shall never again turn backward the flow
Of that human tide which may come and go
  To the vales of the sunset land!

Wherever the coy earth veils her face
  With tresses of forest hair;
Where polar pallors her blushes efface,
Or tropical blooms lend her beauty and grace—
  I can flutter my plumage there!

Where the Amazon rolls through a mystical land—
  Where Chiapas buried her dead—
Where Central Australian deserts expand—
Where Africa seethes in saharas of sand—
  Even there shall my pinions spread!

No longer shall earth with her secrets beguile,
  For I, with undazzled eyes,
Will trace to their sources the Niger and Nile,
And stand without dread on the boreal isle,
  The Colon of the skies!

Then hurrah for the wings that never tire—
  For the sinews that never quail;
For the heart that throbs in a bosom of fire—
For the lungs whose cast-iron lobes respire
  Where the eagle's breath would fail!

XXVIII.

LOST AND FOUND.

'TWAS eventide in Eden. The mortals stood,
Watchful and solemn, in speechless sorrow bound.
He was erect, defiant, and unblenched.
Tho' fallen, free—deceived, but not undone.
She leaned on him, and drooped her pensive brow
In token of the character she bore—
The world's first penitent. Tears, gushing fast,
Streamed from her azure eyes; and as they fled
Beyond the eastern gate, where gleamed the swords
Of guarding Cherubim, the flowers themselves
Bent their sad heads, surcharged with dewy tears,
Wept by the stars o'er man's immortal woe.

Far had they wandered, slow had been the pace,
Grief at his heart and ruin on her face,
Ere Adam turned to contemplate the spot
Where Earth began, where Heaven was forgot.
He gazed in silence, till the crystal wall
Of Eden trembled, as though doomed to fall:
Then bidding Eve direct her tear-dimmed eye
To where the foliage kissed the western sky,
They saw, with horror mingled with surprise,
The wall, the garden, and the foliage rise!
Slowly it mounted to the vaulted dome,
And paused as if to beckon mortals home;
Then, like a cloud when winds are all at rest,
It floated gently to the distant west,
And left behind a crimson path of light,
By which to track the Garden in its flight!

Day after day, the exiles wandered on,
With eyes still fixed, where Eden's smile last shone;
Forlorn and friendless through the wilds they trod,
Remembering Eden, but forgetting God,
Till far across the sea-washed, arid plain,
The billows thundered that the search was vain!

Ah! who can tell how oft at eventide,
When the gay west was blushing like a bride,
Fair Eve hath whispered in her children's ear,
"Beyond yon cloud will Eden reappear!"

And thus, as slow millenniums rolled away,
Each generation, ere it turned to clay,
Has with prophetic lore, by nature blest,
In search of Eden wandered to the West.

I cast my thoughts far up the stream of time,
And catch its murmurs in my careless rhyme.
I hear a footstep tripping o'er the down:
Behold! 'tis Athens, in her violet crown.
In fancy now her splendors reappear;
Her fleets and phalanxes, her shield and spear;
Her battle-fields, blest ever by the free,—
Proud Marathon, and sad Thermopylæ!
Her poet, foremost in the ranks of fame,
Homer! a god—but with a mortal's name;
Historians, richest in primeval lore;
Orations, sounding yet from shore to shore!
Heroes and statesmen throng the enraptured gaze,
Till glory totters 'neath her load of praise.
Surely a clime so rich in old renown
Could build an Eden, if not woo one down!

Lo! Plato comes, with wisdom's scroll unfurl'd,
The proudest gift of Athens to the world!

Wisest of mortals, say, for thou can'st tell,
Thou, whose sweet lips the Muses loved so well,
Was Greece the Garden that our fathers trod;
When men, like angels, walked the earth with God?
"Alas!" the great Philosopher replied,
"Though I love Athens better than a bride,
Her laws are bloody and her children slaves;
Her sages slumber in empoisoned graves;
Her soil is sterile, barren are her seas;
Eden still blooms in the Hesperides,
Beyond the pillars of far Hercules!
Westward, amid the ocean's blandest smile,
Atlantis blossoms, a perennial Isle;
A vast Republic stretching far and wide,
Greater than Greece and Macedon beside!"

The vision fades. Across the mental screen
A mightier spirit stalks upon the scene;
His tread shakes empires ancient as the sun;
His voice resounds, and nations are undone;
War in his tone and battle in his eye,
The world in arms, a Roman dare defy!
Throned on the summit of the seven hills,
He bathes his gory heel in Tiber's rills;
Stretches his arms across a triple zone,
And dares be master of mankind, alone!
All peoples send their tribute to his store;
Wherever rivers glide or surges roar,
Or mountains rise or desert plains expand,
His minions sack and pillage every land.
But not alone for rapine and for war
The Roman eagle spreads his pinions far;
He bears a sceptre in his talons strong,
To guard the right, to rectify the wrong,
And carries high, in his imperial beak,
A shield armored to protect the weak.

Justice and law are dropping from his wing,
Equal alike for consul, serf or king;
Daggers for tyrants, for patriot-heroes fame,
Attend like menials on the Roman name!

Was Rome the Eden of our ancient state,
Just in her laws, in her dominion great,
Wise in her counsels, matchless in her worth,
Acknowledged great proconsul of the earth?

An eye prophetic that has read the leaves
The sibyls scattered from their loosened sheaves,
A bard that sang at Rome in all her pride,
Shall give response;—let Seneca decide!

"Beyond the rocks where Shetland's breakers roar,
And clothe in foam the wailing, ice-bound shore,
Within the bosom of a tranquil sea,
Where Earth has reared her *Ultima Thule*,
The gorgeous West conceals a golden clime,
The petted child, the paragon of Time!
In distant years, when Ocean's mountain wave
Shall rock a cradle, not upheave a grave,
When men shall walk the pathway of the brine,
With feet as safe as Terra watches mine,
Then shall the barriers of the Western Sea
Despised and broken down forever be;
Then man shall spurn old Ocean's loftiest crest,
And tear the secret from his stormy breast!"

Again the vision fades. Night settles down
And shrouds the world in black Plutonian frown;
Earth staggers on, like mourners to a tomb,
Wrapt in one long millennium of gloom.
That past, the light breaks through the clouds of war,
And drives the mists of Bigotry afar;

Amalfi sees her buried tomes unfurl'd,
And dead Justinian rules again the world.
The torch of Science is illumed once more;
Adventure gazes from the surf-beat shore,
Lifts in his arms the wave-worn Genoese,
And hails Iberia, Mistress of the Seas!

What cry resounds along the Western main,
Mounts to the stars, is echoed back again,
And wakes the voices of the startled sea,
Dumb until now, from past eternity?

"Land! land!" is chanted from the Pinta's deck;
Smiling afar, a minute glory-speck,
But grandly rising from the convex sea,
To crown Colon with immortality,
The Western World emerges from the wave,
God's last asylum for the free and brave!

But where within this ocean-bounded clime,
This fairest offspring of the womb of time,—
Plato's Atlantis, risen from the sea,
Utopia's realm, beyond old Rome's Thule,—
Where shall we find, within this giant land,
By blood redeemed, with Freedom's rainbow spann'd,
The spot first trod by mortals on the earth,
Where Adam's race was cradled into birth?

'Twas sought by Cortez with his warrior band,
In realms once ruled by Montezuma's hand;
Where the old Aztec, 'neath his hills of snow,
Built the bright domes of silver Mexico.
Pizarro sought it where the Inca's rod
Proclaimed the prince half-mortal, demi-god,
Where the mild children of unblest Peru
Before the bloodhounds of the conqueror flew,

And saw their country and their race undone,
And perish 'neath the Temple of the Sun!
De Soto sought it, with his tawny bride,
Near where the Mississippi's waters glide,
Beneath the ripples of whose yellow wave
He found at last both monument and grave.
Old Ponce de Leon, in the land of flowers,
Searched long for Eden 'midst her groves and bowers,
Whilst brave La Salle, where Texan prairies smile,
Roamed westward still, to reach the happy isle.
The Pilgrim Fathers on the Mayflower's deck,
Fleeing beyond a tyrant's haughty beck,
In quest of Eden, trod the rock-bound shore,
Where bleak New England's wintry surges roar;
Raleigh, with glory in his eagle eye,
Chased the lost realm beneath a Southern sky;
Whilst Boone believed that Paradise was found
In old Kentucky's "dark and bloody ground!"

In vain their labors, all in vain their toil;
Doomed ne'er to breathe that air nor tread that soil.
Heaven had reserved it till a race sublime
Should launch its heroes on the wave of time!

Go with me now, ye Californian band,
And gaze with wonder at your glorious land;
Ascend the summit of yon middle chain,
Where Mount Diablo rises from the plain,
And cast your eyes with telescopic power,
O'er hill and forest, over field and flower.
Behold! how free the hand of God hath roll'd
A wave of wealth across your Land of Gold!
The mountains ooze it from their swelling breast,
The milk-white quartz displays it in her crest;
Each tiny brook that warbles to the sea,
Harps on its strings a golden melody;

Whilst the young waves are cradled on the shore
On spangling pillows, stuffed with golden ore!

Look northward! See the Sacramento glide
Through valleys blooming like a royal bride,
And bearing onward to the ocean's shore
A richer freight than Arno ever bore!
See! also fanned by cool refreshing gales,
Fair Petaluma and her sister vales,
Whose fields and orchards ornament the plain
And deluge earth with one vast sea of grain!
Look southward! Santa Clara smiles afar,
As in the fields of heaven, a radiant star;
Los Angeles is laughing through her vines;
Old Monterey sits moody midst her pines;
Far San Diego flames her golden bow,
And Santa Barbara sheds her fleece of snow,
Whilst Bernardino's ever-vernal down
Gleams like an emerald in a monarch's crown!
Look eastward! On the plains of San Joaquin
Ten thousand herds in dense array are seen.
Aloft like columns propping up the skies
The cloud-kissed groves of Calaveras rise;
Whilst dashing downward from their dizzy home
The thundering falls of Yo Semite foam!
Look westward! Opening on an ocean great,
Behold the portal of the Golden Gate!
Pillared on granite, destined e'er to stand
The iron rampart of the sunset land!
With rosy cheeks, fanned by the fresh sea-breeze,
The petted child of the Pacific seas,
See San Francisco smile! Majestic heir
Of all that's brave, or bountiful, or fair,
Pride of our land, by every wave carest,
And hailed by nations, Venice of the West!

Where then is Eden? Ah! why should I tell,
What every eye and bosom know so well?
Why name the land all other lands have blest,
And traced for ages to the distant West?
Why search in vain throughout th' historic page
For Eden's garden and the Golden Age?
Here, Brothers, here! no further let us roam;
This is the Garden! Eden is our Home!